Take a HIKE!

Also by Maggie Grant

Fix Them Up

Take a HIKE!

MAGGIE GRANT

Bedford Square
Publishers

First published in the UK in 2026 by Bedford Square Publishers Ltd,
London, UK

bedfordsquarepublishers.co.uk
@bedsqpublishers

© Maggie Grant, 2026

The right of Maggie Grant to be identified as the author of this work has been asserted in accordance with the Copyright, Designs and Patents Act 1988. All rights reserved. No part of this book may be reproduced, stored in or introduced into a retrieval system, or transmitted, in any form or by any means (electronic, mechanical, photocopying, recording or otherwise) without the written permission of the publishers.

Any person who does any unauthorised act in relation to this publication may be liable to criminal prosecution and civil claims for damages.
A CIP catalogue record for this book is available from the British Library.
This is a work of fiction. Names, characters, places, and incidents either are the product of the author's imagination or are used fictitiously, and any resemblance to actual persons, living or dead, businesses, companies, events or locales is entirely coincidental.

ISBN
978-1-83501-412-7 (Paperback)
978-1-83501-413-4 (eBook)

2 4 6 8 10 9 7 5 3 1

Typeset in 10.9 on 13.75pt Bembo Std
by Avocet Typeset, Bideford, Devon, EX39 2BP
Printed and bound in Great Britain by
CPI Group (UK) Ltd, Croydon CR0 4YY

The manufacturer's authorised representative in the EU for product safety is
Easy Access System Europe, Mustamäe tee 50, 10621 Tallinn, Estonia
gpsr.requests@easproject.com

For Ena and Marie –

Who taught me, in their own ways, that people-pleasing is deeply overrated and being fierce is kind of fun.
I hope you enjoyed that glitter bomb.

Lydia

Two Years Ago

The thing about people-pleasing was that it rarely pleased anyone – least of all, me. It felt like running on a treadmill, chasing new, exciting vistas, destined to a view that never changed. Exhausting. Pointless. And yet I couldn't step off. Not even for one of the most important nights of my best friend's life.

The night we celebrated his posh new title: Best Bartender in the UK.

My heart pounded as I paced through the quiet, carpeted hallways of Momentum Fitness, my 'office' for the last decade, legs screaming out after a day lifting, stretching and running alongside my clients. I'd arrived at five in the morning and was leaving as the spring sun was setting behind bright pink clouds. I glanced at my phone. *Shit*. I was almost two hours late. I made my way out of the whooshing doors, across the empty carpark, typing a quick, one-handed text.

Don't hate me. I'm on my way, but it came out as 'Dunt haye me. I in my wsy'.

'Fuck Craig,' I muttered, cursing the reason for all my woes – the newly minted gym supervisor who seemed determined to make my life hell. He'd been promoted a few months ago and acted like he'd been ordained by God himself to micromanage every corner of Momentum. Like tonight, for instance, when he made me stay late to scrub the gym floors, even though we had a whole team of cleaners who showed up before we opened to do exactly that.

I should have said no. I should have pushed back. But Craig had never liked me and, stupidly, I still wanted to change that.

I chucked my fluorescent orange bag into the boot of my Honda Civic, its bright colour not giving me the burst of joy it usually does. I accelerated, navigating Friday night traffic, down Everly Heath High Street, oak trees flitting by. My lip was almost bleeding as I pulled down a familiar street of redbrick terraced houses, finding a lucky parking spot on the packed street.

I heard the sound of metal crunching.

'Shit!' I jumped out of the car to find matching dents on my car and the immaculate BMW that I knew belonged to Jake three doors down. God, he loved this car.

'Fuck, fuck, fuck!'

I fished a pen and a scrap of paper out, shoving the pen cap in my mouth as I wrote.

Jake – sorry – scratched your car. Really sorry!!! I can pay. – Lydia.

And then scribbled down my phone number. He might want to call to shout at me. Or demand my first-born. Or maybe just process an insurance claim. Or all three.

I took a deep breath. I just needed to find Ren, apologise for being late, and then everything would be okay. As I jogged towards my childhood home, I saw our neighbour, Deirdre, was stood outside her house, fag in hand. Her jet black hair, long and thinning, was thrown up into her signature beehive.

'Lydia.' Deirdre's voice was sandpaper.

'Hi, Deirdre!'

'Loud in there.' She nodded her head. 'Quite a knees-up.'

I shoved my key in the door, wrestling with the ageing lock, thumping music coming from the other side. God, Mum and Dad said a few drinks to 'celebrate Ren's achievement'. It sounded like a rave.

'I'll get them to keep it down.'

'Don't on my account, love. You know, I used to throw quite the do's when you were younger.'

Yes, and I could have sworn they involved several couples, keys, and a bowl, but I kept those suspicions to myself. I wasn't going to kink-shame my 70-year-old neighbour.

I eyed the pampas grass in Deirdre's front garden as the door gave way. Discarded streamers and congratulations balloons littered the hallway. Jesus! It was barely 9 o'clock. Mum and Dad's parties could get a bit wild on occasion, like half of the social club kitchen-dancing until the early hours of the morning, but as I passed the lounge full of people I didn't recognise, with empty bottles on the floor, and snogging couples pressed against the wall, I was bemused.

I pushed through the huddles of people, finding Mum in the kitchen drying glasses. I touched her shoulder, and she whipped around, brandishing a glass.

'Oh!' Mum brought her hand to her chest. 'God, you scared me, Lydia.'

'Who are all these people?'

'Oh,' Mum sighed, smoothing her blonde bob. 'Some people Ren invited. They're lovely. But, my God, do they get through some drinks. I've cleaned these glasses twice.'

A woman with spiky blonde hair and a nose ring appeared, looking lost, until Mum handed her a clean glass.

The girl topped the glass up with a huge measure of amber liquid and made her way back towards the pounding music. 'Lola. Lovely girl. Works at a bar in town called Satan's Butthole. Sounds horrible, but I said your father and I would go and have their signature cocktail – Ring of Fire. It's a belter, according to Lola.'

I never thought I'd hear the words 'Satan's Butthole' from my mother.

'Ren invited all of these people?' I looked around, dumbfounded. This didn't make sense.

'Where is he?'

'Outside with Liam, love.'

I headed to the French doors, but then stopped in my tracks, mentally berating myself for being so selfish.

'Do you want me to get rid of these people? Or do you need some help? I can clear some glasses.'

'No, no. Don't be silly!' Mum said, a smile not reaching her eyes. 'I told Lawrence he could invite whoever he wanted.'

My eyes narrowed and I went to search for my best friend, determined to give him a piece of my mind, until I saw Liam had beaten me to it. Ren's face was lit up by the security lights, his face lit in gold and amber. His rich brown hair was styled back off his face and I knew – after years of watching him – that it took an inordinate amount of product to make it look that perfectly carefree. Just like it took an inordinate amount of effort to seem as carefree as he did, because, underneath it all, he wasn't.

His face had hardened over time, but still maintained some of the boyish softness. His nose was slightly crooked from a punch he got from a sixth-former twice his size. Now his face was morphed into anger – his cheeks flushed, his eyes wild. I'd seen this look before, and it always spelled trouble.

'... can't you see what I'm saying?' Liam's voice dropped low, thick with frustration. The strain in it made me still. 'Have you seen the mess you've made of Sandra and Brian's house? They threw this party for you – to celebrate your award. And this is how you repay them?'

'They said I could invite—'

'They said you could invite *some* friends, Ren. Not the entire Hospo scene from the Northwest.'

'Liam, they're here to celebrate me winning the award. But, of course, you don't care about that, do you?'

'Of course I do. But if I see any of them doing drugs—'

Ren flinched. 'They wouldn't do that.'

Here, I could almost hear him add. I was sure Liam could hear it too.

'This isn't the scene I want to surround myself with. These parties, how things can spiral. I have to prioritise Abigail. Now isn't the time for risks, Ren. And this—' *You,* the word unsaid '—is a risk.'

'So that's it? You're going to throw it all in – all the plans we made – because of one party?' Ren spat, then laughed, humourlessly. 'No, of course it's more than that. I can see it in your face. You're scared. Scared of change. Fucking typical.'

'Ren. *Careful.*' Liam's voice was tight, a thread about to snap. But Ren was already chasing the high of a fight.

'It's *pathetic.* You haven't even told Dad about the restaurant, have you? We signed a fucking contract, and you're still at his beck and call, still too spineless to admit you *hate* working for him—'

Ren took a step closer, raising his finger.

'Ren, I'm warning you.'

'You think just because you quit drinking and started acting like a saint, you're better than me. You're not. You're the same washed-up single dad who fucked up his relationship and now—'

Liam erupted.

He launched forward and grabbed Ren by the shirt, slamming him back hard enough that the breath caught in my chest.

'Shut the fuck up!' Liam spat.

I burst through the patio doors.

'Liam!' I barked. 'Take a breath. Think. It's not worth it.'

I'd been pulling these two out of scraps since sixth form, so I knew what to say. Liam stood frozen, fist clenched around Ren's shirt, still breathing hard as he stared down his younger brother.

'Wipe that smirk off your face, Ren,' I said, voice flat. 'You're just proving his point, and you know it.'

Ren's eyes flicked to mine, something in them softening, just enough to know I'd broken him out of his red haze. Liam let go and stepped back. He headed for the door.

'I'm making the call tomorrow,' he said, his voice raw.

And then, just before he shut the door, he turned to me.

'Look after him, will you, Lyds?' he murmured, so low I barely caught it, but I nodded just the same.

I stepped closer to Ren, inspecting him for any marks Liam might have left. Ren's face softened as he finally looked at me, and it was almost painful to see the raw emotion he showed me – only me. He was gutted. Well and truly defeated.

He sighed and opened his arms. 'C'm'ere.'

I stepped into his open arms and felt him exhale, almost in relief.

'I'm sorry you had to see that.'

'I'm sorry I'm late.'

He pulled back, shooting me a dark look. 'Better late than never, right? And at least you didn't miss the main event.'

His tone was bitter, and my heart sank. It had always been like this between Liam and Ren – this push and pull of their personalities that were so at odds. If Ren's face hadn't looked so weary, I would have almost been smug about being an only child.

So instead, I settled on something familiar – teasing him.

I jabbed his ribs. 'What the hell are you playing at, Lawrence? This house is Mum's first rave, I swear. And I swear I saw Dad passing around something that looked suspiciously like a bong.'

Ren took a step back, rubbing his face. I was expecting the usual sly smile, but all I got was a dejected sigh.

'Lydia… I'm really sorry. It just… got out of hand.'

I softened, a smile teasing the edge of my mouth. 'I'm pulling your leg. It's fine. But I don't even know half the people here.' I glanced around at the crowds in the kitchen. 'This doesn't look like your usual crowd.'

Ren huffed, 'Well, that's funny 'cos apparently I've met my brother's expectations perfectly.'

'Ren.'

'I invited Isaac and Imogen.'

I winced. 'You said they were wild.'

'They told everyone they knew. Before I knew it, another fifteen, twenty people had appeared. People I barely know. We're just lucky it's a Friday and a lot of people are working. On a Sunday we'd have been overrun.'

'What are we doing out here? Come on.' I grabbed his hand, leading him back inside. 'Let's kick some people out.'

It took 20 minutes, turning on the 'big light' and unplugging the DJ for everyone to leave. Another 15 to clear the mess and get the house back in order. Mostly. Ren apologised to Mum more times than I could count. Then Mum and Dad giggled their way down the garden to smoke some pot that Isaac and Imogen had brought with them.

I clapped. 'Much better.'

I placed the last glass on the tea towel to dry, turning to Ren, who had a broom in his hand. He gave me a tight, sad smile. The house might have looked in better form, but Ren was still miserable.

'Not all doom and gloom, grumpy.' I walked over to him, poking his cheek.

Come on, smile for me.

'Only because of you.' He ran a hand through his hair. 'I don't know what I'd do without you sometimes.'

I shrugged. 'Get arrested. Again.'

He rolled his eyes. 'It was *once*.'

We smiled at each other, and I shifted on my feet. *Something* always hung between us at the end of evenings, when we didn't want to part. We both wanted to linger longer. Like we wanted to wring a little more time out of the night, twisting every last drop from it like water from an old rag.

'I should go,' Ren said, gesturing to the front door.

'Come on,' I said, slipping my hand into his, ignoring the stupid sparks that shot up my arm as if I hadn't trained myself out of reacting to them. A hangover from my pining days.

Right, and those are totally behind you.

'The night's still young.'

His hand still in mine, I led him through our hallway and up the stairs. I pushed open the door to my childhood bedroom – a little box room, with pink brushed-cotton sheets and old *High School Musical* posters, the ink ageing Zac Efron's face. I climbed into my single bed, gesturing to Ren to join me.

Ren gave a rough laugh. 'I'm not sure we're gonna fit any more, Lyds.'

Ren stood by my door, his eyes shifting between me and the bed, as if he was debating something.

'Oh, come on. For old times' sake. We can watch a film. Take your mind off tonight.'

He paused, unnaturally still. And for a moment, I wondered if I'd made the wrong call. We'd spent sleepovers in this room for as long as I could remember. First as kids, limbs akimbo and full of sugar, then later – as we morphed from kids to tweens to teenagers – things blurred. The lines had softened. And somewhere along the way, I'd stopped looking for them. The nights in this room had been the best memories of my life. Listening to his breath, steady and peaceful, after he lost his mum and shut everyone away. I knew that this room was a refuge for him.

But we were a couple of years away from 30 now, so it felt a bit ridiculous.

'Of course. Silly.' I laughed, my face flushing, throwing my feet to the floor.

Suddenly, I was met with a wall of man – solid, warm, and way too familiar – as Ren launched himself on to the bed, right over me, making me squeal-laugh. His scent hit me instantly, smoky and intense and like home. The touch was playful. Stupid. Harmless. But my stomach still flipped over.

Ren's voice was in my ear. 'Just don't hog it like you used to.'

'I didn't hog it!'

We shifted so we lay side by side. Our faces inches apart. I smiled. 'And you snored.'

'Yeah, well, you used to gob all over my T-shirt.'

'Did not!'

'Did so.'

Ren pulled out my old laptop, pleased when it roared to life, and played the DVD that was already in there – *A Cinderella Story* – and I sighed.

Hilary Duff. Chad Michael Murray. *Heaven.*

'Love this one.' He pulled the laptop closer, because I used to complain about how hot it would get on my legs. 'I'll go after the film.'

I smiled at the familiar promise he never kept. After ten minutes, Ren closed the laptop, throwing us into darkness.

'I just wanna say, before you start drooling on me...' He glanced down at me, his dark eyes simmering with softness. 'Thank you for tonight. For being so brilliant. I – I knew things had got out of control, but I didn't know what to do. I didn't want your mum to think I didn't appreciate the party—'

'She'd throw a party for the opening of an envelope. No offence.'

Ren chuckled, low and rumbling, and I could feel it low in my belly. I shifted, trying to find space in the tiny bed, when Ren lifted his arm.

'Come here,' he murmured and my breath hitched.

I paused a moment before I lay my head on his biceps, his arms cocooning me. I thought he probably just wanted to make more room, but then he pulled me even closer. Ren's lips came down on my temple, a ghost of a feather-light kiss – light and hesitant. My heart hammered so loud I was sure he could feel it thudding beneath his palm pressed against my ribs.

'Today was a shit day,' he murmured, his voice low and rough, so close I could feel his words touch my skin. 'But you always make everything better.'

'You do too,' I breathed, shifting to catch his eyes in the darkness, the faint glow from the streetlights lighting up his face.

And I wished I hadn't looked.

Because Ren was staring down at me as if I was his entire world. His eyes shifted down to my lips. And lingered. We were... so close. We were so close, closer than we'd ever allowed. There was the usual banter, touches and teasing between us, but this? His arms wrapped around me, his eyes fixed on my mouth, his breath warm at my ear – this was something else. Everything was tense and languid at the same time.

'Ren.' I squeezed my eyes shut, preparing myself to put some distance between us. But then my legs grazed against his – warm, bare. And it felt so good.

'Lydia.' His voice dropped, thick and husky.

This – the pull between us – had always been the hardest thing to fight. The way it grew quietly, stubbornly, over the years. I'd convinced myself it was one-sided. But here, tangled up in my childhood bed, with his heat and scent wrapped around me, I could feel it – that same fierce pull from him.

Maybe it wasn't just me.

'How are you so soft?'

His words felt like a snap, an elastic band *finally* breaking. I shifted my legs between his, and he pulled me tighter into him, pressing himself into me, hot and hard.

'Lydia,' he groaned, his breath shaky. 'I've thought about this so many times.'

Have you? I wanted to ask. When? How? Was this always one-sided or did you feel it too?

But the question died on my lips as his eyes locked with mine and his mouth claimed me. Our gasps melted into moans, lips replacing words, and our clothes slipped away. Instead I heard the beautiful things he murmured on to my skin, how I was perfect, exactly how he had imagined. I wanted to ask exactly what he had imagined, but I couldn't form words when his strong body was pressed between my legs, fingertips tracing and marking my skin. Maybe I should have been afraid of the words we should have said.

But as the sweat cooled and our hearts slowed, and he pulled me back into his arms – words felt insignificant.

He was honest about how he felt, eventually.

But when I woke up, he was gone.

Chapter One

Lydia's Diary, Six Years Old

Dear Diary,

Mum gave me this for Christmas. I didn't know what to write. But today something WEIRD happened. Two boys came. Both had brown hair. One was older called Liam. He didn't talk. RUDE. The little one hid behind his mum like a baby.

I said hi. He looked at me like I was evil.

Mum said show him my toys. He ran off.

Rude, rude, rude. His name is ~~Lorence~~ Lawrence. (Mum helped me spell) I told him that's a old man name. He said *PISS OFF*. That is a BAD word! I told Mum.

I just wanted a friend. But I will NEVER be friends with him.

Lydia

'Okay, ladies! Two more minutes, let's finish strong!' I bellowed over Chappell Roan's chorus, holding back a laugh at the collective groan that echoed around the studio from the three women in front of me – Amy, Genevieve and Claire – my dream team.

I wasn't supposed to have favourites, but we'd been meeting at Momentum for three years now, and I looked forward to our sessions every week – bright and early at 7 o'clock. They were more than clients. Some of my best friends, really.

Genevieve – Gen – was half-Indian and curvy, with thick dark hair. Her petite mum had spent a lifetime pushing her to lose weight. Amy, with bright pink hair and a wiry frame, had spent her childhood in and out of hospitals with leukaemia. She fought to keep weight on. Claire, a recent divorcee with immaculate, cropped, grey hair, wanted a revenge body to spite her ex-husband, who'd left her for his younger co-worker.

They'd all come to me to fix something. But over time, their goals had shifted. Now it was about muscle, strength, and mental health. And community.

I wasn't naive enough to think body-image issues disappeared overnight. I mean, I still hated being the tallest woman in every room, a giantess on a hill, but I was proud the gym wasn't just about appearances for these ladies any more. It was about confidence. Achievement. Pride.

It was the reason I got into this business when I was 18 and fresh out of school. It was to bring out the best in people, and I could pinpoint exactly when that passion had begun.

Year nine. When I was caught hiding in the school loos in the worst moment of my week – double maths. Mrs MacDonald, the gym teacher, found me. She was a stern, tall woman. She had brunette hair, always scraped back into a severe ponytail. She was someone I usually avoided during netball but, once I saw how her face softened when she found me, I decided almost instantly to trust her. She didn't shout at me or order me back to class. Instead she angled her head and said, 'Come on – I'm teaching the year sevens how to pass and catch. You can help me.'

I'd almost collapsed in relief. I spent the whole of double maths teaching the young 'uns (by that I mean pupils merely two years younger than me) how to play netball and it was the best two hours of my life.

Afterwards, Mrs MacDonald told me I needed to speak to my Head of Year about how I'd been feeling about maths, but she also said I was a very talented coach. I had a future in it, if I wanted. I remember the way my chest burned with pride. For the rest of my time at school, Mrs MacDonald served as not only an example of a brilliant teacher and coach, but also as a bit of a queer icon for me. When it came up, she spoke openly about her wife and, as a closeted bisexual 14-year-old, that felt huge, to have someone living the life I might lead one day.

'Yes, ladies!' I pushed my arms up. 'Two more minutes and we're done!'

'You said that a minute ago,' Claire hit out, growling at me.

Amy's arms sagged. Gen had abandoned her dumbbells, head thrown back, eyes closed, still jogging. Claire's form was perfect, her face grim with determination. Today's session hadn't been easy. I'd cackled like an evil villain when I'd put the programme together – burpees and lateral rises were killers – but I knew they would thank me afterwards when their heart rate slowed and endorphins flooded their system, leaving their brain nice and quiet for the rest of the day. And that satisfying stretch in your muscles.

'Three... two... one.' I turned down the ear-cracking music. 'Okay, cool down.'

We all collapsed on the mat in front of us. The blood was burning in my cheeks. As usual, I'd joined them in the workout. Some PTs sat on their arses or leaned on equipment while their clients sweated and puffed, but not me. If I was setting you a killer programme, I was doing it with you. Camaraderie and all that.

I starfished on the mat, panting gently, feeling my heart racing down the peak I'd sent it up. The girls' breath echoed around the studio.

'I hate you, Lydia,' Gen panted.

'Liar,' I grinned. 'Okay, stretches.'

I lifted my leg to cradle it to my chest, feeling the stretch in my glutes from our barbell squats at the beginning of the session.

'Oh, that's lovely,' Claire croaked.

Ten minutes later, we sat in a circle, gossiping.

'So he says...' Amy paused dramatically, '... things went from zero to a hundred, and he's not cut out for a relationship. Like I asked him to marry me? It was one date!'

'Ugh,' Gen wrinkled her nose.

'Honestly, Amy,' Claire said. 'If I've learnt anything, men are... What was it again?'

'Trash,' Gen finished, sipping water.

Claire continued, 'Twenty years with my husband. And he leaves me for a twenty-five-year-old. Keep your money, keep your assets.'

'Amen,' Gen raised her bottle.

I huffed, 'Hypocrite.'

Gen just shrugged, eyes smiling. Her lanky, adorably nerdy husband cooked her dinner, paid for her to open a tattoo studio with his lucrative coding job, and every night he played video games while she read Romantasy beside him.

'It can't be all bad,' Amy complained. 'All my siblings are married to their soulmates. So are my parents.'

She picked at her mat, head low. Amy had been single for a while and was desperate to find love. So desperate she let mediocre men mess her around.

She was a romantic, and I'd been like that once.

Until two years ago.

My mind drifted to that night two years ago. The night I thought was a fresh, new beginning until I'd woken alone, with a handwritten note. That's when I lost my best friend and my belief in love, all in one go.

'It doesn't exist, Amy,' I said quietly. 'And even if it did, what's to say they don't leave? No warning. Just gone. All for what – some socially prescribed idea of love? I have you guys. That's all I need.'

Silence. Amy, Gen, and Claire stared at me.

'Lydia—' Gen started.

TAKE A HIKE!

'Are you still not over...' Amy's eyes widened. 'You know – him?'

His name used to roll off my tongue. Now I never said it. And they didn't either.

'We thought you were happy with Casey,' Claire said gently. 'You've moved in together.'

I gave a brittle laugh. 'Of course I'm happy with Casey. I was just saying,' I gestured to Amy, 'maybe we shouldn't put so much pressure on romantic love. Fifty per cent of marriages end in divorce.'

Claire harrumphed in agreement.

'See!' I laughed, eye twitching. 'It's not just me.'

'You used to say I'd find the right person,' Amy said.

'I wonder what made her change her mind,' Gen said.

They knew what happened with Ren. I came into one session after he left and cried my eyes out. I told them everything and regretted it ever since. I wished they didn't know that particular weakness so well.

'It was years ago. I'm totally over it.'

There was a quiet, knowing glance from the girls that made my skin itch, until Claire finally took pity on me and clapped her hands, changing the subject.

'Right. I'd better go. I need to get packing for my trip. I'll see you girls in a few weeks.'

'Oh, I forgot you were going on that trip!' Amy said, tucking her pink hair behind her ears. 'We're going to miss you.'

'I'll be back before you know it.' Claire smiled, gathering her things.

I'd forgotten too – she'd been planning this for ages. Three weeks off, hiking across the country with a bunch of women she'd never met. She'd wanted to do a trip like this for years. Her husband hated nature. He preferred pools and air-con.

Three whole weeks off. I couldn't remember the last time I'd taken three days off. This month alone, I had clients seven days a week. 7 o'clock in the morning to 9 o'clock in the evening. Maybe a nap in the middle. Three weeks off sounded… impossible.

I snorted under my breath, imagining Craig's sour face if I asked him for that amount of time off.

My eyes flicked to the clock. And my stomach turned to lead.

'Fuck!' I shot upright. The girls scrambled to stand too.

'What?' Gen blinked.

'Can you pack up? Shit, I'm screwed.' I was already halfway to the door. 'I'm already fifteen minutes late. Craig is going to crucify me.'

'Go, go.' Claire shooed. 'We'll pack up. Don't worry.'

'But you can't pack up on your own—'

'Don't be daft.' Gen led me by my elbow to the studio doors. 'Get gone, we'll sort the rest.'

'Thank you!' I shouted, as I turned and moved through the gym, weaving past slow walkers on their way to the badminton courts.

'Shit, shit, shit,' I muttered.

Momentum Gym was packed, and I couldn't believe I'd let my class run over – again. I'd spent half the session watching the clock, promising myself today would be different.

I had a meeting with Craig at ten past eight. He always booked appointments at stupid times – never on the hour or half past. Always five past. Ten to. The bane of my life.

I glanced at my watch. Twenty-five past eight.

Fuck!

'Excuse me, sorry.' I swerved past an older lady.

'Oh, Lydia!' Mrs Daniels's eyes lit up. 'My athlete's foot is much better – thank you!'

'Oh, no problem, Mrs Daniels. We've all been there!'

'I've been meaning to ask you—'

Oh, God, please, not now.

Could I tell her I was running late for something? I really should just say it – *Mrs Daniels, we'll have to talk later, I'm running late.* But a voice inside whispered, *She'll be so disappointed.* What if it's something urgent?

The words stuck in my throat. I couldn't say them.

'Sure!' I turned, jogging backwards, palms sweating, even as Mrs Daniels's eyes crinkled with a smile.

'My husband still won't come to the gym. He hates exercising in front of people.'

'Understandable!'

'What can I get him to do at home? For his mobility, you know.'

'Sure. There are plenty of things you could do—'

'Something simple.'

'Sure.'

'Not too challenging.'

'Yep, I've got just the thing.'

'Angel.'

Five minutes later, I'd ordered resistance bands from my Amazon and explained how to strengthen his knees, quads and glutes. I'd never met Mr Daniels, but I knew how much she worried.

'What would we do without you?' she said, patting my cheek.

'Happy to help,' I smiled, twitching.

I bolted up the stairs, past the Olympic-sized swimming pool, dodging Tom and Esme, the inseparable married couple, on the stairs. Me and the other PTs joked they were basically one person now.

'Sorry!' They said at the exact same time.

'Tom. Esme. Tomesme,' I muttered, skidding past Ryan leading a circuit session, giving him a quick wave, and bolted for the staff corridor, until my shoulder hit a hard shoulder.

Quinn Roberts.

He was a wall of a man, with huge shoulders, a bald head and a thick moustache.

'Lydia!' he grinned. 'Meant to ask—'

My eye twitched. I needed to leave. Do it. Tell him you're running late for an appointment. Tell him your nan just died and you need to get to the funeral. Tell him you left the oven on, or you're having an allergic reaction and you're about to swell up like a balloon and float away.

Say anything.

But the words stuck in my throat. Again.

'Shoot!' I squeaked, panic fizzing in my chest.

'I've entered regionals this weekend,' he said, slowly. 'Will you come and watch? I haven't told anyone else, just in case it's a blow-out. It would be so embarrassing—'

'Of course. Text me the details.'

'Ah, I'm chuffed.' He clocked me a strange look as I turned to bolt down the hallway. 'See you, Lydia.'

I hurtled down the hallway, stopping at a door with a STAFF ONLY sign. I paused, nervously, then knocked.

'Come in.'

Craig had his legs up on the desk, a phone in the crook of his ear and a stress ball in his hand. He was throwing it up in the air and catching it.

His dyed-black hair was slicked back, as if it was a nuisance, sharpening his already angular features – a statement jaw, pointed nose, and a mouth that was perpetually angled down like he'd been born disappointed. He gestured for me to sit down, and relief poured into my system.

'Okay, yep,' Craig crooned. 'Well, you know, I wanted to run it past you. Yep, yep, Boss. Yep. Have a drink for me. Yep, ciao, ciao.'

Craig put the phone back on the receiver. His smile vanished.

'Twenty-five minutes today,' he said, looking at the clock. 'That's a record.'

'I'm sorry. I swear it won't happen again. You know how it is – people need things, you can't just walk away.'

Craig stared as if I was a maths equation he didn't understand.

TAKE A HIKE!

Craig had never liked me. When I joined the gym at 18, his eyes had always narrowed when I opened my mouth. Since day one, he'd called me out in front of clients, offered 'suggestions' for their form. I let it slide, thinking maybe he just wanted me to be my best.

But when clients began requesting me instead of him, things shifted. The nitpicking started.

And when he became the general manager six months ago, it got much, much worse.

Suddenly, it was all about numbers.

KPIs. Timesheets. Door codes changed weekly now for 'safety'. The rota switched to 24-hour clocks, and I had to double-, triple-check I'd got the time right for my shifts. I think he knew I struggled – but he never said anything. Just smirked when I counted on my fingers. Or paused too long reading the schedule.

I was diagnosed with dyscalculia at school and had hidden it since I scraped a 'pass' in my GCSE maths and moved on.

But, even now, anything involving numbers filled me with dread. I learnt to mask it, pretending to understand like everyone else. And some days I managed, others not so much.

But I'd kept my head down and tried to keep up with Craig's demands. My disastrous timekeeping – made worse by the fact that I couldn't read the old school clocks in the gym – was the most obvious thing to pull me up on.

Craig leaned forward like a villain in a low-budget mob film. 'We've reached an impasse. Your KPIs are all over the place.'

'I know. I'll improve. I'll set alarms—'

'We're ending your contract.'

Air whooshed from my lungs and my ears rang. Blood desperately tried to pump around my body.

'As in, cutting back my hours—'

Personal trainers were freelance at the gym, meaning I could take on as many clients as I wanted.

'No,' Craig said, shaking his head. 'We're giving you two weeks' notice, as your contract requires.'

He slid over a document. TWO WEEKS, highlighted in yellow.

'Wait... you're letting me go?' I whispered.

'No. We're not renewing your contract. Do you understand the difference?' Craig said slowly. As if he was talking to a child.

'I've been here since I was eighteen. All of my clients. I won't have any income. I'll have to—'

My throat constricted. Tears burned in my eyes when I thought about the idea of building everything again – over ten years of work, ten years of hard graft. It was years of late nights and early mornings. Years of laughing and networking, and making sure every client, every demand, was taken care of. All of it – gone. Just like that.

Without Momentum, I'd have to build everything from scratch again.

I couldn't even form words. Tears threatened to overflow, and I hated crying in front of anyone, let alone Craig.

'Everything has its time, Lydia,' Craig said sagely. 'I'm afraid there is nothing I can do.'

'Niall. Niall wouldn't allow this. We spoke a few months ago about changes. He asked my opinion on the new class structures—'

I'd met Niall, the enigmatic Irish CEO of the gym group, at various times in the last ten years. We had chatted at Christmas parties, and he had always insisted, 'You're exactly what this gym needs, Lydia, someone who cares, a friendly face to keep the gym local.'

Whenever I'd got offers from other gyms, I'd thought about Niall. Whenever I'd felt belittled or bullied by Craig, I thought of Niall and his occasional encouragements.

'That was him on the phone. He agrees. Said this'll be good for you. A fresh start. He asked me to thank you for your many years of service.'

The colour drained from my face but I kept it neutral. My eyes stung, but I blinked it away.

Keep calm. Don't make a scene.

'Look. If you'd prefer not to work the notice,' Craig said, gently, too gently, 'I'll take your clients before they're reassigned. Gives you space to process... and move on.'

I nodded, feeling numb.

I couldn't remember leaving Craig's office, but somehow I made it back to Momentum's cafe, and someone touched my arm. I turned, but tears — tears I refused to let drop down my face — obscured my view.

'Lydia.' Pink hair. Amy. It was Amy. 'We were waiting to check you were okay.'

'What's wrong?' Gen's voice was low and lethal.

'Love, come and sit down,' Claire said. 'Oh, God! What's happened? Tell us.'

'I've been sacked,' I said. I realised then that I was sobbing. 'I've been sacked from Momentum.'

Chapter Two

Lydia's Diary, Six Years Old

Dear Diary,
Mum told me something really, really sad today. Her friend Lily is not feeling well. She has cancer. I know that's really bad because no one wants to say it out loud. They whisper it like it's a secret. It made me feel sad. Lily came over for Sunday lunch. I told her she didn't look sick but then Mum told me off.

But Lily wasn't mad. She smiled and gave me a big hug. She smelled nice, like flowers.

Lawrence was here too but I heard his mum call him Ren, so I'm gonna call him Ren now. Ren brought his toys and we played. His bears fought my Barbies. It was fun.

Maybe he is not so bad after all.

Ren

I was early, too early.

I pushed back on my heels, my legs eager to move. A knot of anxiety ebbed in my chest. The red binder in my hand felt stupidly bright and garish. It was the first time I'd held one since I'd collated my GCSE artwork, one of the only subjects I'd passed because I couldn't be arsed with any of the others.

The spring sun was shining across Everly Heath High Street, lighting up the rain from last night that shone on the tarmac and pavements. I'd always loved living in a small town on sunny spring days like this. While Liam played football with his friends, Mum would glance at me with a conspiratorial glint in her brown eyes and ask, 'Farm?'

Everly Heath Farm was more like a petting zoo on the edge of town, where houses and parks broke out into farms, wide open fields, and woodland. Farm days were one of the only things Mum and I did, just the two of us. She loved the horses and I liked feeding the pygmy goats and watching them bounce from hay bale to hay bale. I'd play on the swings and we'd eat ice cream, and I still remember the feeling of it melting down my arm.

My eyes stung at the memory and I berated myself. There was no chance I'd get through today if I focused on the ever-lingering grief of losing Mum. I had enough on my plate today.

Today I was going to convince my brother to buy Everly Heath Farm.

'Ren!' a feminine voice shouted. 'Ren!'

I glanced around, trying to find the source of the voice, but had no luck.

'God, is that you?'

Pat, Everly Heath's local councillor, Chairwoman of Everly Heath Social Club and borderline busybody rounded the corner, her little fawn pug, Noodle, trotting beside her.

'Fuck!' I muttered under my breath.

I'd successfully avoided Pat for days, but the woman was relentless. She had been calling and texting for weeks now, trying to rope me into one of her schemes, and now I was being harassed in public too. It was all well and good when she was in your corner, but when the warpath was aimed at you, well, you'd better take cover.

I glanced around, trying to find somewhere to hide, but she moved quickly, advancing on me.

Pat smiled knowingly, a little out of breath. Today, her greying braids were styled on top of her head like a crown, and she wore large, statement, red glasses.

'There you are. So glad I bumped into you.'

'Bumped into me? Don't pretend this wasn't on purpose! You've been calling me for weeks and I said no. This is harassment, Pat. Don't make me get Richard involved.'

Richard was the balding local policeman who occasionally came into the social club for a quiet pint. He was 58 and in it for the pension, so I doubt he would do anything, but it was worth a shot.

'Richard?' She barked a laugh. 'You could try but he's in my pocket, dear.'

'*Corruption* from a local councillor.'

'Yes, yes.' Pat waved her manicured hand. 'Scandalous. Now, have you given it any thought? She had nowhere to go and I think you'd be a good fit.'

'Pat, listen. I have no spare time outside of work. In what universe do you think I could look after a dog? I work long hours, Pat.'

I gestured to the brass 'Lily's' sign I was standing in front of. The restaurant that my brother and I opened last year, when I'd come back from Mexico City.

'Oh, it will be fine.' She waved a palm. 'We'll all chip in! Steve and I can help out. Sandra and Brian too.' Pat moved closer, settling her hand on my shoulder. 'We think it would be good for you, dear. You seem so lonely and Peanut—'

'Peanut?' I huffed. 'Stupid name.'

Pat unlocked her phone, showing me a photo of a small golden-retriever-looking dog. Except it had short, stocky legs. Peanut stared at me through the phone. Her soulful brown eyes seemed to say 'I love you'.

Fuck, she was cute.

No, Ren. I thought to myself. *Keep your head.*

'You could rename her if you wanted. She really is lovely.

She has a gorgeous temperament, and the shelter is at maximum capacity—'

'Look, Pat. As cute as Peanut is,' Pat's eyes shimmered with glee. 'I don't have time for this today.'

'Fine. Totally fine. We'll speak tomorrow.'

She backed away slowly, grinning.

'Patricia! I am not saying yes!'

'Fine, fine! But we'll talk tomorrow.'

'This bloody town.'

My brother's van pulling into the bay across from Lily's was a welcome distraction from Pat and her games, but then anxiety shot through me, followed by a jolt of excitement. I'd always struggled to differentiate between the two. My brother climbed out of the van, wearing a 'Fuck off, I'm cooking' cap that Kat had bought him last Christmas, and strode to the restaurant, his eyes widening in surprise at seeing me standing outside like a lemon.

Fuck! I knew I'd been too early. He was suspicious already.

When I asked for this meeting, I said it was about our latest recruitment drive. A year in, Liam could begin stepping back from early mornings and late nights in the kitchen. We could afford to hire some more staff. We could expand the team and be more ambitious with our menu. I launched a new spring seasonal cocktail menu last month.

Everything was going swimmingly.

And I was painfully bored.

I needed something new, a bigger challenge – something beyond the restaurant we'd opened together last year, after Liam finally came to his senses and took a risk. Kat, his fiancée, had been part of the reason for that epiphany. Her energy and enthusiasm were the perfect balance to Liam's grumpy exterior. I loved opening Lily's, named after our mum, but I always felt like it was more my brother's baby than mine. He would argue differently. He'd say a restaurant is nothing without a brilliant front-of-house and bar staff. But the food – that's what people raved about. The food got the attention of local press and national critics, while the service and drinks were given a throwaway mention at the end of the article. I'd always been that, next to my brother – the throwaway sibling. Liam was everyone's favourite, solid and reliable, while I was still seen as the naughty kid at the back of the class, spitballing people on the back of the head.

Which I'd only done a couple of times...

'What was all that about?' Liam asked, nodding towards Pat's retreating figure, before pulling keys out of the black utility trousers he still hadn't got rid of since turning from builder to chef. Liam had always been a creature of habit. I didn't know how Kat dealt with it. I'd never seen her in the same outfit twice.

But then, they say opposites attract.

I wouldn't know.

'Pat wants me to adopt a dog.'

Liam scoffed, 'A dog? That's a big responsibility. You'd have to walk it.'

My hands turned into fists, 'Yeah, I know.' I deflated, because Liam was right. That's exactly why I didn't want a damn dog. But I also hated that he thought I couldn't handle it. Even after a year of solidly working beside him, never being late or forgetting an order (okay, maybe once), he still saw me as his irresponsible little brother.

'What are you doing here so early?' Liam pushed open the door, 'We aren't meeting for another half-hour.'

'I thought I'd come in and do the orders,' I lied. 'But I forgot my key.'

Liam huffed and I could practically hear his unspoken words. *Typical.* I took a deep breath in and out.

Don't let it get to you.

Liam flipped on the house lights, and we made our way through the restaurant, with bistro chairs stacked on top of walnut tables, towards the office – or more like a cupboard – we shared.

'Can we talk now?' I asked.

'Yep,' Liam said, opening the office door and flicking the lights on.

Our office was small and dark, but Kat insisted on infusing it with life by painting it a soft stone colour and hanging framed photos from Lily's opening night. My grinning face, champagne in hand, looked down on me almost mockingly. Liam collapsed in his office chair, which gave a horrible creak, while I sat in the spare chair opposite.

'You need a new chair.'

'You sound like Kat,' he huffed. 'She complains about this chair every time she sees it. "Unsightly", she calls it.' Liam opened his laptop. 'Right, so we've had about fifteen CVs so far for the sous-chef role and twenty for waiting staff. That's not bad, considering it's been up for a few days. Do you want to take a look? It's on the Google Drive.'

'You can pick whoever you want.'

Liam's eyes lifted from the screen. 'You want me to pick your staff?'

I shrugged, 'Sure.'

Liam's eyes narrowed. 'You insisted on picking everyone yourself when we opened. You said I had no idea what it was like to work in a restaurant and that you had the experience of working with – and I quote – "absolute shit munchers", and that there was no chance in hell you'd let me hire them.'

Before we opened Lily's, Liam worked with my dad at the family business, Hunter Building and Construction. Meanwhile, I'd been working in award-winning cocktail bars since I was 18. I had more experience in the trade, even if Liam was an incredible chef. We'd had some teething issues when Liam learnt the ropes of being a professional chef, but I hadn't needed a soft launch. I knew exactly what the menu looked like, what wines

I'd stock, what equipment to order. It was like breathing, really. Easy. And now Lily's was a success, it was a little boring.

'I don't think I said that exactly.'

I said that exactly.

'What's going on? Why are you so twitchy?' Liam's eyes widened. 'Are you moving? Have you been arrested?'

'No.' My jaw tightened. 'I haven't been arrested.'

Irritation – the kind of irritation only a sibling could summon – thrummed in my chest.

'Not recently,' Liam muttered.

My jaw was near cracking. At this rate, Liam would be footing the bill for my dental work.

'Really, Liam? It was one skirmish with the police when I was seventeen. Can you let it go? You'd think I was serving life at Strangeways.'

'What's that?' Liam pointed to the binder.

I took a deep breath. *Okay, here we go.*

'It's a business plan.'

'For Lily's?'

'Yes. Kind of. I know we've discussed new sites. Expansion.'

A huge derelict farm on the edge of town. Just what you expected, right, big brother?

Liam nodded and outstretched his hand. 'Let me see.'

'I'll talk you through it.' But Liam took the binder from my hands and opened it.

His eyes, brown eyes we both got from Mum, scanned the page. They widened when he read 'Everly Heath Farm' and narrowed.

My hands began to sweat.

'It's for the farm. We create a unique destination venue – restaurant, hotel, spa. I've included draft architectural plans, broken down into three phases – the main house, which will be the restaurant, then the boutique hotel, and then the outer buildings. An overview of investment and cash flow. I even put together an example of a crowdfunding page. I think locals would invest for perks, like being the first to dine at the restaurant, especially now that we are more established.' I rushed out, ignoring that we were talking about purchasing a colossal estate.

Liam turned to the last page – the branding and design page that I'd asked Kat, my future sister-in-law, to design. She was a graphic designer until she moved up to Everly Heath to renovate her late father's house, fell in love with my brother, and decided to pursue her dream of being an interior designer.

'Did you ask Kat to do this?' Liam asked, in that scarily calm voice I know he only used when he was furious.

It took me right back to being 19, slipping through the door at 4 o'clock in the morning, still off my face from some rave, and collapsing at the bottom of the stairs – like that was ever going to stop the crash coming. Or 22, when I forgot to order the flowers for Mum's anniversary, so we had to grab a last-minute bunch from the Co-op, and I said – quite rightly – that it's not like you can fit that many in the grave vase anyway. Plus, I knew Mum would prefer orange roses, because they were her favourite. And, of course, it reminded me of when I told him Lydia and I weren't talking any more, and he just looked at me, voice low and quiet and dangerous, and asked, *Why?*

'Yes.'

'Did you discuss this with my fiancée before me?' Liam was lethally calm. 'Is Kat your business partner?'

'I – yes. But I know Kat designed the original logo for Lily's, so I asked if she might mock up one for the farm too.'

'The farm,' Liam repeated. 'You're talking like this is a done deal, Ren.'

I felt like a sprinter in the last few moments of the race, seeing the competitor in the corner of my eye, pistolling forward.

'Well, I've spoken to the owners.' My voice broke a little. *Pathetic.* 'Bert wants to sell quickly and is open to a deal. Mabel died last year and, well, it sounds like he's accepted he needs to sell. His kids have been trying to get him to sell for years with no hope.' I rubbed a hand across my face, trying to block out the sadness I saw in Bert's eyes when I spoke to him about selling. 'We'd need to raise the capital, but I think we could get them down on price. I can sell my flat,' I offered.

I hated my two-bed flat in Manchester anyway. I'd bought it with money Mum and Dad had put in a trust for us before she died. I'd wanted somewhere cool, completely different from this quaint little town. But now, the drive after a shift was hellish during rush hour, and it was too quiet, too still, when I got home. It reminded me of how alone I was. It reminded me that I last felt joy in my flat with *her*. The last time I felt anything, really.

Nope.

I'm not going to think about Lydia right now.

'And where would you live?'

'At the farm.' I took the binder from him. 'I'll convert one of the outhouses into a studio apartment. Then we can convert the other two into Airbnbs or even small offices for start-ups. People will come from all over for the hotel and restaurant in the main farmhouse. Looking at the architectural plans, you can see the plan for adding an orangery for the restaurant to double our covers. Then we add on extras, like weddings and wine tasting. Corporate parties. Stuff for kids in the holidays.'

'No,' Liam said, closing the binder with a snap.

'Liam,' I laughed humourlessly. 'Come on.'

'This is more than a second site. This is a huge project. A massive risk. I expect you're thinking HBC will help with the renovations. Even though Dad is only working three days a week? Jack is run off his feet as it is.'

When Liam left the family business, he enlisted Jack, Liam's right-hand man, to run it with Dad, who was pushing 70 now. Dad's body was beginning to show the wear and tear of years on the job, though he stubbornly refused to slow down.

'Well, obviously, we'd pay them.'

'Ren.' Liam rubbed his face. 'Kat and I are getting married next year. She just opened her shop. Abi is starting her GCSEs. Dad has recovered from that knee op, but I'm battling with him to keep to three days a week. It's too much.'

I felt a stab of pain when Liam summarised his life like that – a life marked by love, chaos, and milestones. I'd never cared much for domesticity but a new, strange pressure was creeping in as I faced turning 30. I kept laughing off questions about my love life or whether I'd settle down, but when I got home, I couldn't deny the gnawing emptiness in my chest. No business ventures or flights to exotic locations could keep it away. I'd tried both. And my reputation as the flighty, fun, irresponsible brother of Liam Hunter was chafing like too-tight clothes.

The farm was a way to prove that I was different.

I'd changed.

Or even better, I wasn't the loser they thought I was, to begin with.

'I can do it,' I said, snatching the binder from Liam's desk. 'We can recruit someone to replace me here. I can train them, make sure they aren't shit.'

'We'll spread ourselves too thin.' Liam returned to his laptop.

This was it. I'd taken my shot and missed. Frustration twisted in my chest and this felt strangely like déjà vu. Memories from two years ago lingered in my consciousness. The day I'd fought with Liam about Lily's and sought refuge in Lydia's small bedroom. Now Liam and I had opened Lily's, but I still hadn't made up for the shitty mistake I'd made when I left Lydia in her bed, and left a cowardly note on her pink bedsheets as she slept.

God, she'd looked so perfect.

'I've got a decent application from a guy called Theo for the kitchen,' Liam said, his attention already back to the matter in hand.

'You won't even *think* about it.'

Liam glanced back to me and softened. Like he pitied me. Like he knew exactly what memory I was thinking of. Like he knew how much this hurt.

'Look. This proposal is brilliant, Ren. It's thorough and I can see what you're trying to make happen.' His tone didn't bring any sense of relief. 'So bring me back another site. Something simple, more practical. Then we can talk.'

I sat there for a moment, letting the words sink in.

We were supposed to be partners. Fifty-fifty on profits, risks, losses. Liam had been clear about that when he called me in the airport in Mexico City, not knowing I was already heading back home anyway, saying he was finally ready to set up Lily's. He said he couldn't do it without me.

And, besides that, we were brothers. Before anything else.

But after I had spent months pouring everything into this proposal, here he was, speaking to me like an intern. Like this was his company. Like I worked for him.

I stood and headed for the door.

'Ren,' he called after me.

Hope flared, soothing the sting of rejection. He was pulling my leg, taking the piss. He was going to say *gotcha!* He believed in me and the vision I'd outlined.

'Don't speak to Kat about this without telling me first, okay?'

Hope deflated, my eyes burned.

I left the restaurant, threw the binder in the bin outside Lily's, and walked home to my empty, soulless flat.

Chapter Three

Lydia's Diary, Seven Years Old

Dear Diary,

Mum said the Hunter boys are gonna stay with us for a bit because their mum is in the hospital. Mum asked if I would let them sleep in the spare bed in my room. I was mad. I didn't want a boy sleeping in *my* room.

Yuck!

Liam had flowers and said thank you and Mum cried. That was so weird! Ren looked really, really sad. I asked if he wanted to play in my room. I told him it could be his room too if he wanted. And he smiled. Ren NEVER smiles. He's always so sad. But I liked it when he smiled because he looked happier.

I gave him all my favourite things. My new Barbie car. It felt nice to make him happy.

Love,
Lydia.

Lydia

'I've had the day from hell,' I murmured, clinging to Casey, savouring the smell of her musk perfume, my pulse quickening as I pressed her closer, almost afraid to let go. My fingers brushed lightly against her arms before pulling back. She looked a little perplexed, but she had a warm, open expression as her eyes scanned my face.

Yes, this is what I needed. Casey. She made everything better.

'You're not going to believe it when I tell you.' I lowered myself into the seat.

Lily's, Everly Heath's best restaurant, was packed and I couldn't help but smile at the unmistakable touch of my cousin, Kat, woven into every inch of the restaurant. She helped Liam design the space before its grand opening last year. After re-inventing herself as an interior designer, she opened her own interiors shop just a few doors down from Lily's, filled with fabric samples, wallpaper and little brass door handles I was a little obsessed with. Kat had slipped into life here so seamlessly, it felt like it had been inevitable all along.

'Yeah?' Casey frowned.

She looked impossibly cool, wearing a cropped brown leather jacket, black wide-leg jeans and her favourite cherry-red Doc Martens. Casey loved dark colours and sharp tailoring, which meant we were probably the only same-sex couple who didn't share a wardrobe. She couldn't stand athleisure, and I couldn't stand stiff clothes. They were suffocating, and I needed to move.

The only thing we shared was her lipstick, because Casey liked to kiss it on my cheeks, blending it with her fingers, giving my complexion a soft pink glow in more ways than one.

Casey and I met at Momentum Fitness, and celebrated our six-month anniversary last week. Supposedly, Kat had clocked that Casey liked me when we had ordered from the cafe. I was convinced she was just being friendly and, from experience, it was always harder to tell when women were flirting with you. So I took a risk, asked Casey out, and Kat had been right. Casey had blushed pink, asking for my number.

Our first date was almost too perfect. I met her at a cocktail bar, and we drank orange wine and laughed about people we worked with. I was hooked on the scent of her perfume and the sharp black of her eyeliner. Things moved fast. We spent all our time together, so I asked her if she wanted to move in after a few weeks. She had laughed, eyes crinkling, and said yes. That night I bought us champagne – and tasted it on her skin. I wasn't sure I would forget how her lips had pressed to mine that night, soft and daring. My fingers tracing the curve of her neck, then I traced it with my lips. We hadn't moved out of bed for hours that night.

I might have lost my job, but at least I had Casey, right?

'Hey, you know I'm so lucky to have you, right?' I said, leaning my hand across the table.

Casey pulled her hand back, biting her lip, 'Lydia, I have some... news too.'

'What's up?'

Casey could look anywhere but at me.

She didn't answer, making blood rush to my head. My system was already on high alert after everything that had happened with Craig.

'Casey, you're freaking me out.'

Her fingers twitched nervously with the gingham napkin, but when our eyes finally locked, a soft sadness settled there.

'I—' she stuttered, her big brown eyes shifting down. 'I wanted to tell you at a good time. But we haven't seen each other all week. You've been so busy and now I'm thinking this is a mistake, maybe we should talk at home.'

'It's fine—' I leaned across the table, grazing her soft hands. 'You can tell me any—'

'I'm moving to London,' she blurted out, pulling her hand back from mine.

Blood drained from my face for the second time that day. I took a breath, leaning back in my chair. It felt like someone had just hit me in the stomach.

'What do you mean? What do you mean you're moving to London? Josh,' I called over the young waiter. 'Could I get some wine, please? Anything really—'

'Sure, Lydia.' Josh smiled.

Casey reached out, stilling me with a touch. 'Lyd.'

'I'm fine. It's just,' I squeezed my eyes shut. 'London? Really?'

Casey exhaled, her brown eyes steady and warm. 'I got a place at Central St Martins.'

'Oh, my God.' I suddenly felt like the worst girlfriend on the planet. 'Casey, that's amazing! I knew you could do it.'

Casey had been developing her craft as a print-maker for the last year. She started making greetings cards, wedding invitations, and now she made handmade prints that Kat loved and stocked in her store a few doors down. But Casey really wanted to train formally, and she had mentioned applying for Central St Martins, the world-renowned arts and design college in London, a couple of times. But then she'd said it as a throwaway comment, like she hadn't liked her odds. It was competitive, not to mention expensive.

Casey gave me a tight smile. 'Thanks.'

'It's a full-time course. Two years. My uncle has offered me a room at his to stay, rent-free. So I'd only need to get a part-time job to pay the fees, plus I can use some money I have saved.'

I nodded, my mind whirling, trying to keep up.

'Okay. That's fine,' my voice squeaked, but my heart was clenched tight, an ache blooming in my chest. 'We can make that work.'

'Lydia.' Casey's face was marred with sympathy, her fingers squeezing mine gently before pulling away. 'I don't think we should do long-distance.'

'Long-distance,' I scoffed. 'It's three hours on the train, Casey. That isn't long-distance.'

'You work evenings and weekends. It wouldn't be fair. I know how much you love your job.'

I should have told her about my day, about the pain aching in my chest. But I couldn't shake the feeling I'd ruin her day and sour her good news.

'I can work around it.'

It's not like I have a job now anyway.

'I really like you, Casey. I think we could make this work.'

She paused, studying my face. 'I don't think that's a good idea.'

For the second time today my stomach bottomed out. She was serious about this. She was going to end it. My pulse thudded.

'I don't think we should do long-distance.'

'But why?' I leaned forward. 'Things are so good. We moved in together.'

'I moved out this morning.'

My breath caught in my throat. 'What? When – when did you find out about the uni course?'

'A couple of weeks ago.'

'Casey,' I croaked.

I could barely swallow. Casey had been planning all of this – plotting all of this – while she'd been sleeping next to me. While we discussed what to make for tea or idly chatted about our day. She had been plotting to leave me the entire time.

'I know, I'm sorry.' She rubbed a palm over her face, smudging her eyeliner a little, but then she reached across the table, brushing a stray hair behind my ear with such tenderness it took my breath away. 'I didn't know how I felt. I didn't know how I felt until now, and now I'm sure.'

'You're sure about breaking up with me,' I repeated, needing the information to sink in.

'I think it's best,' Casey said with a tight-lined mouth.

'Why?' I croaked.

'Because we're not able to come to this restaurant on Tuesdays and Thursdays. Because we have to cross the road when you see him coming. Because you murmur his name in your sleep.'

Blood drained from my face.

'Casey, you can't be serious.'

'You aren't over *him*.'

'I was never with him.'

The corners of Casey's mouth pulled down. 'Don't give me the same line. Something happened. I know it in my gut. And you won't share, fine. You don't want me to know. But the air is thick when you're in the same room.'

'We're never in the same room.'

'Exactly. And you won't tell me why you're so obsessed with avoiding him. Even if you're deluding yourself into thinking you don't have feelings for him, I'm certain he has them for you.'

'He doesn't.' I closed my eyes, forcing the words out like a prayer. 'Trust me, he doesn't.'

But, even as I said it, my mind betrayed me and pulled me back to a moment from a year ago, carried on the scent of magnolia and musk.

'Lydia, wait. Let me explain,' Ren said, shutting the patio doors behind him.

'How was your trip?' my voice detached, ghostly, 'Those long-haul flights can be a pain. Did you get those mini-bottles of gin, though? I've always loved those.'

'Lydia. Look at me. I'm trying to explain.'

'You don't have to explain anything. It's fine.'

'It's not fine. I know none of it's fine.' Ren rubbed a palm down his face, then pulled a scrap of paper out of his back pocket. 'I wrote it down, so I could get this right. But the words don't work now.'

I allowed myself to look at him. He was different. He was tanned, for one thing, with lines on his temples where his sunglasses had sat. He looked a little skinnier, as if he hadn't eaten properly and had hiked across the Andes or backpacked through crowded cities.

'Lyd, I'm so sorry. I know I fucked up.' He stepped forward. I took a step back. He flinched. 'You have to believe that I didn't mean to hurt you. I know I did, I know. Trust me, I know I fucked up. I know. I didn't know how to tell you because I suppose I didn't want your doubt, doubt that I could do it. After the fight with Liam, I was so low.'

I wanted to scream that I would never doubt him, but I held it back.

He took a shaky breath. 'So that night I panicked. Lydia, you have to believe me that that night meant everything to me—'

Just smile, Lydia.

'You don't have to explain anything.' *I smiled, keeping my rage at a distance. He didn't deserve to see my pain and embarrassment.*

'What do you mean? Of course I do. We're best friends—'

I meant to give a dry laugh, but it was a hysterical giggle. Ren's face moulded into confusion.

'We're fine, Ren. We can just move on. No harm, no foul.'

'Lyd. I understand you're angry. I do. I fucked up, massively.' *He exhaled, his brown eyes meeting mine.* 'But I came back for you. Not for Liam or the restaurant. I came back for you. When he called about the restaurant, I was already at the airport. I knew it was a mistake when I boarded the flight, but I was so hurt, and I'm sorry—'

I couldn't listen to this any more.

'I'm glad you're back,' *Ren's eyes softened until I said,* 'Because we can get back to normal. A new normal.' *I nodded to our families inside.* 'They don't know what's happened. So I'd prefer no one knew, you know? We can just keep things amiable. Cordial.'

'Cordial?'

I gave a breezy laugh. 'I'm fine, you're fine. We're all okay. Okay?'

'Lyd, you can't be serious. You're shutting down on me. I know you are. You're giving me the sunshine act, but you forget I know you—'

'I'm seeing someone.'

'Oh—' *Emotions flickered across his face like a flip book.* 'That's good.'

'It's going well. Just thought you should know.'

'Then can we at least be friends?' *Ren asked, morphing into something that looked like desperation.*

I gave him a pat on the shoulder, knowing it would hit home. 'Cordial, Ren. Let's leave it at that.'

Before tears threatened to roll down my cheeks, I headed back into the warmth of my family home and for the next year I ignored Ren's gaze boring into the side of my face.

'Sauvignon blanc?'

I almost thought it was him – him offering me the glass of wine, until I looked up to find Josh's youthful, smiling face.

'Thanks, Josh!'

Silence fell over the table, and I didn't know what to say. How could I convince her it was nothing when I couldn't convince myself?

'I think I should go.'

I watched as Casey carefully picked up her leather handbag, rising from her seat. She paused next to me, debating how to say goodbye. Then, she planted a kiss on my cheek, her lipstick leaving a mark on my cheek for the last time.

'You'll thank me eventually. I know it.'

Chapter Four

Lydia's Diary, Eight Years Old

Dear Diary,
  Lily died today. Ren was picked up from our house. They went to the hospital.
  Mum got a phone call and fell on to the kitchen floor. Dad hugged her really tight, but she was still crying. I watched from the dining table, where I was doing my cats-and-dogs puzzle.
  Ren wasn't at school. I kept asking Mum if he could come over. She said he was really sad. I said that was the point but she just smiled in that way grown-ups do.
  On Friday, after school, Ren was sitting at our dining table. He looked quieter, and smaller. I ran over and hugged him tight. He let me. Even though it's a bit weird for boys and girls to hug, he didn't push me away. We finished my puzzle together, not talking much. Then, we watched *Spy Kids* because it's my favourite, and I told him he looked just like the boy in it. He didn't say anything, but I think he liked that.
  Later, when Dad took him home, I saw him and Ren's dad hug on the driveway. Grown-up hugs always last longer than kid ones. I think they might have been crying, but I wasn't sure.
  Ren waved at me through the car window before he went back inside his house. I hope he comes over again soon.
  Love,
  Lydia

Lydia

A burst of light hit my face, hitting my corneas.

'Wakey, wakey!'

Mum, in her signature Skechers and silk blouse, flung the window wide. A gust of air swept over me and I burrowed under the duvet.

'Come on. We're doing things my way now.'

'Mum,' I groaned. 'Leave me alone.'

She picked up a pink thong from the floor and tutted, 'Lovely.'

'Lev Mh Ahlne,' I groaned into the pillow.

'Was that "Mum, please save me from my pit of despair since I lost my job and got dumped?"'

I sat bolt upright, my bird's-nest hair sticking up. 'I did not lose my job. My contract wasn't renewed.'

A very pathetic technicality.

'And have you called that chap – the CEO? The one you were pals with?'

'His name is Niall.' I shrank back. 'And no, I haven't.'

'You should. From what I hear, you practically ran the place.'

'That's not how it works, Mum.'

She crossed her arms. 'You know, Ravi's storage unit at the industrial estate is free. You should look into it. It would make a marvellous gym.'

'Mum,' I sighed. 'You know why I can't.'

'Why not?' She put her hands on her hips. 'Your father agrees you'd be marvellous. We could help if you needed it—'

'You know I couldn't. You know why,' I said gently.

'Oh.' She waved a hand. 'You worry too much. We could find you a good accountant—'

'Mum,' I said, a little more sharply than I meant to. 'You know it's not just about an accountant.'

She sat on the bed beside me, running a hand down my matted hair.

'I know, love. I know you struggle with numbers and you always will. Your teachers told me as much.' She said it softly, and I almost wanted to cave into her chest and let her rock me. Her lips tugged up in the corners. 'But you have people to support you. People who love you. We wouldn't let you fail, you know that.'

A headache threatened at my temples. We'd had this discussion a handful of times. Mum and me. Dad and me. Mum, Dad and me. It always left me thrumming with anxiety, because they didn't get it. I couldn't run my own business. I couldn't even do my four times table, for fuck's sake. I couldn't count coins without the feeling that someone was grabbing me by the throat. I certainly couldn't be responsible for thousands of pounds, for wages, for suppliers relying on me to get it right.

I didn't want to risk that – risk that failure, or, even worse, risk having to rely on others. No, all I needed was to rely on myself and what I could do. And that certainly wasn't running my own business. But no matter how many times I explained this, it seemed like no one fully understood the all-encompassing shame I carried around about my disability. The looming feeling that it was silly, even trivial.

Oh, you're scared of the oogy-boogy numbers.

There was one person who took it seriously from the start.

But I couldn't say his name out loud.

'Thank you, Mum,' I said, hugging her around her middle, as I used to when I was a kid. 'But it will be fine. I promise. I'll find a new gym.'

I pulled back, gesturing around the room. 'Besides, I haven't got out of bed in a week and you want me to hop up and open a gym?'

Mum clicked her teeth. 'Well, I suppose it would be motivation to get up and get dressed.'

'I don't need my own gym. I need to apply for jobs.'

'Not in this mess, you won't.' She angled her head. 'Come on.'

She wasn't taking no for an answer. I flopped back on the bed and groaned.

Half an hour later, and some more mithering from my mum, I was clean-ish. I'd not bothered to wash my hair because who could be arsed? So I just threw it up in a bun. Meanwhile, Mum had begun cleaning the whole flat and made surprising progress. With a bin bag in hand, she cleared the pizza boxes and noodle cartons from the living room. I remembered crying as Julia Roberts stood before Hugh Grant, a wide, tragic smile on her face.

I'm just a girl. Standing in front of a boy, asking him to love her.

Love was bollocks.

'You look better,' Mum said, inspecting my bun. 'Could've washed your hair.'

'Mum!'

'All right, all right. Baby steps. You're lucky I didn't invite the whole lot up.'

I narrowed my eyes. 'Who is "the lot"?'

'Operation Sunshine. Ren said—' She stopped herself mid-sentence.

My stomach dropped. 'Ren? Mum...'

'No, no. He's not here. I know you two are like chalk and cheese... God knows why. You know, a lot of people thought you'd end up together one day.'

Heat rushed to my face, my heart kicking into overdrive. Does she know? I fought the urge to deflect – to steer us away from anything Ren-shaped.

'Right,' I said, forcing my voice sharper. 'Because bisexual women are just secretly into men. Only men.' I rolled my eyes. 'As if they're so annoyingly irresistible, we must all fancy them.'

Mum gave me a level look, folding her arms. 'That is not what I meant, and you know it. I don't give a shit who you shag.'

Guilt throbbed at my temples. I knew that. Mum and Dad had never blinked at who I dated. But I was raw, and the high horse was right there.

'I know, Mum,' I muttered.

She kissed my forehead. 'I just want you to be happy.'

Ugh. Cue more guilt.

'Now.' She pushed the door open. 'Chop, chop.'

We stepped into the stairwell and, when she opened the front door, five familiar figures waited. Amy, Claire, Gen, Kat, and her best friend, Willa.

'Operation Sunshine is go!' Mum declared, clapping. 'I'm off to work. Claire, see you at book club next week.'

'If I finish that dreadful World War II book,' Claire muttered.

'Peter is never picking again. It's a bloody doorstop,' Mum nodded, waving as she vanished into her car.

'What are you guys doing here?' I stared at the five women in front of me. 'It's a Tuesday morning.'

'Wednesday, actually, love,' Claire corrected. 'We took the day off.'

Amy smiled proudly. 'We cancelled our memberships after that toad sacked you.'

'And I've told anyone who will listen,' Gen said. 'Quinn is in bits, bless him. He sends his love.'

'Oh, and Mrs Daniels gave Craig a piece of her mind in the cafe the other day – in front of everyone!' Claire laughed. 'It was quite a scene. So don't think we've forgotten, Lydia.'

'Guys,' I said, my voice croaking. 'You don't have to do that. Cancel your memberships or become vigilantes. I don't want you to lose your love of the gym—'

'We can find another gym.' Gen cut me off.

'We can't find another Lydia,' Claire said, pulling me in to her side. 'You know, I never liked that man. He always looked so slimy.'

Claire let me go and I was pulled into a hug from Kat, the top of her curly ginger hair brushing my chin.

'We're so sorry, Lydia. Liam wanted to come,' Kat said. 'I told him it was girls-only.'

'I'd like to see him try reformer Pilates,' Willa said dryly.

I froze. I could almost smell the pine of the machines, the smell of eucalyptus and the soft click of springs.

My happy place, now turned into a reminder of what I'd lost.

I choked out. 'Guys, I appreciate this, but I'm not up for Pilates.'

'Ha!' Gen barked. 'Since when did you let us get away with that?'

Kat jabbed a finger. 'I did hungover yoga for you.'

'And when I cried over that guy with all the snakes—'

'Fifty snakes,' Gen and I said solemnly.

'*Fifty* snakes,' Amy shuddered. 'You picked me up. Made me rage-lift to Taylor Swift, and I forgot all about it. Now it's our turn. We are *your* Lydia today.'

I looked around at the expectant faces. All of them were waiting for my enthusiastic 'Hell, yes!' and I should be proud. They were preaching what I'd coached into them for the past few years – pure positivity. Look on the bright side of life. Get up and out, and seize the day. But it was one thing practising what I preached when I wanted nothing more than to climb back into my hovel and rot there for a few centuries.

Just smile, Lydia.

I could smile for one day and give my friends what they wanted – a revived Lydia with all the bells and whistles. I stood up straighter, plastered on a smile, and faced them.

'Okay, let's go.' I ignored how my stomach sank.

An hour later we pulled up to the Serenity Rooms, a spa hotel just outside Everly Heath. Then I was stretched out in Pilates, fed a full breakfast in the cafe, massaged within an inch of my life, and now we were all floating around a serene spa pool, even though I felt anything but relaxed. I'd had to explain everything that happened with Casey to a chorus of 'But you seemed so solid, so secure', and 'Her loss'. Now I was quietly torturing myself by imagining her in London – sitting outside an art gallery, sipping coffee across from a girl with no face. I'd always sort of known I wasn't quite educated enough for Casey. Not cultured. She was a creative, while I was loud, tall, and strong. Sometimes I felt like the barmaid from *Shrek*.

'How's the job hunt going, Lydia?' Kat's soft southern voice echoed off the tiles of the spa pool, oblivious to the way the question made my heart pound.

My friends turned towards me with interest. Gen's eyes snapped to mine from under the waterfall, where the pounding spray beat down on her shoulders. Claire looked up from her book, carefully lounging on the poolside bed to avoid getting her hair wet. Willa sat beside Kat, their feet dangling in the water. Amy rose out of the pool where she'd been floating serenely on her back, the motion sending ripples towards me.

I gulped and drifted towards the deep end, dragging my fingers through the water as if it could anchor me.

'Good,' I choked.

The waterfall shut off with a soft clunk. Silence filled the space, save for the gentle drip-drip-drip of water echoing off the tiled walls. Claire's gaze flicked back to her book, and she turned a page with a delicate swipe.

'Good,' Kat repeated, smiling awkwardly, her heart-shaped face tilting in concern.

'Good is good,' Willa offered with a nod, her tone light but not quite convincing.

The silence was going to kill me. I hated it. I had to fill every single bit of empty space in a conversation.

'Okay, fine. It's a disaster. I haven't applied for any jobs. I just can't bring myself to do it.'

'That's fine, Lydia,' Amy said. The youngest in our crew sounded the wisest as she said, 'It's been a traumatic experience being dropped at Momentum. It's okay to take some time off.'

'Amy's right.' Gen said, her voice deep and smooth. 'You need to take some time to think about what you want to do next.

When I quit my job to start Everly Ink, I took two months just to think about what I wanted.'

'Yes!' Amy said, glee entering her expression. 'You should open your own gym! It would be *brilliant*. A women-only gym.'

'I would be down for that,' Gen nodded.

'I would go to the gym more if you ran it, Lydia,' Kat smiled. 'And I'd happily design a space for you if you wanted.'

'We do websites at Horizon,' Willa offered.

Panic rose in my throat.

I croaked, 'I – I'm not opening my own gym.'

Amy deflated and even Gen, who kept her emotions under close guard, looked a little disappointed.

'I can't,' I laughed rustily. 'I'd never be able to run a business like you guys. I—'

Would I admit to it? Could I? My eyes landed on Kat, whose ADHD diagnosis later in life had shaken everything up, but she seemed to know herself better now. Why couldn't I be that brave? Kat gave me a light frown and cocked her head, as if to say, 'What's up?'

I hated that she was so intuitive. If my cousin could be so honest about her diagnosis, maybe I could too?

I took a deep breath. Something about the water was soothing, so I concentrated on the way it rippled as I dragged my hands through it.

'I have dyscalculia. I was diagnosed at school as a kid. It's a problem processing numbers, of any kind really. I can't tell the time. I can't read a clock. I know it sounds stupid—'

'It's not stupid,' I heard Kat murmur, and I gave her a soft smile, knowing she had battled these feelings too.

'Even basic addition. Or counting coins. I just can't.' I let out a shaky laugh, the kind you make when you're trying not to cry. 'And let's say I could do it and, by some miracle, the numbers are right. I still manage to convince myself I'm wrong.'

The others stayed quiet. Listening.

'Even with a calculator, I think I've messed it up somehow. Like I've pressed the wrong button or read the number backwards. Sixes and eights blur together. Twos and fours swap places. Everything just... gets mixed up.' I dragged a hand through my damp hair. 'So I get anxious. Really anxious. Like, heart-racing, can't-breathe anxious. I know that if I ran my own business, I'd wake up at three o'clock in the morning, convinced I've got something wrong. Something basic. Like I've invoiced someone for the wrong amount or scheduled a class at the wrong time.' I swallowed. 'And maybe no one else would notice. Or care. But I would. I always do.'

Claire placed down her book, bringing her legs to sit up. Amy and Gen floated a little closer, as if they wanted me to know they were there if I needed them.

'Does anyone else know?' Kat asked. 'I didn't really tell many people about my diagnosis.'

'Mum and Dad. And Ren,' I said, my voice breaking at the mention of his name. 'He was pretty good at school, so he used to help me with my maths homework.'

'Ren was good at maths?' Kat's eyebrows shot up. 'Wow!'

'Yes!' I snapped. 'He was a lot smarter than anyone gave him credit for.'

My face burned when I realised I had come to the defence of a man I couldn't stand to be in the same room as.

'Lydia, I'm sorry. I didn't mean—' Kat brought her hands up to her face. 'I can't believe I just said that. I'm sorry.'

'It's okay, it's okay.' I waved a hand. 'You didn't mean it.'

It was hard to stay mad at my cousin. She was so... herself. I was envious of the way she moved around in her body, with an air of confidence I don't think she realised she had, and the way she said what she thought. Even if it got her into trouble. I was always trying to keep myself back.

'I was terrible at school,' Kat explained. 'I guess I just presume everyone else hated it too. But that comment was ignorant.'

'Well,' I shot her a wry smile. 'I was the same, Cuz. At least when it came to the numbers.'

Kat's smile was tilted and knowing, like she was happy to have me in her exclusive club.

'So I can't open my own gym.' I turned back to Amy. 'And I'm yet to get a job. And I have rent to pay on my apartment, so it looks like I might need to move back in with Mum and Dad and, as much as I love them, they will drive me insane. So, in conclusion, no job, no girlfriend, no place to live.'

I gave a hysterical laugh, but it was sharp and jagged.

All I could hear was the drip, drip, drip of water.

Claire clapped her hands. 'Right! Only one solution. You're coming with me on the "Wild Women Walk" trip this week.'

I blinked. 'Claire…'

I didn't want to be surrounded by strangers, exposed to the elements like some kind of Victorian orphan. Torn away from my sofa, my sanctuary, and the deliciously bi-panic-inducing combo of McDreamy and Dr Addison Montgomery.

'We'll all go,' she said with finality.

Gen nodded. 'I'll find someone to take my appointments at the shop.'

'I could do with a break,' Amy added. She worked as a marketing manager for a law firm and they were pretty relaxed when it came to last-minute annual leave requests.

'Guys… you don't have to do this.'

'It'll be good for us all,' Claire said firmly.

My gaze darted to Willa and Kat. *Help!*

Willa raised a brow. 'I need to be back in London. Horizon needs me.'

Willa was struggling to get new clients at her graphic design agency, Horizon, and Kat mentioned she had had to make her two employees redundant recently. It had destroyed her and Willa was half-killing herself to make the business work. I suspected that her regular trips up to Everly Heath were a form of escapism for her.

Kat chimed in, 'Busy at the shop. And Abigail and I have plans.'

Traitors.

Claire, Gen, and Amy all turned to me expectantly, as if I was about to hold up my score on *Strictly Come Dancing*. Spoiler: it was a big, fat zero from me. But they'd gone to so much trouble today. They'd planned a whole day to pull me out of my rut. So I should be grateful, right? Who was to say a hiking trip wouldn't help? Did I have a better plan? I'd just admitted I had no idea what I was doing. I could hardly claw back those words now. If I wasn't such a pushover – if I could quiet the ravenous guilt gnawing at my insides – I might be more like Willa or Kat. I'd say, 'Hell, no!' I'd tell them camping was my actual nightmare, because it was. I'd remind them I like my workouts in a perfectly air-conditioned room, earbuds in, heart rate monitored, no insects in sight.

But I wasn't that person.

I was a stupid, cowardly people-pleaser.

I dipped under the surface of the water, smoothing my wet hair back, then faced the girls.

Just smile, Lydia.

'"Wild Women Walk", here we come.'

The girls whooped, Amy's arms coming round to hug me. Claire launched into all the equipment we would need to buy. And I ignored the way my stomach sank like a stone straight to the bottom of the pool for the second time that day.

Chapter Five

Ren

I *was* enjoying a quiet pint at the social club, disassociating as much as mentally possible, when Jack's smug face appeared in front of me.

'God, you look shit,' he grinned, setting his pint down on my table. Internally, I groaned. It wasn't that I hated Jack. He was a good guy, and I've known him decades now. He'd worked for my dad since he was barely out of school, eventually stepping up to run the business after Liam left to open Lily's with me. These days, he practically *was* the business – and he was proving trustworthy and reliable. His face was tanned and weather-lined, and he had the kind of crooked grin that spelled trouble. His hair was sun-streaked and always messy, as if he'd just taken off a hard hat. Or more likely rolled out of someone's bed.

Not many people realised Jack was a few years older than Liam – so he was in his mid-thirties now, though he never acted like it. He was more accident-prone than an apprentice, and spent a lot of time in A&E. But, like Liam, he worked ridiculous hours, drove a knackered Land Rover he refused to part with, and had three older sisters who half the town fancied at one point or another.

But I could do without Jack today – with all of his energy and optimism.

Until now, it had just been me and Peter, the local curmudgeonly grouch, and I'd been pleased with that for once.

Peter sat at the table opposite, a scowl on his lined face. He looked how I felt. And, other than Peter's burning stare, it was uncharacteristically quiet for a Saturday night. Usually, there would be terrible karaoke or a crooning performer in a shiny waistcoat. Maybe a darts competition. But I'd been in luck. It was quiet and I could sulk in peace.

'Who is this?' Jack asked as he gestured to the dog lying beside me. Jack's face morphed into glee. 'Pat got to you, didn't she? She tried to drop this one off at my house a few weeks ago.'

'Great,' I said sarcastically. 'I'm second choice for a dog I didn't want.'

Peanut's head lifted, as Jack leaned down to rub her belly. She rolled over, exposing the pale fur of her belly. I'd arrived back at my apartment to find Peanut sitting on my sofa, lightly panting. She had an expectant, eager expression on her face, as if she'd been waiting for me to get home. Pat had used the spare key I kept under my doormat for emergencies, to let herself in, drop off Peanut, her bed, and a month's worth of food. I'd been furious, determined to call her and give her a piece of my mind, until Peanut cantered over to me, giving my hand a welcoming lick, and that was it.

I was a goner.

Now Peanut was stretched out on the red, patterned carpet of the club, content after our muddy walk and a handful of pork scratchings.

I hated the way it made me feel... useful. Worthy.

'God, she's cute,' Jack smiled. 'What's her name?'

'Peanut.'

Jack paused, his sharp blue eyes meeting mine, then burst into laughter. I sighed as Jack lowered himself into the seat next to me, still laughing at my expense.

'You can't be shouting Peanut across the park, mate.' Jack wiped his eyes. 'Why don't you rename her? What about Pippa? Pickle. Poppy.'

Peggy.

The name hit me, laced with a memory from ten-year-old me. Lydia leaving her worn, well-loved toy on the bus. Her face distraught. So I ran. She shouted for me to stop but I kept going, sprinting after the bus to the next stop. I launched myself on board, ignoring the driver's protests, and retrieved the floppy plush dog. Then, I reunited it with its smiling owner.

I'd felt like Tom Cruise that day. But, you know, without the religious cult stuff.

'Peggy.'

Peanut – or now, Peggy – lifted her head.

'There you go. Peggy is much better than Peanut,' Jack said, scratching behind her ears. She sighed as if she'd been waiting her whole life for this exact moment.

'Traitor,' I muttered.

Jack chuckled. His dirty-blond hair was cropped short, his usual crooked grin looked as if he had pulled a prank and was waiting for you to find out. But recently, he had an air of confidence as if he'd found his purpose. Not that he needed it.

'What are you doing here?' I asked, 'Haven't seen you in the club for a while.'

'Meeting your brother for a catch-up about work,' Jack said, taking a gulp of his pint.

As if he'd been summoned, the social club door swung open and Liam strode in, eyes searching, until he found Jack at my table. He nodded and ordered his drink with Sandra. I bit my lip. Jack and Liam were going to talk shop about HBC and, after he'd shut down my idea for Everly Heath Farm, I wasn't in the mood to hear my brother's demonstrative orders about what Jack should or shouldn't do. Liam couldn't help but stick his oar in, even though he didn't work with Jack any more.

'Ey up. Pat got you in the end then.' Liam plonked his pint of

Coke Zero on our table, pulling up a chair next to Jack. Peggy sat up, nuzzling her head into Liam's legs, and he gave her a scratch behind her ears. My eyes narrowed.

Double traitor.

'You can keep the lecture about how a dog is a huge responsibility to yourself, big brother,' I muttered, sounding as petulant as I felt.

Liam's eyebrows rose and Jack stifled a laugh.

'He's been seething away since I got here. What's got you so miserable, Lawrence?' Jack cocked an eyebrow. 'Someone woke up on the wrong side of the bed.'

'Yeah, your mum's.'

Jack laughed, and I was envious of how open and free he was. I used to be like that. I could pinpoint exactly when that stopped. When I boarded a flight to Mexico and made the cataclysmic mistake of leaving *her* behind.

'Come on then,' Liam said gruffly. 'What's up?'

'We're sharing now, are we?'

Liam shrugged. 'What can I say? Kat and Abi have made me more open.'

I huffed. 'Sure. How is my niece?'

I was asking because I'd not seen Abi in weeks. But also so I could steer Liam away from asking questions I didn't want to answer.

'Currently at a paint-and-sip party with Kat and Yas.'

My eyebrows shot up. 'Mum and Stepmum. Wow. Very modern.'

From what I could sense, Kat and Yasmin hadn't started out as friends. Yasmin, my brother's ex-childhood-sweetheart had been protective of Abigail, and was worried about bringing another woman into her life, for her to leave it. But once Yas realised Kat wasn't going anywhere, they seemed to be getting on like a house on fire.

'Oh, they're the best of friends now,' Liam muttered into his pint. 'Terrifying is what it is. They gang up on me, the three of them.'

I chuckled, despite myself. I could picture the three of them wrapped around my brother's little finger. Particularly Abigail, who was playing her part of surly teenager so well I was sure the academy would be in touch any day now. Suffice to say, I was proud.

'She still rinsing you for that face stuff? Pissed Giraffe?'

'Drunk Elephant. She's rinsed my bank account and I'm ninety-nine per cent sure she doesn't need the stuff.'

'Well, isn't that lovely? Everyone playing happy families.'

Jack and Liam exchanged looks as I gulped my pint.

'Right. This is an intervention,' Liam announced. 'Starting now, we're having a very frank conversation about your... mental health.'

'My mental health,' I repeated.

'Yes. We've done it before. So we're doing it again,' Liam said, in a strangely formal way, like he'd prepared a speech.

Liam wasn't wrong. We did talk about my mental health, now and then. He took me to the GP in the worst bouts of my depression when I was younger. He kept me fed and watered through it, even when I didn't have the energy to bring a fork to my mouth. I couldn't deny that one of my brother's best qualities was how he looked after the people he loved, even if he rarely understood me.

'No depression. I'm still on my meds, and they work better than the ones I was on a few years ago.'

Peggy sat up, nudging my thigh with her nose. I sighed and scratched her, the warmth of her solid presence grounding me, even just a little.

Liam nodded. 'Good.'

We took a sip of our drinks.

Jack glanced between us. 'That's it? That's the big intervention, big strong men talk about their feelings?'

Liam shrugged. 'He said he's fine. And I believe him.'

'We made an agreement years ago that as long as he knew the necessary details, then he wouldn't pry in my head.'

Jack looked at us like we'd grown four heads, respectively.

'You can't be serious. That's all you're going to say?' Jack pointed at me. 'He's not depressed. He's lovesick, Liam. It's Lydia.'

I hissed, shooting looks over at the bar. 'Will you keep your voice down?'

'What? 'Cos her mum is six feet away from us? Newsflash, mate. She already knows. Everyone does. Everyone is talking about how fucking weird the vibe is between you. Pat almost scheduled a super-secret emergency meeting when you came back so that everyone was on the same page, but it got cancelled 'cos of the rain.'

My gaze swung to Liam. 'Did you know about this?'

Liam looked anywhere but at me.

'You did. Some brother you are.'

'Look – I know what it's like being under the scrutiny of this bloody town. Last year, they were salivating whenever Kat and I were in the same room. Plotting to get us together.'

'But you *are* together,' I shouted, my fist landing on the table. Liam's and Jack's eyes widened in shock. I dropped my voice. 'There is no hope for me and Lydia. Case closed. She doesn't even want me as a friend, let alone… anything else.'

Liam's eyebrows shot up. 'And you want… anything else?'

Jack raised his hands. 'Of course he does. Are you blind? Those two have been joined at the hip since school for a reason. They've been pussy-footing around it for years now, but everyone knows they're meant for each other. You could even ask Peter and the miserable bastard would agree.'

Our heads swivelled to Peter, who grunted, and lifted his huge newspaper, blocking him from sight.

'See? Peter's a big softie really. And Ren's been in love with her for years, even if he didn't realise it. And I'd guess she is with him too.'

I gave a humourless laugh. 'You're wrong. So wrong.'

Liam's voice was low. 'I've just never heard you admit it. I suspected, obviously. But I'd figured you were just messing with her. Flirting.'

My stomach sank. This was my brother, and this was his low opinion of me. Some dickhead who'd mess with Lydia just for the fun of it.

But isn't that what you did? A dark, gleeful voice echoes around my head.

Yes, I did. I deserve this. I deserve this feeling of worthlessness.

Lean into it. Feel it. The voice chanted.

'You did something.' By some miracle, Liam's perception decided to rear its head. 'You made a mistake and now you don't know what to do.'

'Bingo. Would you like your prize? It's a front-row ticket to my pathetic life.'

'God, you're dramatic.' Jack's lip twitched, but he had the sense not to laugh directly in my face.

'Have you tried to fix it? Make it up to her?'

'Liam, she won't even speak to me. How am I supposed to make it up to her when she won't stay in the same room? She's literally nicking the rota off Kat just to avoid me at Lily's – tell me that's not extreme. And if we do accidentally bump into each other, she keeps me at arm's length with that sunshine routine she saves for charity fundraisers on the high street.'

'Come on. You've got to think bigger. When I wanted Kat to move up here, I didn't just *say* it – I renovated her house based on her designs and built her a studio in the garden for her business. It wasn't about promises. It was about action. I gave her a reason to stay.'

I wanted to point out that, judging by the look on Kat's face when she looked at Liam, she would have lived in a yurt if it meant being with him.

'One word,' Jack announced. 'Grand gesture.'

'That's two words, genius.'

Liam nodded. 'Grand gesture is the way forward.'

'If I go with some big grand gesture right now, when she can barely look at me, she'll destroy me. No. No way.'

Jack chewed his lips, and Liam was thinking so hard he looked constipated.

'Fine. You're probably right. But you need to find a way to get through to her.'

'Pssst.'

The hissing sound had all of us looking around the room.

'Psssssst.'

'Are you hearing that?'

'Oi!' Sandra barked, coming out from behind the bar. 'I was trying to be subtle, but you lot have thick skulls.'

Sandra wore her half-pinny to keep her smart trousers clean from spilt beer. Her short, quaffed blonde hair was in its usual style, and today, she wore a striped white-and-black jumper and a scowl on her face, as if we'd ruined her fun.

'All right, Poirot.' Liam's voice was laced with humour. 'What's up?'

'Ren.' Sandra angled her head. 'A word.'

She said the last word firmly, transporting me back to when I refused to eat my greens or when Lydia and I had stolen sips of port from the sideboard in their front room.

'She – she wants to speak to me?'

'She said your name, so I'd say yeah.'

'Go on. I'll watch the dog.'

Liam took Peggy's lead and shooed me up from my seat. I walked like a zombie over to Sandra, heavy-footed. It wasn't that we weren't talking, per se. Sandra had welcomed me back from my travels with a big hug, demanding she wanted to hear stories from my trip. But we both were navigating around the Lydia-sized elephant in the room. We were both ignoring it, probably out of respect for our past. Sandra had been like a surrogate mum for me after Mum died. Sandra picked us up from football practice, cooked us tea and made sure that Dad had the 'birds and the bees' talk with us, only to repeat it for good measure, ignoring the hands over our ears in protest. She kept Dad's head above water after losing Mum, the love of his life, to cancer. She brought food and did the washing when Dad couldn't get out of bed.

There was a real, deep history between our families that meant the rupture – the crack between Lydia and me – was more obvious. More painful.

Sandra shuffled into the little kitchen at the rear of the bar, where Liam helped prepare food for events now and then. It was a tight space, and being in such close quarters with a woman whose wrath I'd faced more than once was a little intimidating.

Why did I feel 12 years old again?

'I've had enough,' she announced and shoved a letter into my hand. 'Here.'

I glanced down at the letter, my brows drawn together.

'What is this?'

'It's a ticket to a hiking trip. They leave on Monday.'

'A hiking trip?' I racked my brain for the missing details. 'What hiking trip?'

'The one Lydia and her friends are going on on Monday. You'll need to buy some supplies, but I've covered the cost of your ticket. You should have enough time to pack your stuff and drive to the Peaks on Monday.'

No. Surely Sandra isn't serious.

'Sandra, I can't just join on to a hiking trip, without telling her. Lydia doesn't want me there.'

Sandra raised a finger at me, her eyes flashing. My stomach dropped through the floorboards into the cellar below.

'You. Will. Fix. This. Lawrence Hunter,' she went pink. 'You will fix whatever you broke. I'm sick of it. We're all sick of it. I don't care if you're friends or an item. Yes, don't act so surprised. I'm not a bleeding idiot. I don't care how or what you do, but you will make it up to her and bring back my daughter.' Her voice grew thick. 'You will swear that you'll make her happy, whether as a friend or more. Because she needs you, you blithering idiot. You need each other. She doesn't want to admit it and I don't want to either, but she missed you. She misses you. And I don't know all the details – I don't want to, frankly, because I'm worried I'd kill my best friend's son, and God knows I swore to Lily I'd look after you – but I know you messed something up. So you'll fix whatever you've broken. Swear it to me.'

My throat was dry, my eyes stung.

'Ren. Swear it to me.'

'I swear.'

Sandra wiped the back of her hand across her face, plastering on a smile her daughter would be proud of, before gently patting my face.

'Good. Thank you.' She kissed my cheek before exiting the little kitchen, leaving me with no choice but to follow her wishes.

'What was that about?' Liam asked, as I sat back down, a little dazed.

'Have you heard about this hike Lydia is going on?'

'Kat mentioned it. Something about dodging a bullet.' Liam huffed. 'A big group of them are going – some of Lydia's friends from the gym. Gen, Claire and – who was the other girl?'

'Amy,' I said. My bones felt all soft and weird. 'And me.'

Liam coughed into his Coke Zero. 'You're going?'

Jack chuckled. 'Well, that's something.'

My eyes widened. 'I – I can't go, can I? I mean, we have Lily's to run—'

'Hey, we can sort something out if you want to go—'

'No,' I scoffed. 'This is ridiculous. I can't join her on some hiking trip like a stalker. I'm going to tell Sandra I can't do it.'

I rose from my seat until Liam pulled me down in a sharp tug that reminded me of playing (losing) touch rugby with him when I was a kid. Liam's eyes were wide, as if I was missing the point.

'Sounds like one hell of a grand gesture, Ren,' Liam said slowly.

'Or a way of getting yourself chopped up into little pieces and buried in the woods,' Jack grinned, shrugging. 'But yeah. Let's go with grand gesture.'

'You're serious? You think this is a good idea?'

Liam lifted an eyebrow. 'Have you got anything better? Are you going to keep moping around for the rest of your life? Or are you going to try and win her back?'

For the first time since I came back to Everly Heath – and saw Lydia's cold, distant expression – something stirred in my chest.

Win her back.

I repeated the words in my head, turning them over. Vignettes juddered to life, like an old cinema reel. Lydia on a trail, the sun turning her hair golden. A backpack strapped to her, that wide smile breaking across her face as she turned to find me behind her.

The feeling grew so much that I could finally put a name to it.

Hope.

Chapter Six

Lydia's Diary, Nine Years Old

Dear Diary,

I pushed Liam over today in the garden. He was arguing with Ren about something, and then he called me Ren's little girlfriend – but in a mean way. Ren went all pink and looked upset, and I got SO angry.

So I pushed him.

He stumbled back, and I really wanted him to fall in the grass – but he's 12, and I'm only 9, so I don't think I was strong enough.

One day, though.

One day, I'll be big enough to beat him up properly.

Love,

Lydia.

Lydia

The knock on the motel door came at 6.30 in the morning.

'Coming!' I mumbled around my hair bobble, shoving my hair into a high ponytail.

Not my best work, but I was late. Last night, the group of us arrived at the Peak Inn, and Mandy, the hike leader, introduced us. The inn was a bustling pub, with low beam ceilings, deer antlers, and locals sipping pints of dark ale. The group of us –

eight women in total – were staying in the cosy rooms above the pub. Some had to share but, luckily, I'd bagged a single room with a little, log-burning stove. Blue and green plaid cushions and curtains gave it a cosy, worn-in look. Once we'd checked in and dropped our bags in our rooms, we went downstairs for a pub dinner and introduced ourselves to the rest of the group.

Unsurprisingly, Claire, Gen, Amy, and I made up a big chunk of the group. Mandy was in her forties, with shoulder-length, dark brown hair and an athletic build that said she hosted hiking trips for a living. Then there was Amara, an environmentalist who had recently accepted a job in conservation at the Peak District National Park. She was short and slim, with a soft-spoken voice. She seemed a bit shy to me, but also the type that would love to quietly observe every detail of the trail. Jade and Clara were the only couple on the hike, so they arrived together. Jade had deep-brown skin, wild curls, and a camera slung over her shoulder. She was a freelance photographer, Mandy told us excitedly, as she was always looking for more photos of the trips. Her partner, Freya, was tall and composed. She spoke with a soft German accent, had poker-straight blonde hair and a calm demeanour, which made sense when she shared that she was a psychologist.

We ate and drank and, despite Mandy's warnings to get an early night, I stayed up too late with Amy and Gen, the three of us a little giddy, as if our parents had let us have a sleepover. Claire had headed to bed with the rest of the crew, much too sensible to stay up with us.

While I wasn't hungover this morning, I couldn't deny that my tongue was stuck to the roof of my mouth, and there was a light throb at my temples that said I was almost 30 and really shouldn't be surprised I got a hangover after four pints of lager.

I shoved open my creaky hotel door to find Claire, a massive backpack on her shoulders, and her short grey hair perfectly blow-dried.

'You ready, love?'

'Yes, yes. Coming.' I headed back into the room and hastily threw my thermal sweater over my head.

'Oh, I don't think you'll need that,' Claire said, her mothering tone coming through. 'It rained last night, but the sun is coming through this morning. Spring is in the air.'

'About time,' I mumbled.

As much as I loved Christmas, I hated the weather that January and February brought. I was over grey skies and drizzling rain. It was early April and, finally, we were blessed with some decent weather. And I was excited to see it on these hikes up mountains and across fields in the Peaks.

'Okay, I'm ready,' I beamed, my backpack on and my shoes tied. 'Are you and the girls?'

'Girls.' With a weird undertone, Claire repeated, 'Yes, the *girls* are all ready.'

'Okay then, let's go.'

'Lydia, before we go—'

'Come on, I'm already late.' I shooed Claire out of my room, locking the door behind me.

'Wait a second—'

'Let's walk and talk.'

I strode down the corridor, a renewed excitement bubbling in my arms and legs. As we wove through the pub and on to the gravel carpark, I noticed the girls had convened on the grass outside the main hotel building, with a gorgeous view of the peaks behind them. The morning smelled like spring and promise – grass, moss, and fresh air. I drew in a deep breath, closing my eyes as if I was in a film.

Yes. I was the main character today.

'Lydia, would you slow down?' Claire complained, on my heels. 'I need to talk to you.'

The girls were laughing – no, giggling. They were giggling.

'What are they laughing at?' I frowned.

'Well, I tried to tell you—'

'Tried to tell me what—'

Amy moved out of the way and I saw exactly what – or who – was making the commotion. Dark brown eyes snapped to mine like magnets.

Ren stood in the centre of Amy, Genevieve and the other ladies. Amara and Jade were crouched in front of a little golden dog that looked like a golden retriever crossed with a corgi, fussing over her. My heart began to pound, my head a little dizzy.

Ren wore a casual, lazy smirk that dropped an inch when he saw me standing there. His eyes flickered around me, like he was scanning my outfit. He wore all black. Black walking trousers, jumper, backpack, and black and green walking boots. His hair was coiffed perfectly, and the wind was his biggest fan as it ran through it. He was dressed to walk. To hike. But he couldn't be on *our* walk. There was no way.

'Ren.'

I hated the way my words sounded raspy.

'Ah, so you've met Ren.' The programme manager, Mandy, came striding over to the green, smiling. 'He's a last-minute addition, but I didn't think you ladies would mind another camper. Especially since he told me he's a professional bartender and has his travel cocktail shaker with him.'

Mandy delivered the news as if we'd won the lottery. Jade grinned, nudging Freya, and Amara was smiling softly, but her eyes were shifting between Ren and me, as if she noticed the energy shift.

But all I could focus on was one word.

Camper.

He was going to camp with us.

'He can't come with us,' I blurted out.

Ren's eyebrows shot up. The golden dog stopped panting, its eyebrows quirking. Do dogs even have eyebrows? Well, this one did. And it looked forlorn, as if they'd picked up on the words.

The girls – my girls – looked at me with a mixture of sympathy and concern.

The smile I plastered on teetered on manic.

'It's called "Wild Women Walk",' I gave a fake, rich laugh. 'Not "Wild Women Walk with a Man".'

'Well,' Mandy frowned, aware there was more to this situation than seemed on the surface. 'We don't have rules against men joining the groups, as long as most on the trips are women and the men joining us know this is an open, safe and accepting environment for women.'

'And he's agreed to that?' I lowered my pointed hand, realising I was revealing too much.

Just smile, Lydia.

'Yes,' Ren replied. 'Of course I have, Lyd.'

My eye twitched, and I stared at Ren, smiling, whilst I tried to imbue all of my rageful thoughts through his thick skull. This can't be happening.

'Mandy,' Ren smiled. Mandy gave a soft smile. Ugh, she practically melted. I wanted to stick pins in my eyes.

'Do you think I could have a minute with Lydia before we head off?'

'Of course.'

'Come on,' Ren said, pointing his head towards the tree at the edge of the hotel carpark. It provided shade and was far enough away that no one could hear us.

'What makes you think I'll go anywhere with you?' I whispered through a smile.

Ren's face grew closer, his smell enveloping me. 'Lydia, come on. I'm not some big scary monster. It's just me.'

'Fine.'

We stalked over to another tree in the middle of the green, feeling the eyes of the women behind us.

I whipped around. 'What are you doing here?'

Ren's eyes shifted around. 'I'm coming on the trip.'

'Why?'

'Why what?'

Just smile, Lydia.

'*Why* are you coming on this trip?'

'Because—' he pulled his hair. 'I wanted to get out of Everly Heath, just like you. I could do with a new challenge.'

I knew this expression – the eye shifting, the frenetic energy, the vague statements. Something had happened and he wanted to escape. I knew better than anyone.

'Surprise, surprise. You're on the run again. What are you avoiding now?'

Ren's voice was steady and sure when he said, 'I'm not running. I told you I'm not going anywhere again.'

'So why are you here?'

Ren cursed under his breath. 'I said I'd find a way to make it up to you.'

My eyes widened. Surely this wasn't happening. I was dreaming. This was something I was going to wake up from in a cold sweat.

'You don't have to look so horrified, Lydia,' Ren's voice warbled. 'I just know you've been going through a hard time, and I thought you might need some… support.'

Ren scratched his jaw and shifted his feet.

I folded my arms. 'And following me around like a lost puppy will do that, huh?'

That riled him out of his coy performance. Good.

He said, through a clenched jaw, 'Well, you've been avoiding me for months, so I'd say it's worth a shot.'

'That's a little pathetic, don't you think?'

'Almost as pathetic as stealing my rota so you can avoid me.'

My stomach lurched. Shit. I didn't know he knew. I'd told Kat to keep discreet.

Ren said, low and rumbly, 'You think I wouldn't notice? A little childish, don't you think, Lydia?'

My cheeks flushed, blood rushed in my ears. 'Oh, give over, Ren. I'm allowed to avoid you if I want to. You made your own bed. Or should I say, left mine?'

I would never usually bring up *that* night. But the thing about Ren was he was always able to expose me like a live wire. He could tease laughs out of me in the most inappropriate moments. He could pull the truth from me, even when I insisted I was fine. And, mostly, he could rile even the most easy-going people-pleaser who never wanted to rock the boat.

Ren's eyes flashed and I knew instantly I'd walked straight into the trap.

His voice dropped, low, rough, and sinful. 'You say you're over it, that we're fine, but then you throw that night back in my face. Tell me, Sunshine… is it still in your head? Like it's in mine?'

Heat surged up my neck, traitorous and hot. I hated the way it gave me away.

'In your dreams,' I bit out. 'I haven't given it a second thought.'

His mouth curved – not quite a smile, more like a challenge. 'Liar,' he murmured. 'Your blush says otherwise.'

At some point we had drawn closer, our faces mere inches apart, as we argued in hushed voices. Our chests were rising and falling. At some point, I tilted my head to meet his gaze. And, God – his eyes burned into me, intense and unyielding. It made me think of the last time I was this close to him. And, before I could stop myself, my gaze flickered down to the fullness of his lips. I couldn't help but think about the last time I'd touched them, in the dark of my bedroom, under covers – shit!

Don't go there, Lydia!

I glanced up to see Ren's mouth curved up at the edges of his lips.

Ren leaned in, emboldened by my stupid mistake. I should have stepped back, I should have moved, but I couldn't, because I was pinned by the way his eyes were tracing my face.

He murmured, 'Good to see you've dropped the sunshine act,

Lydia.' He chuckled. 'You don't get it, do you? I want your anger. Firstly, I deserve it. Secondly, it means you still feel something. And thirdly, I know, deep down, that you want to shout at me. You want to bang your fists against my chest and shout.'

I clenched my fists like, on demand, I was ready to do just that. I consciously relaxed them. He wasn't the boss of me.

Ren stepped back, and I almost sighed at the relief of it. 'And I'm prepared to wait for you to do just that.'

I flushed. He didn't get to make these big, sweeping statements that made me feel as if we knew each other. I felt as if I was losing this conversation. I needed to get back on an even playing field.

'What's your end game here, Ren?' It was my turn to step forward into his space. 'Do you think I'm going to fall back into bed with you? Like you're *so* irresistible, that I'd forgive and forget the last two years?' I scoffed. 'You're deluded if you think that's ever going to happen—'

Ren cut me off. 'I want your friendship back, Lydia. Nothing more than that. I know I fucked up when I left. Massively. But when I heard about you going on this trip, I knew you'd be dreading it.'

I rose to full height. 'I was not dreading it.'

Ren huffed. 'Come on, Lyds. I know you. You're terrible with the outdoors. You'll smash the hike, sure. But the camping.' He raised an eyebrow. 'No posh showers out here, Sunshine.

'I'll be fine,' I said through clenched teeth.

'I know you will be,' Ren said in an annoyingly soft voice. 'But... well, I thought if I was here and if I could help you through it... I don't know.' He palmed his forehead, like he was trying to find the source of this stupid decision. 'We used to help each other through shit times before. I thought maybe I could do that now.' He scratched the back of his neck, a self-deprecating smile tugging at his lips. 'Like I could help you pitch your tent?' He winced, his eyes squeezing shut. 'God, that sounds so dumb now that I say it out loud.'

Ren stepped back, the sad smile on his face looking more painful than anything. It was clear he didn't know what to say any more.

'This was stupid. I'll go,' he muttered, his voice quieter. 'I don't know what I was thinking, honestly.'

Ren brushed past me.

I squeezed my eyes shut. I hated that I felt myself soften towards him, this man who used to mean everything to me – the comfort, the home and fun. But he was also the one who had broken my heart. And still... I couldn't look at his awkward, pained face and not soften, just a little. It was like he was in my bloodstream.

I turned and called out, 'The dog.'

He froze. I saw the muscles in his back shift before he turned around, a neutral expression on his face.

I looked at the little golden dog, still being fussed over by the ladies.

'Is it yours?'

'Pat decided I should get a dog,' he said dryly. 'Who was I to disagree?'

I gave a huff, nodding. Of course Pat had something to do with it.

'Her name is Peggy.'

My eyes snapped to his and I could swear his ears went pink.

Grainy memories developed before my eyes. A little brown toy dog, worn but cherished. The scruffy thing had seen it all – teddy-bear picnics, dirty puddles, classrooms of children. Then, one day, I left it on the bus. I burst into tears. Ren hadn't hesitated, sprinting to not one but two bus stops, ignoring Mum shouting after him. He was determined to catch the driver and rescue it. He retrieved it, running back to me, clutching the dog like a prize. His grin had been so wide, so proud, that I'd broken the sacred ten-year-old rule of 'boys are gross' and kissed him on the cheek.

'Peggy,' I muttered idly. The toy's name had been Peggy.

Ren's brown eyes flickered with awareness as if we were both watching the same film.

As if we'd summoned her with her name, Peggy appeared, having wrestled out of the grip of Amy, who shouted an apology. Ren crouched down and Peggy wagged her tail, licking his face.

'She's naughty. But she's cute, so she gets away with murder.' Ren ran a hand through her long fur. His eyes were soft and gooey. God, he was gone for this dog already.

I crouched down too, unable to resist her big brown eyes and panting face.

'She is very cute. Aren't you?' Peggy nuzzled her nose into my palm. 'Yes, you are.'

I could feel Ren's eyes on me.

'Peggy is another reason I came on the trip. She loves off-lead adventures, and her recall is good, so Mandy said she could just canter along with us. Wales and Scotland might be a bit of a push, but the Peaks is dog-friendly enough.'

Peggy rolled on to her back, her stubby legs waving in the air, her tongue lolling out. I rubbed her belly and her tail wagged. Shit! I was a sucker for a cute dog. If I sent Ren packing, Peggy would probably go with him. Her sweet, panting face might be the only thing keeping me from losing it out in the wilderness.

I stood up, my hands on my hips. Ren stood too, his hand wrapped around Peggy's lead.

'Did you bring enough food for her?'

Ren's lips quirked. 'Yes.'

'Treats?'

He nodded, his smile shy but genuine, making something inside me stir despite myself.

I sighed, 'Then you can't disappoint her. You can come along. But,' I raised a finger, daring him to challenge me, 'that doesn't mean we're friends, Lawrence. I'm serious. *Stop* smiling. Give me my space and I'll give you yours. If you can respect that, we'll make it through this without your murder making the front page of the *Everly Heath Gazette*. You know Bob loves a story.'

'New carpets at Everly Heath High was the last front page,' Ren said, his eyes glinting in amusement. 'Just think how excited he would be about my death.'

I hummed. Joking about Bob and his boring stories was teetering too near friendly for my liking.

'We're in agreement then. Keep out of my way and I'll keep out of yours.'

I ignored the way his words echoed back to me.

I want your friendship back, Lydia.

I ignored the way it made my palms sweaty, turned sharply on my heel towards the group of women, examining trees and guzzling water like they hadn't been watching our every move.

God, I was going to get a ton of questions after this.

I looked back at Ren.

'Promise me one more thing.'

'Anything.'

'Don't tell me you've missed me.'

His face softened, that unreadable look flickering behind his eyes.

'Lyd—'

'Just promise.'

He muttered something under his breath, something about promises, but I couldn't catch the words.

Then he exhaled, long and slow, and met my gaze.

'I promise.'

Chapter Seven

Ren

What the fuck was I thinking? The question looped in my head as we set off from the hotel carpark into the Peaks.

I'd followed her on to this trip like a dog, panting after her, surrendering what was left of my dignity, only for her to walk six feet ahead of me at all times. All I could do was stare at her swinging blonde ponytail, knowing exactly how those silky strands felt between my fingers. This was pathetic.

Sandra and I were going to have serious words when I got back. She had conveniently left out that this was a women-only hike. Wild Women Walk. I'd wanted to groan and leg it back to my car the second I realised I was *that guy*. I was the guy crashing their space. I'd been ready to pack my bags and vanish before Lydia even spotted me. But Mandy had smiled and waved me over. She hadn't seemed fazed when I turned up. If anything, she'd looked... expectant.

Like someone had tipped her off.

My eyes narrowed. Sandra. Meddling as usual.

Plus, I was a goner as soon as Lydia's eyes met mine — God, she looked so riled. Gloriously furious. And I couldn't help myself. I had to stay.

But it didn't mean this wasn't bloody awkward, though, as I trailed alongside the eight other women, wondering if I was the giant elephant on the hike.

The saving grace so far was Peggy. She was my icebreaker, as she wove between everyone, tail wagging. She stopped every few feet to sniff a tree stump or patch of grass as we left the gravel and hit the path, wide fields stretching out ahead.

At least someone was having fun.

The rest of the group was welcoming, thankfully. Freya and Jade asked me what I did for a living, and commented on the weather. Classic British chat, although Freya had a German lilt to her voice. Amara trailed next to us, quiet but observing, her hand passing along the shrubs and bushes as we went. Amy, Gen, and Claire kept their distance from me so far, and I couldn't blame them. They probably hated me.

Mandy brought everyone to a stop in a clearing and clapped her hands. Her bright, encouraging smile could give Lydia a run for her money.

'All right, everyone, listen up! Today's a relatively easy start, but we've got some challenges ahead. We'll head through Edale Valley and up to Jacob's Ladder. It's a rocky ascent, so please watch where you walk. The climb up might get your legs burning, but the view from the top will make it worth it. Remember, this is the first location and the easiest. It's designed to warm you up and prepare you for more challenging hikes in Snowdonia and the Highlands.'

She paused, making eye contact with a few of us. 'But we're not in a race. We're in the peaks for another four days, so take it slow and enjoy the walk. We'll stop for a break at the top, have snacks, take pictures, and then continue along the ridge towards our campsite. The terrain's tricky in places, so watch your step. All right, let's get going. The sooner we hit the top, the sooner we can sit back and enjoy the view.'

Excited conversation rippled through the group and I felt a stab of loneliness. Lydia laughed with her friends. God, I hoped I'd made the right bet coming on this trip.

Grand gesture, Liam had said.

'So what's your deal?'

The voice beside me was deep and smooth, cutting through the sound of boots on gravel as we wound through Edale. The trail was well-trodden, the path stretching ahead.

I turned to see Gen beside me. She'd appeared without a sound and, from the look on her face, she wasn't here to make friends. Gen had light brown skin, long dark hair that was braided today, and an expression that said she was perpetually unimpressed with you. Or maybe that was just for me.

I cleared my throat. My palms were already sweating. 'What do you mean?'

Gen levelled me a look. 'Don't play dumb, pretty boy.'

'You think I'm pretty, huh?'

'If you break her heart again, I will kill you,' Gen said, low. 'And I'm very good at making things look accidental. It's amazing how many accidents happen on hikes, you know.' She gave me a lazy smile. 'And we're headed to very remote places. Slippery rocks, a gust of wind...'

She held my gaze. My stomach dropped.

'Jesus,' I gulped, like a goofy cartoon character. This woman was effective. I felt oddly comforted, knowing Lydia had her in her corner.

'Look, I'm not—'

Gen held up a hand. 'Don't care,' she said flatly. 'I came here to threaten you and leave.'

Gen was a few steps in front of me when I called, 'Does she know about the tattoo?'

She turned, giving me a sharp look. 'No. It would have been confusing for her, after you left that note. And I don't chat shit about my clients, even ones I don't particularly like.'

Gen picked up the pace, returning to Amy and Lydia. Lydia turned, a curious look on her face as she scanned me like she was worried Gen had left scratch marks.

I gave her a tentative smile, but she turned away fast, her blonde ponytail swinging.

'This isn't going to be an easy trip, Peggy,' I said, but even she left me to sniff a tree stump.

The sun broke through the clouds in bursts, lighting up the wet grass and woolly sheep as we crossed Edale Valley. I kept my distance, as Lydia had asked. Still, there was something grounding about being near her again – watching her attentive expression as Amara explained the birds of the Peak District or her face tilting to the sky like she was savouring the sun on her face.

But then some things began to grate on me. As Jade began to snap photos, Lydia offered to help carry some of her equipment, even though she had the biggest backpack of everyone here. Then she began walking on the grass verge or at the edges of puddles, her boots squelching through mud, just so everyone else could stay dry. She offered Claire the last of her water when Claire upturned her flask, bemoaning that she'd run dry.

Classic Lydia. Always making herself uncomfortable so others didn't have to.

Two hours in, as we reached Jacob's Ladder, I noticed her slowing, her smile fading.

'Tired?' I murmured, as the others pushed on ahead of us.

'No,' she said quickly. 'Just warm.'

She adjusted her pack, sweat glinting on her brow. She was a little pink, still carrying Jade's kit bag, because of course she was.

'Give me your pack,' I said.

'It's fine.'

'Lydia.'

She looked at me then – defiant, exhausted, and, of course, beautiful. There was an ache in my throat. Would she ever let me in again?

'Let me help,' I said, more quietly now. 'Just this once.'

She handed me her pack. I misjudged the weight and it dropped straight to the ground. Lydia gave me that smug, little smile she wore whenever she beat me at anything – Wii tennis, downing pints, life. She was a born competitor, and I was happy to be her favourite rival.

'Too heavy for you, huh?'

'Take off your top.'

The smile vanished. Colour bloomed in her cheeks and crept down her neck. Her eyes softened, hazy, and I knew exactly where her mind had gone. Same place mine had.

'You're warm,' I added quickly, voice a little rough. 'Take off a layer.'

'Oh, right. Yeah.'

She peeled off her long-sleeved top, revealing a bright pink tank that made her flushed skin glow. Her biceps flexed, collarbones catching the light. She ran a hand through her ponytail, and I forced myself to look away as she pulled the pack back on to her shoulders.

'Wait. Take it off again.'

She narrowed her eyes. 'What is your obsession with telling me to take things off?'

I swallowed a grin.

'Let me put this under your shoulders. So your pack doesn't rub.'

'Oh.'

She turned, letting me step in close. I picked up the pack and eased it over her shoulders, fingers brushing her skin, sun-warmed and soft, and I had to grit my teeth not to linger.

'What the hell do you have in this pack, Lydia?' I muttered. 'A dead body?'

She shrugged, 'Just the essentials.'

'Ten-step skincare routine?'

She bit her lip. It was cute. 'Maybe.'

I held back a smile, not wanting to scare her off. We turned to join the group. I was unsurprised to see Gen staring, her eyes like pointed daggers, and Amy next to her, with a softer, curious look on her face.

I coughed. 'We have an audience.'

Lydia glanced up to see her friends' stare.

'Do they know? About... that night?'

Lydia's shoulders tensed.

I ran a hand through my hair. 'I'm just curious. Gen was particularly vicious earlier. Threatened to throw me off a cliff.'

'They know,' she said, staring at the gravel path.

I hesitated. 'I'm surprised you didn't tell more people. Get them on your side. Everyone would hate me.'

She stopped mid-step and swivelled, her expression thunderous.

Her voice dropped. 'Let's get something straight. I'm not talking to you about that night. Not here. Not now. Not ever.' She took a step closer. 'You lost the right to ask me questions the second you walked out of my life that night like—' She slammed her mouth closed. 'Like I meant nothing. So don't you *dare* try and play the victim.'

I opened my mouth but she was already turning away, striding back to the others as if she hadn't just gutted me with a single look.

Some dark, arrogant part of me felt almost relieved. Because for the second time today, what I'd seen wasn't indifference. It was fury, sharp and unfiltered. And fury, at least, meant she'd cared once.

And maybe she still did.

We reached Kinder Scout by two in the afternoon, after a few stops from Amara to collect plant samples for her pressings. A few helped, making sure she collected the brightest flowers, and I couldn't help but marvel at the way women made friends so quickly. Peggy was a little tired now, so she sat in the shade next to a water bowl I'd set up for her. Freya and Jade went to sit next to her, giving her fuss she was growing accustomed to.

Jade took photos of the group at the top of the mountain but I held back, not wanting photographic evidence of my hijacking of their tour. I offered to take a photo of the group, including Jade, but she waved me off, saying she preferred to be behind the camera. Some gathered on the grass, opening snacks and lunches, while others admired the view.

And a view it was.

The clouds had broken away, and I wiped the sweat from my brow and stared at the uninterrupted view of the moorland and rock formations. It was so green, with so much wide-open space. Birds circled above us in formation.

A bittersweet thought popped into my head.

God, Mum would have loved this.

The familiar sensation followed, as it always did when I thought of my mum — nose burning and eyes stinging. Then an image of her dark brown hair and the smell of her perfume. The memory of her face was blurry now, as if someone had placed a drop of water on a photograph and it had rippled the ink. I wanted to scream at someone, anyone who was responsible for taking her likeness away from me. It was all I had left.

'Ren?'

Lydia's voice sounded beside me, soothing like a hot bath. I turned to see her adjusting her ponytail with a confused expression on her face. For a moment I decided to forget that she hated me, and just take her in as she was now. Lydia was angles and sharp edges — lean, quick, built for movement. Her dirty-blonde hair was scraped back into a ponytail, though a few loose strands had escaped on the hike up, framing her face in a way that made her look a little windswept.

Lydia had a narrow face and a strong jawline that brought out the elegance of her neck. Her features were softened by a button nose and full lips that could crack open into a beautiful, wide smile if you were lucky. A faint dusting of freckles stretched across her cheeks and forehead, the kind that only showed up in the summer when she spent more time outside. When she smiled, her slightly pointed canines peeked through, giving her grin an edge of mischief. Her eyes were my favourite: bright blue and searching.

'What's wrong?' she asked again.

It took me a moment to respond, as if talking about Mum was a muscle I hadn't used in years.

'Just thinking Mum would have liked this.' I nodded to the view.

A shadow of a smile graced Lydia's face, and I could have collapsed at the sight of it. God, I was pathetic.

'She would have.' She nodded. 'She would have been a step ahead of everyone else, though.'

I frowned. 'What do you mean?'

She tilted her head slightly, as if trying to make sense of something ridiculous.

'Ren, she worked out, like, all the time. Almost every day, and she had young kids. She loved tennis and badminton and netball. I reckon she could have given me a run for my money with the weightlifting.'

I racked my brain for this memory and came up with nothing.

'How... how do you know that? We were six when she—'

Lydia nodded, not making me repeat the word she knew I hated.

'Mum offered to watch you and Liam if she wanted to squeeze a workout in. Then, when we were a bit older, Lily *tried* to get Mum to see the joys of fitness.' Lydia huffed. 'Tried. Mum hated it. But I suppose it stuck with me somehow. Someone new and fresh, bringing in these new passions. She took me to Momentum for the first time. When I was a kid. A kid's taster to tennis. I loved it, even though I was shit.' She huffed. 'And then I guess it grew from there.'

I frowned. 'You mean that Mum...' I paused, not able to continue with what I was saying.

'She's the reason I became a PT,' Lydia concluded, as if it was the most obvious thing in the world.

'You never told me that. How have you never told me that?' I bit down the annoyance rising through my cheeks.

Lydia's eyes scanned me, her brow furrowing. 'Sorry. It didn't seem important at the time. And I didn't want to imply I had some big connection with your mum when I really just thought she was cool. I didn't want to be a try-hard.'

'You're never a try-hard. I would like to have known.'

We paused for a second, staring at the horizon.

'I like it,' I announced. 'That she might have influenced you or your career.'

Lydia smiled. 'Yeah, me too.' She stared up at the sky. 'But it would be good if you could get me a bleeding job now, Lily.'

'Yeah, Mum. Any time now would be good.'

We chuckled and then, as if she was watching us, a cloud broke away from the sun, sending a huge golden beam across the landscape before us. My eyes burned, but there was a lovely, bubbly feeling in my chest.

'Thanks. It's nice to talk about her. With someone who knew her.'

Lydia nodded, a guarded expression back on her face.

A moment later, I almost missed the muttered 'Any time'.

Chapter Eight

Lydia's Diary, 11 Years Old

Dear Diary,
 I start big school tomorrow and haven't told anyone, but I'm really scared. I keep looking at my uniform on my bed, and my stomach won't stop flipping over.
 The only good thing is that Ren will be there too, so at least I'll know one person.
 We spent the whole summer climbing trees in his garden. He has this huge oak tree, and he dared me to climb it one day. I was scared, but I did it anyway. Ren looked impressed.
 Maybe school will be okay.
 Love,
 Lydia

Lydia

We reached the little campsite as the sun began to set.
 On the descent from Jacob's Ladder, we went past Kinder Downfall, a waterfall amidst craggy rocks. After the steep climb, the sound of the rush of water had been soothing, relaxing even. Peggy dipped down towards the stream, taking in gulps of water. I smiled, glancing over to Ren as Mandy described how the rock formation had come to be. I found him looking at me, a slight smile on his face, as if he knew exactly how much I liked the

sound of the water, Peggy's tentative paddle, and the view of the waterfall. I glanced away quickly.

'Okay, ladies.' Mandy's booming voice carried on a gust of wind across the campsite. 'And gentleman. Sorry, Ren. This might be your first time camping, but let's try and get the tents up as soon as we can, as the sun will be gone in …' She glanced at her Fitbit. 'About twenty-five minutes. So I'd like everyone to pair up. That is your tent buddy. If you are already sharing, like Jade and Claire, then just get your own tent up before helping others.'

The campsite smelled of cut grass and damp earth. It was empty apart from us, and I wondered if not many people liked the idea of camping on a random Monday in April. It was a wide open, secure field, which meant Peggy could roam free, with some brick buildings at the rear that housed the toilets and showers I'd been promised.

Mandy continued her speech, but my mind was spinning about the tent shoved into my backpack. God, it was at the bottom of so much crap I'd packed. I threw my pack to the floor, shifting through the stuff – changes of clothes, toiletries, and enough snacks to get me through an apocalypse.

'So I guess it's just us left.'

A deep voice next to me sounded, and my stomach dropped. I'd been teetering far too close to being friendly with Ren at the top of the mountain earlier. I blamed the beautiful view and the talk of Lily. I couldn't be a bitch with that combination. I glanced up to find Ren's tentative expression, which made him look so young and boyish. God, I hated that his hair flicked in front of his forehead, making me want to push it back.

'For the tents,' he said. 'Everyone else is paired up. I thought we could choose that spot over there. Far enough away from the toilets to avoid the stink, close enough if we need to run through the dark for a wee in the night.' He shuddered. 'Not looking forward to that.'

'Still scared of the dark?'

He gave me a droll look. 'Terrified.'

'We're not pitching our tents next to each other.' I pointed to the spot he'd picked. Annoyingly, it was the perfect spot. High enough ground and flat too. A tree was nearby so that might provide shade from the morning sun.

'We have to. Mandy said,' Ren summarised.

'And since when do you listen to authority?' I arched a brow.

Ren was perfectly happy challenging authority. He'd talk back to teachers, then don an amused, triumphant smile when he was ordered out of the room. I was almost envious of the casual way he slung his backpack and slunk off to the head teacher. Sometimes, he would bunk off school, declaring he had lost his way to the office.

'I like a bit of authority. Of course, it all depends on who's in charge.' His eyes danced and my mind flashed an image of his palm wrapped around my wrist. My body flushed. Stupid, stupid hormones.

'Fine.' I said, my voice a little uneven. 'But only 'cos it's the best spot.'

Ren's lips twitched as he held his hand out for my backpack, which in a cowardly fashion I handed over, mainly because I was knackered, and despite being strong enough to deadlift Ren's entire body, I *had* packed too much for the trip.

Ren strode to the spot and began taking out his tent, laying it flat on the floor with all the poles and pegs. Peggy came over, using Ren's proximity to the ground as an excuse for some fussing, which he gave her until she trotted off elsewhere. Ren turned back to the tent and began assembling it. I bit my lip. He'd clearly done this before, and I hated feeling out of my depth. I pushed away that feeling and copied him, laying my tent next to his, but far enough away that I was sure I wouldn't hear his breathing at night or the odd time I knew he sleeptalked.

Ren cocked an inquisitive brow at the distance between

our tents but mentioned nothing. I began to put up my tent, wrestling with the poles, when I felt a warm hand come over mine.

'Here, let me help.'

'I've got it.'

'Lyds.'

'Don't *Lyds* me, Ren.'

'Okay, okay.' Ren backed off, returning to his own half-erected tent. At another time, in another world, I would have made a hilarious, inappropriate joke about 'erected tents', and I felt a bit sad that I couldn't do it now.

Ten minutes later, the sun was almost down, and Mandy gave a five-minute warning that made me want to burst into tears. I crouched beside the pile of tent poles, glaring at them as if they had personally offended me. How hard could this be? The 'instructions' were crumpled beside me, the diagrams doing nothing to help. I shoved a pole into what I thought was the right slot, only for the entire structure to collapse in on itself.

'Need a hand?' Ren asked, taking a bite out of an apple as he watched the pitiful mess of my tent.

He'd put his up in record time, but then it was a small two-person tent. Peggy was sitting in it now, with some treats Ren had given her, her bum on display as her little legs splayed half out of the tiny tent. It only had two poles when I'd opted for a more... elaborate choice. It was a four-person tent with a little gazebo at the front, where I imagined I'd sit and have a flask of tea in the morning, watching the sunrise.

'I'm perfectly capable of putting up a tent.'

I blew a strand of hair out of my face.

'Okay.' Another bite of the apple.

God, he was annoyingly smug.

I made some progress until a gust of wind swept across the campsite, sending the half-assembled panel into my face. I stumbled back, swatting at it like an idiot, while Ren watched.

'You sure?' he asked, his face innocent, but I could hear the smirk in his voice.

I inhaled through my nose and exhaled slowly.

'I'm a grown woman. I can put up a tent. If Kat managed it, surely I can.'

Ren cocked an eyebrow. 'Didn't hers collapse?'

'At least she got it up!' I half-shouted.

Ren's lips folded in as he held back a laugh.

'Immature.'

'Let me help,' Ren asked, his tone softer.

'I can do it myself.'

'I know.' He smiled softly. 'But you don't have to. I'm here to help you.'

I battled with the pros and cons of letting Ren help, until Ren muttered a soft plea.

'Please.'

I stared at his eager expression, and stepped away from the tent.

'Go sit there with Peggy.' He nodded to the little entrance of his tent, where Peggy was sitting. 'She hasn't had any fussing in half an hour. She'll keel over.'

As if on command, Peggy, her treats gobbled up, turned, and curled up on the cool grass in front of the tent.

'Fine. For Peggy.'

Relief flooded my body, and I couldn't even feel the shame of it. My feet were raw from a day of walking in new boots I hadn't broken in, and I wanted to rip my hair out because it kept sticking to my face. If Ren wanted to help, and it was easy for him, why not? For some reason, I thought of my dad, who always emptied the dishwasher and took the bins out religiously. Mum didn't touch them ever. When I asked if he hated it, he just replied, 'Your mother smiles every time. I think it's well earned, don't you think?'

God, they were insufferably in love, my parents.

'Done,' Ren announced two minutes later, in front of a perfectly erected tent.

'Well, I guess travelling teaches you some things,' I said, bitterness laced in my tone.

'Ah—' he scratched the back of his head. 'Well, I actually watched a load of YouTube videos last night.'

I glanced up, frowning. 'But – you did camp on your trips, didn't you? Dad said.' I shut my mouth, not wanting to express how much I lived for the tiny morsels of information I was given when he was away, even as I clung to my anger. 'Or did you stay in hostels?'

Ren scratched the back of his head. 'Well, about that, I didn't really—'

Mandy's single clap interrupted him. 'Right, well done, everyone. I promise it will get easier on the trips. Now, they don't usually allow campfires, but I got to know the owners, and they stipulated that as long as it was just my group...' She stepped aside, revealing a collection of logs and twigs. 'So I thought we could roast some s'mores. Very American, I know, but if they got anything right, it's melted marshmallows.'

We all gathered around the fire, to the sound of it crackling and popping, and everyone helped themselves to a stick, a marshmallow, and a digestive. Peggy was desperate for a bite, but I had to explain that chocolate and marshmallows were bad for dogs. She didn't look convinced, and I glanced up to find Ren smiling at us both. I glanced away quickly.

Claire lowered herself on to the makeshift logs we were using as seats. The warmth of the fire flickered across her face.

'How are you doing, love?' Claire ran a hand over my ponytail, and it made me ache for my mum. I felt like a shaken-up bottle of pop, just ready to explode, and I knew Mum would know what to say. 'You look a bit... strained?'

Shit! I needed to sell this better.

'Are you joking? I'm great.' I plastered on a grin. 'The hike was amazing today – the view was gorgeous. And I've got my tent all set up.' I gestured around the campfire. 'Plus, I'm spending time with my friends. What could be better?'

My voice was high-pitched and Claire looked at me with a concerned expression. Great! Academy-Award winner I was *not*.

Claire lowered her voice. 'Maybe it's that your ex, no, I know he's not your ex. He's your ex-whatever. And maybe it would be better if he wasn't sitting opposite, shooting you those puppy-dog eyes.'

I whispered, shooting a glance to Ren, who was thankfully in conversation with Clara. 'We're – it's not like that. We weren't together. Just friends who—'

'Who fell into bed?'

My eyes snapped to Claire. I hadn't really told her the full story, as I had to Gen and Amy. A bit of me wanted to hold back the full truth from her, because I didn't want her to be disappointed in me. But she proved I shouldn't have worried with the next sentence.

'Oh, love. Don't look so panicked. We've all been there. God, the list of men I wish I hadn't gone to bed with, well.' Claire pouted. 'When I think about it, the list isn't that long. I should have more regrets really.'

I chuckled. 'There are apps for that, Claire.'

'Oh,' Claire waved a hand. 'I'm not interested in the apps. And I don't think he is, by the way.' She nodded at Ren. 'He's always got an eye on you…'

I followed Claire's eyeline, and found Ren glancing over at the same time, a tentative smile on his face. I glanced away quickly, then my face burned.

'Really, Claire, it's not like that.' I scratched my arm. 'We talked, cleared the air. We can just keep out of each other's way.'

She hummed, then a slow grin took over her face.

'What are you thinking?' My eyes narrowed. 'You look like you just had a very evil idea.'

'I was just thinking that as long as he is here – he ought to earn his keep, don't you think?'

'Earn his keep? What, like put him to work?' I laughed, disbelieving. 'Like a butler?'

Claire's eyes glinted in the firelight. 'Exactly like a butler. How better to show he's earning back your trust?'

Wow! Never underestimate the creativity of a woman scorned. Claire's cheating ex-husband had a lot to answer for.

I laughed, shaking my head. 'I couldn't do that.'

'Why not?' Claire shrugged. 'He's invited himself on this trip. The least he could do is make himself useful. I saw him help with your tent. And he looks like he'd do anything just to get you to look at him.' Claire bopped my nose. 'There is power in that, you know.'

The idea of having power over Ren made me feel a little lightheaded. I'd always felt like the one on the back foot – he had always been the cooler one, the one with more social currency. I'd been the peppy, overexcited best friend who usually made a fool of herself at some point during the party. But Ren had said he would do anything – anything to make it up to me. Maybe if I pushed him far enough, he would realise it was doomed. *We* were doomed. And he'd leave me alone.

'Ren,' I barked across the fire pit. Ren's head shot up. The ladies looked between us curiously.

'Lydia,' he said, a little amused.

I almost lost my nerve, tempted to make something up, but I was keen to swipe the smug look off his face.

'Mandy said you brought a cocktail shaker,' I said, tilting my head. 'But I don't see a drink in my hand.'

A ripple of laughter passed through the camp, low and knowing.

Bold. Maybe too bold. God, did that sound bitchy?

Ren's face flickered and he didn't look offended. Quite the opposite, actually. His eyes were a little glazed, as he took me in.

'What can I get you?' he asked, his voice gentler than I expected. 'Name it – I'll make it.'

An hour and a half later, we were four cocktails deep, all giggling, Joni Mitchell drifting from Amy's phone as the fire crackled between us.

'Another cocktail, ladies?' Ren asked with a grin, leaning across the flames to top up Gen and Claire's glasses from the metal cocktail shaker he'd packed, along with a million tiny bottles of spirits, like some kind of wilderness bartender.

'Yes, please,' I said, feigning innocence as I leaned forward, a mischievous glint in my eye. 'Could I have a margarita this time?'

Ren's eyes twinkled. 'Of course. At your service, madam.'

He worked the cocktail shaker and, with the spirits thrumming through my veins, I couldn't help but track Ren's arms, and the way they flexed. He looked handsome with the firelight flickering off his face, at ease, even as we ordered him about. He came around the fire to stand behind me, leaning over, his arms brushing my shoulder as he went to pour the drink.

'Oh, Ren.'

He paused, eyebrow raised, looking down at me expectantly. 'Yes, Lydia?'

I bared my teeth in a smile. 'We need more firewood.'

Ren's answering slow grin made me wonder if I'd bitten off more than I could chew. He leaned down, to top up my drink.

'Careful, Sunshine,' he murmured under his breath. 'You keep barking orders like that and I might start enjoying it.'

My breath caught and I held his gaze and took a sip of the drink, the tequila coming through strong, giving me that boost of confidence I needed around this version of Ren. Then his hand wrapped around mine and he lifted the glass to his lips.

'Just a taste test,' he said, sipping from the exact spot I had.

'Want to make sure it's up to scratch for my most... demanding customer.'

The flush bloomed across my cheeks before I could stop it. I blamed the booze. And the fire. And the bloody audacity of that smile.

He handed the drink back, his fingers lingering just a moment too long – as if he wasn't quite ready to let go. Then he turned to fetch the firewood, leaving me flustered and wondering who won that round.

I suspected it wasn't me.

By the time we hit drink four, Gen was on her feet, clinging to Amy, who was already struggling to keep Claire upright.

'Come on,' Gen said, the most sober of the three. 'Let's get to bed.'

'Night, ladies,' Ren said, his voice laced with amusement. 'I hope I passed the test.'

'Oh, yes.' Amy hiccuped. 'I think so.'

'With flying pigs,' Claire added, her eyes pointing in different directions.

'Flying colours,' Gen corrected. 'I think you've proven yourself. For now.' Gen pointed her fingers at her eyes, then flipped them around to Ren. 'But we're watching you, remember.'

'Yeah.' Amy hiccuped again, then pouted. 'I got a forty-five and a shovel. I doubt anyone would miss you.'

I stifled a giggle. Amy was steaming drunk but still managed to quote *Clueless*. She was an encyclopedia for any form of entertainment with a whiff of a romantic subplot. The girls dissolved into laughter, then wandered off to bed in a chorus of yawns and whispered good nights, leaving Ren and me alone in front of the dying fire.

'Thank you. For tonight.'

'You're thanking *me*?' My brow furrowed. He'd just been at our beck and call for hours. Gen almost got him to give us foot rubs, but I drew the line there.

'I know it was meant to be some sort of public humiliation, but you let me earn my keep. I already felt bad enough being the only bloke on this trip—'

Our eyes met. The fire crackled between us.

'And it was nice,' he smiled, that irritatingly tentative, soft smile. 'Seeing you have fun. Letting yourself go. I like being your victim, Sunshine. You can use me however you want to.'

Use me.

My face couldn't help but flush. Ren didn't look away and neither did I and I realised how close we were sitting. Not touching, but I could feel the heat radiate from his thighs to mine. His eyes flickered around my face, then lingered a beat too long on my lips. It was just a second but long enough for me to clock it. Long enough for it to feel like a caress.

Then a log cracked loudly. I jumped, and stood. Ren did the same, still looking at me with that searching expression.

I cleared my throat, laughing lightly. 'Right. I better sleep off these cocktails.' Hoping I came across unflustered. Unbothered.

I brushed off my leggings, heading for my tent.

'Night, Lydia.'

Chapter Nine

Lydia's Diary, 12 Years Old

Dear Diary,

I've been at this school for a few months now and I *hate* maths. My teacher, Mr Nichols, is an old dragon. His breath smells like stale coffee, and he shouts at me when I can't do my times tables. He says I should know them all by now, like it's *so obvious*. He keeps telling me I can do better, but wouldn't I already be doing it if I could? He scribbles all over my work in red pen, and I HATE it.

Numbers don't make sense in my head. Fractions are a nightmare. And double maths on Mondays? As if Mondays weren't already bad enough.

That's why I skipped double maths a few weeks ago and hid in the toilets until it was over. It worked – until lunchtime, when Mrs MacDonald found me. She is the gym teacher, and was actually nice.

She didn't shout at me, but let me help with year seven netball. Then, she said that I could be a good coach one day. The bad part was that she insisted I go see the Head of Year, Mrs Smith. But I didn't want to disappoint Mrs MacDonald, so I went.

Mrs Smith sat me down, and suddenly, everything just... came out.

How I'm rubbish at maths. How I don't see the point in even trying. It's not as if I'm going to *need* maths. I'd rather just avoid numbers for the rest of my life. Ren said he would help – he doesn't mind numbers, so he said he'd do them for me. I don't know if he was joking, but I might take him up on it.

But Mrs Smith actually listened. She said she thought I might have something called dyscalculia. Mum's booked me in for a test in a few weeks. She said it's expensive, so she really hopes Mrs Smith is right – or else she's marching down to the school to demand they pay for it.

Honestly? I kind of hope Mrs Smith *is* right. Because if there's a reason why I find maths impossible, maybe – just maybe – it's not all my fault.

Love,
Lydia

Lydia

A bird squawked in the early hours, startling me awake. For a moment I forgot where I was, and then it all came rushing back. I took some deep breaths, calming my nerves. My hair smelled of smoke, and I found the smell strangely soothing. My heart rate slowed, so I checked my phone and spotted a missed call from a random number. *Suspected spam*.

Who the hell makes phone calls these days? Probably people I owe money to and that could wait until I found a decent job.

I listened for snores or murmurs but couldn't hear anything, besides the odd noise of birds. In fact, the campsite is eerily quiet. I groan when my bladder shouts – no, screams – at me. I drank a lot of water after the hike up Mam Tor yesterday. Along with Ren's cocktails, that was a deadly combination and I was paying for it now.

I zipped open the tent and almost gasped at the sight of the moon – a brilliant crescent glowing in the middle of the sky, stars flickering around it, lighting up the campsite. The sky is so clear. Everly Heath didn't have the benefits of avoiding all the light pollution from Manchester, so I rarely saw skies like this. Ren probably saw loads on his trip, I thought bitterly, and chastised myself for the thought. I didn't need to be resentful, because I didn't care.

Plus, I'd already bitten his head off a few times yesterday and hadn't liked the sensation of my true feelings coming to the surface. It felt so... vulnerable.

I climbed out of the tent, ignoring the low call of an owl in the distance as I ran to the block of loos. As I left the outbuilding, I heard loud snores coming from Gen and Amy's tent and made a mental note to find out who that was, so I could take the piss out of them tomorrow.

'What are you smiling at?' a voice whispered from next to me, and I let out a short, sharp whisper-scream. My heart pounded, my hand clasped at my chest.

'Ren.' I hissed.

Ren was leaning against the block of loos, a smirk on his face. His dark hair looked wild, like he'd run his hands through it in his sleep. He seemed so familiar like this. It brought back all of our childhood sleepovers. Sleepovers that had wandered far too long into our teen years, when they became marred with hormones and yearning and *skin*. At least for me. Ren had been oblivious to my changing feelings.

He was laughing now, his shoulders shaking. It made him look so handsome it hurt my heart. I'd not allowed myself to look – really look – at him since he'd come home.

'It's not funny.'

'Sorry,' he whispered back. 'Was a bit funny, though.'

'What are you doing up? Where's Peggy?'

'I heard you wake up. She's still snoring in the tent. Today knocked her out.' He paused. 'I just wanted to check you got back to your tent okay.'

He said it frankly, as if he had no intentions or ulterior motives to hide – just frank concern for my well-being.

'You braved the dark?' I cocked an eyebrow.

'I'd brave a lot more for you, Lyds.'

I blushed and glanced away, unable to cope with how my stomach threw around butterflies like confetti.

He doesn't actually mean that.

'Well, thanks.'

'No problem.' He smiled, then nodded to the sky. 'I'm glad I woke up. *That* is gorgeous.'

'Yeah, it is, isn't it?'

We stared up at the sky, scattered with stars, for a moment.

'Gorgeous,' he murmured, but he wasn't staring at the sky now.

He was staring at me. I begged my cheeks not to flush and glanced back at the sky, avoiding the intensity of his gaze. I should have moved back to my tent and stayed away from him. But something about the quiet, the dark and being far from our home made me feel bold. Standing side by side. Pretending we weren't some sort of adversaries with complicated history.

'I could get used to this.' Ren sounded... wistful.

I turned to see his face leaning up to the sky, his eyes closed. His shoulders looked relaxed for the first time in weeks.

'What, camping trips?'

He shrugged, turning to look at me. 'I guess somewhere quiet. Remote. No cars honking, people meddling. I love our hometown, but sometimes, it can feel a bit...'

'Much.'

'Yeah.'

'I know what you mean.'

Is that why you left? I wanted to ask. So, I used the security blanket of the dark to ask another question I'd been dying to ask since he got back.

'How have things been, you know, upstairs?' I tapped my forehead.

He smiled. 'I forgot about that.'

'What?'

'Our weird repressed way of asking if I've slipped into the pits of depression recently.'

'Well, when you say it like that,' I said, dryly, 'it sounds bad.'

He chuckled. 'Nah, I like it. Makes it feel less like a doctor's appointment. And things are fine upstairs. Good actually. I haven't had an episode in a while. Some days I can wake up and it can feel like I'm walking through treacle. But it's not all-consuming like it has been in the past. And I've still got my therapist.'

'Jan.'

'Good ol' Jan.' He nods, smiling. 'I had a wobble a couple of weeks ago. But it was mainly triggered by work.'

I frowned. 'Work? I thought things were going well at Lily's.'

Ren smiled ruefully. 'It is. Going brilliantly, actually. We can open a second site.'

Pride expanded in my chest. 'That's great.'

'Yeah. And I've picked out a second site,' he said, kicking the grass. 'I put an offer in on Everly Heath Farm a few weeks ago.'

Shock rippled through me.

'The derelict one we used to go to as kids?'

Ren nodded.

The farm was a popular local haunt, especially for families. I remembered running riot, goats chewing the paper bag of the feed Lily had bought us, and our ice cream melting down our arms. It smelled of earth and manure but always felt so… alive with activity, kids shouting and the animals bleating, shouting parents urging us to slow down. Ren had adored the place, even more than me and Liam. We'd go every year for his birthday. Lily had party hats and cake in the cafe. Then, after Ren's mum was gone, Ren's dad made sure to book it every year. But it wasn't the same. Ren confessed as much on the first birthday without his mum. It's not the same, he'd repeated. It's gone. I'd hugged him, far too young and naive to understand his pain, but I tried to be there for him anyway.

TAKE A HIKE!

Ren nodded, aiming a sad smile at the sky. As if he was confessing his secrets to the moon... and me.

'Bert is selling it. After his wife died years ago—'

'Mabel died?' My voice was thick, thinking about the smiling woman who sold tickets in the little shed at the front of the farm in long floral dresses. She'd felt ancient to me in the nineties, but she had probably only been in her forties then, her dark hair always pinned up in a bun. 'I didn't know.'

'Bert keeps to himself. And since Mabel's been gone, he hasn't been able to keep up with it, so it's in bad shape. But I want to keep it going. I want to turn it into a destination. Food, drink, boutique hotel. We could get local farmers involved and lend them some of the land to grow food or keep cattle – a farm-to-table menu. Then, as a homage to Bert and Mabel, run events for the kids in the holidays. Pumpkin patches, strawberry picking.'

'Christmas trees.' My heart squeezed. 'Easter-egg hunts! Oh, my God, craft making. You could do wreath making at Christmas!'

I shut my mouth, realising I'd got carried away and shown too much. But Ren didn't notice my slip. He just shot me a wry smile.

'I knew you'd be good at this.'

I ignored the way my chest expanded at his words.

'That sounds amazing, Ren. I—' I paused, not knowing how to word the following few sentences, which veered too close to friendship, back to *us*. 'I think it would be brilliant. I'm proud of you.'

He smiled then – slow and a little bit crooked. The kind of smile that used to make me feel as if it was just us two in the room. And for a second I felt it again – that little flutter, low in my stomach.

'Thanks, Lyds.'

I dropped my gaze, cheeks suddenly warm. 'No problem.'

'Too bad it's not going to happen.'

My head shot up. 'What? Why? Is it the cost?'

I couldn't imagine wrapping my head around the figures, projections and losses for that kind of project. This is why I'd never be able to run my own business. I couldn't trust myself with numbers. I could move my body and chat with clients. I was good at that, but I didn't want to deal with numbers, with the responsibility. Just the thought of getting it wrong made my chest tighten. It was why, even as I despised Craig, I was honest enough to admit that I could never do his job.

'Liam said no. I'd need his sign-on to do it. We'd need to build on the success and reputation of Lily's to make it happen.'

'He thinks it's too much of a risk?'

'Yep.'

'Sounds like Liam.'

'He's probably right. It would tank. And I'm not sure I can risk failing.'

'Ren—'

He raised a hand. 'Don't try to comfort me. I'm being a mardy arse. I'm just trying to say that I wanted something for myself, I suppose.'

He shifted his head, finally looking at me rather than the sky. 'Something that's *mine*.'

The word hit me in the chest, and time stretched between us. His eyes flickered, and I could feel Ren reaching out with his expression as if his eyes were grazing my hands and cheeks. I didn't move my eyes, feeling bold enough to hold his gaze as the darkness and the silhouette of trees against the skies cocooned us.

'Lydia—' his voice was pained and stretched out. It snapped me back into place. It reminded me where and what we were to each other.

I cleared my throat. 'I get it. It's brave.' I huffed. 'God, I don't think I could ever do anything like that. I couldn't trust myself not to mess up,' I say, staring at the giant oak tree, and back to the topic at hand.

I knew that, without saying it implicitly, Ren would understand what I was getting at.

My lack of ability to grasp basic numbers — even as simple as addition and subtraction — would always hold me back. And it wasn't as simple as using a calculator. Numbers gave me anxiety. I avoided them at all costs. I never carried cash because the idea of having to count at the till, someone's eyes tracking how I couldn't add up the coins, made my palms sweat and my heart pound.

Ren shook his head. 'Even with the dyscalculia, you'd do brilliantly. I've always said Momentum didn't deserve you. Craig.' His voice dropped. 'What happened with all of that? I got the gist from your mum—'

'I knew it,' I sighed. 'I knew you'd been in cahoots.'

Ren had the decency to look sheepish.

'I was worried. You looked so... lost. And people were talking about what happened with Momentum... and Casey.'

I shifted my eyes away. Casey had texted me a few times to check in over the last few weeks, to let me know that she'd settled in at her uncle's house, and then to let me know she had started her course and was doing well. The texts were courteous and removed, like she was ticking off a to-do list. I missed her, but not as much as I'd thought I would.

In fact, I felt more than a little guilty that I actually missed my job more than her. And, God, if she knew I was on this hike with Ren. I remembered that knowing look she'd given me when she left me in Lily's.

You murmur his name in your sleep.

Ren continued, thankfully snapping me out of that memory. 'So, yeah, I texted your mum to check you were okay.' Ren's voice turned low and a little lethal. 'So what did Craig do?'

He shifted to face me, his shoulder against the brick wall. I turned my head, and... God, he looked... good. I could just about make out his dark eyes and his tangled hair pushed back from his face. His face had gone serious, with a flicker of something fierce underneath and somehow it made him more handsome.

Ren had always been so unattainable to me, even when he was the most familiar of faces. He'd been reserved when I'd been outgoing. Then, he'd turned flirty and cocky when I'd been unsure, clinging to my rules like a life raft. It always felt like we were in parallel worlds, with a golden cord pulling us together every so often.

'You know we're all freelance at Momentum.'

Ren nodded, quietly waiting for me to continue.

'Well, he didn't renew my contract. He said I'd been late too many times. That I wasn't keeping up with timesheets or hitting all the KPIs.' I shrugged, like it was a full stop.

'Those bloody KPIs only showed up when he did. Who actually cares how many of those disgusting protein balls you can flog in a month when you're a brilliant trainer with a full client list?' Ren glared up at the sky like it owed him something. 'God, he was such a prick. I still can't believe they promoted him over you.'

I huffed out a laugh. 'I wasn't in the running.'

Ren frowned. 'Why not? You're more than qualified—'

Because I didn't put myself forward.

Ren angled his head to the side, and I was relieved when he changed the subject. 'You can't tell me anyone actually likes working with Craig.'

I chuckled, hollow. 'No, most of the PTs hate him. Ryan was already looking for new jobs before I got canned.'

'Exactly. It doesn't make sense.'

I shrugged, trying to play it off. 'One time I messed up my schedule and turned up two hours late. Craig had switched everything to 24-hour time, and I've always struggled with that kind of thing.'

Ren's jaw tensed. 'Did he know? About your dyscalculia?'

'No.' I shook my head. 'I've never told anyone I work with.'

'When he got promoted... did he get access to staff files? If you told HR?'

My breath caught. My stomach dropped. Shit. I had disclosed it – back when I had started, during onboarding. It was meant to be confidential.

Ren's expression darkened. 'That's what it is. He knew. And he used it against you.'

My mind whirled, things falling into place.

'He did start focusing on KPIs and spreadsheets. And he used to track when I'd clock in at work. I thought it was just because of the promotion...'

'That piece of shit,' Ren muttered, turning to me, his eyes shimmering. 'I'm sorry, Lydia.'

My mind was whirling, trying to wrap itself around this new perspective – Craig might have been sabotaging me. On purpose. Maybe it wasn't all my fault.

The thick tar of shame that had sat heavy on my chest for months loosened. Just a little.

Craig was an ableist arsehole who had used my disability against me. Cruel, and far more cunning than I ever gave him credit for. And even if he got away with sacking me, it still wasn't my fault. He'd built a whole system just to shove me out – because he saw me as a threat. I'd almost be flattered, if I hadn't also wanted to curl into a ball and cry at the fact I still had no job. No career. Nothing.

And then, it all came bursting to the surface. Everything I'd been swallowing down for weeks. All of it.

'You know what? I don't even care about Craig. He's always hated me and I was stupid to think I could convince him otherwise.' I raised a finger. 'It's Niall I'm upset about. I thought he respected me, you know? I put my blood, sweat, and tears into that place. And it was fine because they loved me, right? Niall used to meet me to chat about the business. He has thirty gyms all over the UK but wanted *my* advice. He wanted me to train people. He had me run an HIIT workout with the head office at their AGM. He said I was the example of how classes should be run. So surely it was worth it? To be wanted, to be appreciated. But then, poof.' I clicked my fingers. 'Gone.'

'He'll be regretting it now, I know,' Ren said. 'I bet everyone is leaving.'

I shook my head. 'You think that but the world keeps spinning, even when it stops for you. And I didn't tell my clients. I wish I could have, but it was too much. Too messy. I'd lost ten years of graft overnight, and suddenly I didn't know who I was without it. All of those hours spent giving people advice about their knees, or not invoicing people who said they were struggling—'

Ren tutted.

'—I know, I know. I shouldn't let people walk all over me. But I just... struggle to say no.'

'I know you do.' Ren's hand twitched, as if he might reach for mine. My breath snagged. But then he dropped it, fingers curling into a fist. 'I interrupted, sorry. Go on.'

'I didn't know what to do. I couldn't get out of bed. I had no reason to. And then things started getting bad – I'd wake up feeling this crippling panic about what to do with my day. Too many options – apply for jobs or change my whole life. Both feel impossible.'

'I think change sounds good,' Ren said, crossing his arms. 'For both of us.'

'Well, I'm not really one for change.' I shrugged. 'I like routine. I like reliability.'

I hesitated, then added, more softly, 'But, for the record – I think Liam's making a big mistake.'

Many people didn't realise that Ren's passion and drive for the things he truly cared about were utterly infectious. I knew the farm would thrive because he had this remarkable ability to make others believe in his vision. It was the same way he could talk me into sneaking out at 16 to join a house party or convince me to go skinny-dipping on a midnight walk on Kynance Cove on our family holiday to Cornwall. His enthusiasm was always impossible to resist.

Ren held my gaze, something unspoken flickering behind his eyes. Sadness maybe. Gratitude. A little bit of hope.

Then finally, he said, 'Thank you, Lyds.'

We stood silently for a moment until my feet got cold and we slowly walked back to our tents. I bent to unzip the tent, but Ren's hand landed on mine, warm and familiar. I froze, eyes fixed on the veins across his skin, too aware of how close we were. And too scared to look up and see what was written on his face.

'I just want to say I'm sorry about what happened with Momentum.' Ren took a deep breath. In and out. As if this was painful to say. 'And thank you for listening about the farm. And not laughing.'

'I'd never laugh, Ren.'

'I know. I just wanted to tell you to prove to you I'm not leaving again. I'm here to stay. Whether I get the farm or not. I'm here to stay.'

'Okay,' I said, too quickly.

Later, back in my sleeping bag, I felt the words catch up with me.

I'm here to stay.

They echoed in the dark, steady and dangerous, until I drifted off to sleep.

Chapter Ten

Ren

The last hike in the peaks took us through Bleaklow and Snake Pass, with 11 miles of walking through heather-clad moorlands and up limestone cliffs. The glow of the first-day hike had worn off, and the ladies were quiet on the journey but bonded enough that the silent offering of snacks and water was met with a small, appreciative smile. Peggy continued to weave around the group, loving her off-lead freedom, her blonde tail wagging. It should make me smile, but I didn't take my eyes off Lydia's swinging ponytail as she walked across the desolate moorland.

It had been two nights since our midnight chat, and I swear she was letting me in – just a little. She'd let me refill her water bottle, even accepted the cup of tea I made from the camp stove. After catching up on what we'd missed – like the farm and Lydia losing her job – it felt as if we'd struck a quiet understanding of why we were both out here.

But that made it even harder to watch the slight limp from the blisters I knew were on her left ankle. I grimaced at the rub of her shoulders and imagined the red skin underneath. I gritted my teeth when she gave a bright smile to Mandy, who asked after her ankle.

I finally snapped when Lydia offered to hold Amy's pack as we ascended Bleaklow Head, passing World War II aircraft wreckage sites Mandy has a Wikipedia-like knowledge of.

TAKE A HIKE!

'I'll take it,' I said, offering my palm to Amy. The three of us stopped as the rest of the group walked ahead up the hill. Peggy turned around, searching for me, then cantered back to where we stood, and I gave her a little pat.

Lydia's face was like stone. Gone was the woman who had smiled at the idea of pumpkin patches and Christmas trees last night. We had both shared a moment last night under the star-lit sky, but she avoided my gaze this morning. God, she'd looked so beautiful, the light of the moon hitting the side of her face, giving me just a glimpse of her blue eyes and painting her blonde hair silver.

'It's fine, I can handle it,' Lydia said, her jaw set, her eyes flashing.

Oh, I'm in trouble. Good.

'Oh, I don't want to make a fuss.' Amy's face turned pink. 'I can do it, just sometimes I get a bit tired up the hills. Silly, I know. It was my fault for packing so much.' Amy rolled her eyes. 'I never pack light.'

'You two have that in common.' I raised an eyebrow at Lydia.

'Amy, you don't have to explain.' Lydia shot me a death glare. 'I can carry it.'

I knew from Lydia that Amy had some lingering fatigue from her cancer treatment as a kid. I overheard Mandy chatting to her, saying she could skip out a day if the fatigue hit. But I knew she never held back from training hard with Lydia too. Lydia's Instagram posts detailed Amy's journey, a story of her milestones, despite her challenges with fatigue. I admired her for it. I knew Lydia did too. That's why Lydia would sacrifice her short-term pain for Amy. She knew Amy was perfectly capable, but needed support now and then.

'Amy, why don't I take the heavier stuff from your backpack?' I smiled, trying to put her at ease. I kept my voice low enough that the other members of the group didn't look over. I didn't want to embarrass her. 'That way you can keep your pack on. I know how much you like a challenge.' I lean in, a little conspiratorial, a little cheeky. 'I've seen Lydia's Instagram. You could probably bench-press me if you fancied.'

Amy went a little pink. 'No – I couldn't.'

'Trust me, you could.'

Amy lit up. 'Did you hear that, Lydia?'

'Yes,' said Lydia, her voice flat. I turn to see Lydia's arms crossed, her eyes shifting between Amy and me. 'And I'm not surprised. Ren has never been one to *commit* to training.'

'Maybe I just need to commit to a good trainer.' I leaned towards Lydia to whisper, 'Put me in, Coach.'

'Don't call me Coach.'

'Why?' I grinned.

A beautiful blush was creeping up Lydia's neck. I was throwing her off. So I used that opportunity to seal the deal.

'What's the heaviest thing in your bag, Amy?'

I threw my bag down, clipping it open.

'Are you sure?' Amy's eyes shifted between Lydia and me, as if she were worried there was some underlying tension she was unaware of.

'Amy, come on.' I gestured around. 'It's the least I can do for crashing this trip. Right, Lydia? You were fine with putting me to work the other night.'

I'm not ashamed to say I added a flirty edge to my voice. It's got me out of more than one scrape in my life – from a business-class upgrade to weaselling my way out of a parking ticket. Liam always hated the way I did it. He said consequences bounced off me. Like it wasn't a skill in itself to be bold enough to try.

Don't ask, don't get, Mum used to say.

Lydia's eyes narrowed, but she nodded to Amy.

'Okay, if you're sure,' Amy said, a little dazed. I took some of her items and, by the time she put her backpack back on her shoulders, she sighed with relief.

'Thanks, Ren.' Amy smiled. 'That's much better now.'

'It's nothing.' I smiled, my eyes on Lydia. 'Maybe I need to go up a weight, *Coach*.'

Lydia rolled her eyes, but I knew I'd made her smile. Even internally.

Amy made her way back to the group, moving faster than before. Peggy followed her, cantering to rejoin the group.

'Why did you do that? Take her stuff?'

My eyes shift to Lydia's ankle. 'You're in pain. Your boots are rubbing, and so are the straps on your backpack. You were going to make it worse carrying both of those packs.'

Lydia raised her chin. 'I could have done it.'

'Of course you could.' I raised an eyebrow. 'But would you push your clients through injuries?'

Her silence was a quiet victory I refused to rub in her face. I would have done it years ago, but we weren't there yet.

'It's pretty simple, Lyds,' I said quietly. 'I don't like seeing you in pain. And if I can do something to avoid that, then I will.' Her head snapped up, eyes locking on mine, searching. Maybe to see if I was joking, maybe for a way to explain away my words. But I didn't give her one.

I saw the exact moment she absorbed my words. Something in her softened, just for a second, before she blinked it away.

She swallowed, then nodded. 'Okay.'

We walked silently for a few beats before she muttered, almost too quietly, 'Thank you.'

My chest tightened, expanding with something warm and insistent.

'No problem.'

'Right, if everyone wants to stop here for a second.' Mandy brought everyone to a halt. 'There is a time-honoured tradition on these trips of doing a little race up the last of the hill, up to the summit of Bleaklow. Now, anyone too tired can walk with me, but I suspect we have some people ready for a challenge.' Her eyes shifted to Lydia, and I huffed a laugh until her eyes landed on me too.

'This path here,' Mandy gestured to the grassy path littered with stones, 'leads to the peak. First to the top wins first shower at the campsite.'

My eyes flickered to Lydia, who was biting her lip in a way I know is assessing her likelihood of winning, weighing up the effort and reward. I knew she had decided to go ahead when her eyes flicked to me, her natural opponent since she was six. Lydia never had any siblings to fight against, to beat, to give her the first taste of victory. And Liam had been too old and weary after losing Mum for games by the time I'd been ready to compete. So it was Lydia and me. And I loved it. We'd compete over the last slice of pizza, or who could run to the end of the garden the fastest or who could down the pints the quickest. I usually lost, even when I actually wanted the prize, but I was soothed by the glorious look on Lydia's face – flushed and victorious.

But she was injured.

'Lydia,' I warned. 'Your blisters.'

'I'll do it,' Lydia blurted out, then faced me with a challenge in her eyes. God, I missed that look.

Fine. If she was going to run, I was going to run with her. At least I'd be on hand to help if she made her blisters worse.

'Me too,' I added, and her eyes narrowed at the contented smile I knew drove her crazy.

Mutters through the group told us that there weren't any other takers. It was just us and my chest roared. If I could see that beautiful blush on her face, I was going to win either way.

'Okay. Looks like its Ren and Lydia for the last stretch, then we'll follow up and see who wins.' Mandy turned to us. 'No sore losers.'

I whistled. 'In that case, Lydia will have to drop out.'

'Excuse me!'

'Come on. You know you're the biggest sore loser, Lyds.'

'Am not!'

'You stomped on my foot after I won that hundred-metre race at school.'

'Because you cheated! You started early and moved into my lane.'

I held up my hands. 'It wasn't my fault you weren't ready.'

'You liar. You just had the teacher wrapped around your finger!'

We were breathless, throwing accusations back and forth, a barely suppressed smile on my face, a blush on her cheeks, when we turned to find the group staring at us, in various states of shock and fascination.

'Oh, Jesus,' Gen muttered loudly to Amy. 'They could be more subtle.'

'Let's get this over with.' Lydia rolled her shoulders.

I put Peggy's lead on to keep her from running after us, and thanked Amy, who offered to watch her.

I shot Lydia a grin as she rolled her shoulders, earning a droll look that clearly said, *you're an idiot*. Mandy drew the line to start, and we immediately started bickering about whose foot was too far over it.

I was in heaven.

Mandy shouted 'Go!' and I pelted down the path but Lydia, as usual, was too quick and pulled in front of me down the narrow path. The trail opened up and I picked up the pace, my thighs burning and screaming as we climbed higher. My chest begged me to stop. I hadn't done a workout like this in months but I kept pushing on, just to keep up with the Lycra-clad woman in front of me, the tight material hugging her curves. She always looked so invincible when she ran or shifted heavy weights. I craved to watch her at work. Sometimes I'd just turn up under the guise of meeting her for a coffee break, just to watch her pick up dumbbells and move them over her head with ease, as her poor class groaned in front of her. She was superwoman.

I almost tripped over a tree root and muttered a filthy word that had Lydia glancing behind her, grinning.

'Careful, Lawrence. Looks like you're out of steam.'

'Yeah, yeah.' I pretended to be pissed off, cos I knew it would make her happier. 'We're not at the end yet, Sunshine.'

She picked up the pace but I did too and, by some miracle, I kept close behind her, close enough that I could stretch my hand out and grab her ponytail, or her waist, pulling her back to me, hold her close, feel her heart race against my chest—

No.

She wasn't even close to being my friend again, let alone to deal with all the other feelings that had awoken on the night we spent together. The feelings that had me running away from her.

Lydia was still ahead as we reached the peak of the hill, but I was close enough to hear her breathless, manic laugh as she pushed forward, somehow pulling out all the stops at the last minute. She slapped her palm against the stone marker, and then spun around to face me, wild-eyed and grinning. Her hair had escaped the ponytail and her chest was rising and falling rapidly, her whole body buzzing with triumph.

I hunched over, hands on my knees, gasping for air, but I couldn't stop looking at her – the flush to her cheeks and the look of victory on her face.

'I won.' She threw her arms above her head. 'I won. First shower is mine. Suck it, Hunter.'

I huffed out a laugh. 'Well done.'

'You were slow.' Her eyes narrowed. 'Did you let me win?'

'I didn't let you win, Lydia,' I scoffed, gesturing to myself, sweating twice as much, barely standing upright, while she fixed her ponytail. 'Would I look like this if I'd let you win?'

'I've seen you in better shape.'

I snorted. 'Charming.'

'Did you mean what you said earlier?' She tilted her head.

'About lifting less than Amy? Or did you say that to make her feel better?'

'Lydia. You have that girl deadlifting a hundred and twenty kilos. I work in a bar five days a week and shake cocktails for a living. What do you think?'

'You make a good point. But they are good cocktails,' she said, kicking a stone.

'Thank you.' I managed to pull myself upright, staggering closer to her. 'And you're a good coach.'

My smile was soft and tired, and she allowed me close enough to smell the perfume and sweat radiating off her.

'I—' She glanced away. 'I could put you together a training plan if you wanted. I have them already, so it wouldn't be much for me to send one over.'

Warmth spread through me. I knew she was holding back, but her instinct was still there – to help me.

'Thanks, Lyds. I'll make you a deal. What do you weigh?' I asked, assessing. 'What – seventy kilos?'

'Seventy-six.' She corrected me, extending her biceps with a grin. 'Give me some credit. I'm stronger than that.'

I grinned, stepping forward and wrapping my hand around her arm. Her skin was soft, but the muscle underneath was strong.

I hummed. 'I stand corrected.'

My hand stilled there and I watched Lydia's throat bob.

'Why don't we make a deal?' I said, my voice low. 'If you send me a plan, I'll make sure I can always deadlift seventy-six.' My eyes shifted up and down. 'And squat it… bench-press it.' I glanced up to find her cheeks flushed pink. 'Just something to keep in mind.'

Lydia's eyes flicked up to mine, then – for just a second – dropped to my mouth.

'Deal,' she said, her voice husky.

I ran my hand down her arm, marvelling at the feeling of her hands, running my fingers along hers. I hadn't touched her in so long. It felt like a cooling bath after a day under the sun. I'd always loved the power of her hands and what they could do – they were a perfect combination of lithe and strong. I brought her hand up to my mouth and kissed it. Lydia inhaled, sharp and quiet.

I knew she was remembering the last time I'd kissed her palms, that night in her bed, when everything had blurred and contorted into something new. Something scary. But something I was ready to face now. Lydia should have pulled back by now, like she had before. Throw harsh words at me or make a cutting joke. I would have welcomed that over the icy sunshine she had given me for the last year. But she didn't. I stared at her, trying to tell her I was hers for the taking.

I raised an eyebrow.

Your move next.

Her blue eyes narrowed in challenge and my lips twisted up. I should have realised a challenge would get her to play. She stepped forward into me, close, close, and closer.

Yes.

All I could feel was the heat of her body, the touch of her hands.

She crowded my senses and it was all I wanted.

Her nose grazed my jaw, her breath warm, as she ran her fingers through mine, clasping them at my side. My pulse hammered against my ribs. It was as if we were animals circling each other in the wilderness. I inhaled her perfume, the sweat on her skin, the smell of Lydia, and something in my chest tightened, twisted, and ached.

'You look beautiful when you win.' My voice was soft, but the words landed heavily. 'I've always loved when we compete. But I love it when you beat me even more. You looked like an avenging goddess.'

Lydia stuttered – the sound mangled, choked, as if her brain had short-circuited mid-word.

'You shouldn't say stuff like that, Ren.'

'I know.' I watched her throat bob as she swallowed, her hands clenched at her sides. I gave a slow smile. 'Doesn't stop me thinking it, though.'

I didn't finish my sentence because my hands slipped out of hers to hold her waist, hold her back from torturing me any longer. I pulled her in to me, planning on the ways I could get her up against a tree and press her further against me. Lock her there, keep her.

A rustle of leaves.

A girlish laugh.

A stomp of boots.

Lydia pulled away as if a bucket of water had been thrown over us just as Gen, Jade, and the others came into view. Peggy walked over to greet them, her bum wiggling.

Lydia turned to them, jumping away from me, as if we'd been caught doing something truly scandalous. If I'd had it my way, we would have been.

Mandy came into view, a conspiratorial smile on her face, 'So who won?'

Lydia slipped on a smile, pretending the last 30 seconds hadn't just happened.

But I saw it.

The way her smile didn't quite meet her eyes.

'She did, of course,' I said, keeping it light. 'Lydia always wins in the end.'

Her eyes flicked to mine, narrowed slightly.

'I don't,' she said quietly.

Chapter Eleven

Lydia's Diary, 13 Years Old

Dear Diary,
 Ren came over last night, and we went to my room to watch a film on my DVD player. It felt... different. Not bad, just a bit strange, like maybe we were getting too old for this.
 Did it mean we were... together? Like boyfriend and girlfriend?
 Annabel has a boyfriend at school, but they never even hold hands. Honestly, I don't think they've ever spoken outside of lunch. It's weird. But Ren and I actually talk. We hang out all the time. He helps me with my maths homework, and I help him with English, but I wonder if he actually needs the help. He's a lot smarter than people realise, he just doesn't like to make much effort.
 I thought about asking him, but what if he laughed? Or worse – what if he stopped coming over? Sometimes he looks so sad when he gets here, like his whole day has been heavy, but he always cheers up when we put a film on. That's why I always pick the funny ones. *Shrek* is one of his favourites.
 After he left, Mum said it was fine for him to come into my room, but the door had to stay open now, and there would be no more sleepovers. I told her I didn't care, but I did a little bit. It felt like something was changing, and I wasn't sure if I liked it.

Oh, and he smelled nice.
Love,
Lydia.

Lydia

The water scalded my skin, a hum catching in my throat – even as guilt thrummed in my chest for taking the only hot shower.

Mandy explained on our arrival to the camp, which was much smaller and more rustic than the last, that while there was a shower block, there was only one cubicle with working hot water, despite her appeals to the owners to keep it in working order. I'd offered it to Amy as she sat outside her tent with a dazed look that told me she was knackered. She looked desperate to shower and to hit the hay, but she waved me off with a smile. I didn't hold back the victorious, smug look I shot Ren as I grabbed my microfibre towel and headed to the shower block, and I heard his huffed laugh.

I shifted my shoulders, shaking them under the hot water, feeling it burn on my cold skin. I had a complicated relationship with showers – I hated the idea of them, the wet floors, hair sticking to my skin. But once I was under the hot spray, the smell of my shampoo in my nostrils, I never wanted to leave. You could call it a love-hate relationship of sorts. It was worse knowing I'd leave this warm shower cubicle, my wet hair hitting the fresh air, covering me in a chill.

But what I truly hated, even more than cold, wet skin, was washing my hair. I exercised for a living. There was never a perfect day for it, never a guarantee I wouldn't blow-dry it only to sweat through it minutes later. It was the bane of my career – but also a reminder that my problems were, on the whole, pretty minimal.

My throat thickened. Hair washing wasn't a problem now. I had no job, no gym, no clients.

I squeezed my eyes shut as the panic tried to push itself through my blood.

Just don't think about it.

I shut off the water, rubbing my skin dry with the thin, pink towel. I wrapped the towel around myself, berating myself for not just bringing my clothes in here and changing – it would be a cold run across the campsite back to the tent. I braced myself, opening the door, preparing to run, until a warm, firm body slammed into mine.

Ren had come out of the cubicle opposite me, his body colliding with mine, almost making me drop my towel. I held on tighter, my hair still around my shoulders, and looked up to find Ren...

...topless.

He ran a hand through his damp hair, stray droplets sliding down the hard planes of his chest. My eyes traced the tanned skin down to where his dark-wash jeans sat low on his hips. My eyes followed his forearms as they flexed, clutching a flimsy towel in his right hand. Ren was lean, never bulky, but there was strength in the way he moved. As if he could hoist me up without thinking twice, pin me where he wanted, and make me feel how strong he really was.

Surprise rippled through me when I saw dark ink swept from his upper arm, curling over his clavicle and dipping on to his chest. Flowers bloomed in fine lines, delicate, intertwining, anchored by a sun and moon nestled across his pec. It was intricate and beautiful.

I couldn't help but stare.

'God, Lydia. I'm a person, you know. Not a piece of meat.'

His voice yanked me out of my horny trance, my stomach flipping as if I'd been caught doing something I absolutely should *not* be doing. God, the moment at the top of Mam Tor, and now this. Heat crawled up my neck, but I kept my gaze locked on his smirking face as he ran the towel thrown over his shoulder through his damp hair.

Do not look at his chest. Or his arms. Or the V-cut disappearing into the waistband of his jeans.

I glanced up to find that I wasn't the only one staring. Ren's smirk was gone now, as he made his own perusal. His eyes were darker now, dragging over me with a slow, deliberate stare, as if I'd given him permission to look. As if he wasn't about to waste the opportunity.

A pulse of something electric shot down my spine.

'Lydia. You look so...' His voice was rough, and I hated that my breath hitched, waiting for the next words.

'Tattoo,' I croaked, desperate to change the subject. Or just have a subject, because I hadn't said a word since he'd walked out of the shower.

Ren's expression flickered and a flush crept up his neck. My eyes snagged on the flowers, something about them seeming familiar. I stared at the swirling ink.

'Lilies,' I murmured, reaching out before I could stop myself. 'You got lilies for your mum.'

'Yes.' Ren's voice was husky, strained, and I glanced up to find him staring at where my finger was touching his skin. I pulled away as if I'd been burned.

'Sorry.'

'Don't be,' he said, his voice low. His gaze dropped to my mouth, lingered, then swept down to where the towel clung to my damp skin. 'It's just... I've thought about this. You. And me. What I would do if I had a second chance – and none of those thoughts included a busy campsite or shared shower cubicles.'

Heat bloomed across my cheeks. That voice, that look on his face. It sent me spiralling back to that night in my childhood bedroom, when we'd done very adult things. The sweep of his tongue between my thighs. The way his fingers gripped my hips, held me still as he groaned into my skin. His murmured encouragement, raw and reverent, as I shattered beneath him.

All of those memories played, and I could see from the way Ren's eyes darkened that he had gone there too.

Ren stepped forward, heat radiating off him in waves. And, God, I wanted to crash into him and press my mouth to his, forget everything but the feel of his hands on me. But a voice, small, sharp, and impossible to ignore, sliced through the want.

I had to get a grip. Change the subject. Anything to pull focus from the fact that he was inching closer, his eyes scanning my face as if he was looking for a crack in my resolve.

I forced the words out. 'What does the rest mean? The tattoos.'

He reached for my hand, his fingers wrapped gently around mine, guiding them over his chest. I wasn't breathing. I wasn't even blinking. I was touching him, but it felt like he was touching me – every nerve alight.

'This is for Mum, like you said. And this—' he traced my hand lower, '—this is magnolia.'

My breath caught.

'Because your dad loves telling the story of planting that tree when Sandra was pregnant with you. She cried when she saw it, remember? And he always says it bloomed—'

'—the day I was born.'

Ren nodded. Then he drew my hand across his chest, over the sun and the moon.

'And this... this is me. Dark. A little moody.'

'You're not dark, Ren—'

'Shush,' he said softly, smiling. 'Not finished. This,' his fingers brushed the sun, 'this is you.'

My heart thumped.

'Me?'

'Sunshine,' he said, his gaze lifting to mine, steady, intent, like he needed me to hear this. 'You've always been the light I needed. So I thought I'd keep you here.' He pressed my palm flat against his chest, holding it there. 'Right over my heart. Where you've always been, even when I was too much of an idiot to say it.'

His voice was hoarse now. His eyes flicked down, just for a second, then back to mine. He shifted closer. Just a fraction. If I angled my head up, just slightly—

His breath brushed my cheek. My pulse pounded in my throat. His hand tightened around mine, as if he wanted to keep me there.

'When,' I managed, 'when did you get this?'

'The day before I flew out. Gen squeezed me in. Rushed appointment.'

It was like a bucket of ice-cold water was thrown over me. I stepped back, wrapping my towel around me.

While I'd been spiralling, confused and heartbroken, he'd been inked with secret messages he didn't have the guts to tell me. He didn't get to do this – show up with pretty words and art etched across his skin. He didn't get to tell me that it had been there all along, while I lay in bed alone, reliving whatever I'd done wrong that night. While I agonised over what I should have done differently.

'Lydia.'

'It looks good.' My voice was distant, light.

Just smile, Lydia.

'Lydia. Talk to me.'

'I'm a bit cold,' I gestured to the tent. 'I better—'

'Lydia, wait.'

I stopped, but refused to turn around. I couldn't look at those tattoos.

'We're going back to Everly Heath,' Ren said. 'Before the Wales trip.'

'Yes.'

Mandy gave us a weekend between trips to refuel and rest before we trekked four days across Wales and climbed Snowdon.

Ren said, his voice thick, 'If... if you were open to it, we could go to Wales together. I'm driving there anyway and I can pick you up.'

I didn't turn back, as I said, 'I know you think we're okay. I know we've shared a few laughs. But I'm not there yet. Nowhere near. There is so much—' my voice cracked.

There is so much I was still angry about, and I couldn't even put it into words.

'I know and I'm here if you want to shout or scream at me. I get it—'

I turned, meeting his gaze.

'Ren. Are you listening to me? I'm not there yet. The more I'm around you, the more I realise that I haven't processed anything. You leaving, what happened between us. Losing my job. None of it. So you need to stop pushing me.'

His nod came immediately, flooding me with a confusing combination of relief and guilt.

'Absolutely. I totally understand. I'm sorry I pushed you. I won't do it again.'

He ran his hands through his hair, keeping his eyes on the grass. He was growing quite a bit of stubble on the trip, and I hated how it made him look even more handsome, more rugged, although I'd always liked his boyish features. I got up to leave, feeling the need to put distance between us. But even then, I couldn't completely dismiss him.

'Ren—' I spun to face him, and he stood upright, like an eager Boy Scout.

He turned, his eyes eager. 'Yes?'

My lips twitched. He looked like a Boy Scout.

'It hasn't been completely terrible. You know, having you on this trip.'

The small, hopeful smile he offered me in return threatened to crack my resolve in half.

Chapter Twelve

Ren

'You pathetic coward,' I shouted across the gym floor.

I'd timed it perfectly. Peak gym hours. Maximum audience. The echo bounced off the high-gloss walls and polished mirrors of Momentum's main training space – a posh, pristine set-up, all reflective and stainless-steel. Craig was barking instructions, leading a packed-out circuit training group in the centre of the room, until my voice cut through it like a dropped barbell.

Metal weights clattered to the floor. Treadmills slowed. Heads turned. Every eye in the place shifted to me as I made my way towards Craig's ratty face.

I'd been planning this since Lydia told me what he'd done – since I saw her face fall as she pieced it together. The subtle, devastating discrimination. The way he'd used her disability against her, knowing exactly what he was doing.

'Excuse me?' Craig rose to his full height – all five foot seven of it.

His black hair was slicked back, just like the first time I'd seen him. Lydia had been showing me the new equipment and he'd called her over just to embarrass her. He'd told her we'd been too loud, and that she wasn't allowed to have non-members in the gym without his approval. She'd come back with her cheeks flushed and her spark dimmed. He'd always seen her light – and wanted to snuff it out. I should have said something then. God,

I wanted to, the second I saw that look on her face. But she'd begged me not to.

Don't make a fuss, she said. *It's fine.*

Well, it wasn't fucking fine now.

Craig cocked his head. 'Do I know you?'

He knew exactly who I was.

Because every time I swung by the gym to pick Lydia up — whether we were headed to the cinema or out for the night — his beady little eyes tracked me like a threat. Craig had always been weirdly fixated on Lydia in a way that made my skin crawl.

'She worked here for years,' I snapped. 'Put up with your bullshit daily. You kept her late to clean the gym. You undermined her in front of her clients. And now you sack her? Just like that?'

All eyes swung to Craig, whose face was turning a beautiful shade of puce. Craig's jaw twitched. He was trying to stay composed, but his eyes flickered like a cornered animal.

'This is a private matter between myself and a staff member,' he said stiffly.

'Oh, so *now* you know who I am.' I stepped forward into Craig's personal space.

The thing about being at the edge of your emotions at all times was that it was easy to step into them. They were always there, simmering at my fingertips.

Love, hope, rage, frustration.

I'd always felt so much. I hadn't learnt to manage my emotions until I went into therapy at 16 and, slowly but surely, I developed better ways to deal with the surging North Sea that was my feelings. But the best bit? Was letting it go when someone deserved it.

Don't get me wrong — I wasn't some alpha dickhead. I'd always been the one to get punched. Admittedly, it was because I knew exactly how to push someone's buttons to make them see red. Although I hadn't leaned into this particular skill in a while —

not since my brother had me by the scruff of the neck two years ago. And my brother didn't count, surely? Who didn't wind up their siblings until they wanted to strangle you?

I had matured. Mostly. Now I was the one de-escalating fights in bars.

But I was more than happy to reprise my role as chief shithouser for Lydia. I was happy to do this for her, say the words that I know she wouldn't have thrown in his face – yet. And I'd be more than happy to drive her to this gym when she was ready to say them herself. It took Lydia a while to process how she felt, but when she was ready... well, Craig better duck for cover. An angry Lydia was a rare sight, and *much* scarier than me.

'I think everyone here deserves to know why Lydia Williams isn't working here any more,' I said, addressing Craig's class. Half of them had been Lydia's clients once upon a time. 'I don't know what he's told you – probably something about new pastures, new opportunities. But he effectively fired her. No notice. No reason. Just blindsided her.'

Craig sputtered, 'I didn't fire anyone. Our personal trainers are freelance—'

'Fucking semantics,' I spat. 'You terminated her contract out of nowhere, blindsiding her. All because you were jealous that she did your job better than you. All because she was more likeable than you. You were threatened – because talking to you is like trying to have a meaningful conversation with a toilet brush.'

Out of the corner of my eye, two women looked at each other and shrugged, like, *he's not wrong*.

'Our pal Craig here planned to get her out – and waited until her contract was due for renewal to do it.' I clamped a hand on Craig's shoulder, which was admittedly solid.

'I just thought everyone should know what a piece of shit you are,' I whispered. 'And what dirty tactics you're more than happy to use. I'm not as quiet as you, huh? She worked her arse off here for years,' I said, voice rising. 'And you nitpicked every bloody second of it. Timekeeping, formatting, her invoices not matching your weird little spreadsheet template.' I shook my head. 'You were never managing her. You were waiting for her to mess up.'

I took another step forward, lowering my voice.

'You knew she struggled with numbers. And, instead of supporting her, you used it as a reason to push her out. You made her feel small for something she can't control.'

Craig opened his mouth, but I didn't let him speak.

'Tell me, Craig. Did you document that properly? Did you make reasonable adjustments? Because, from where I'm standing, it sounds a lot like discrimination. And wouldn't that be fun to explain to Niall?'

Craig's face flickered with panic, and I knew it then. I grinned, showing my teeth.

'Ah! Now we're getting closer to the truth. Interesting.' Craig's eyes grew dark and empty, making me shudder, thinking of Lydia working with this man. 'He doesn't know, does he? I wonder what Niall would have to say about his golden employee being shoved out without a word. What did you tell him, huh? That she'd gone to work for some other gym? That she'd been too emotional about leaving Momentum to tell him to his face?' I hummed. 'Naughty, naughty, Craig.'

I booped his nose, and that's when I saw it – the final wave of anger. Craig launched for my hand, pulling it with force away from his face, and pulling his other hand into a fist, aimed directly at my face.

And there we go, ladies and gentlemen.

I could always make them throw the first punch.

The class gasped, and people leaped off their treadmills.

'Take it easy, son,' an older, grey-haired gentleman said to Craig.

'Easy does it,' another added.

Craig's face morphed into embarrassment, with a nice hint of shame. Good. I hoped he felt even an inch of what he'd made Lydia feel.

'Yeah,' I said, my voice low enough that I knew only Craig could hear me. 'Take it easy, Craig. Don't want to have evidence of you punching a paying customer.' My eyes shifted to the CCTV cameras behind Craig, with a perfect view of his attempted punch. 'I think that might be a sackable offence. God knows, you whip them out of your arse,' I added.

Craig shoved me away, and I smiled, stepping back with my hands up, as if I hadn't been the antagonist of this whole interaction.

'Have a good day, Craig.'

I swivelled on my heel, practically skipped towards the exit, but not before I asked for Niall's email and phone number at reception.

I thought he'd be very interested in what I had to say.

Chapter Thirteen

Dear Lydia,

I know this letter isn't enough. Nowhere near enough. But I'm too much of a coward to say this to your face – to see that look in your eyes. I'm leaving tomorrow morning.

This isn't about you. It isn't about us. I need you to believe that.

I'm trying to be someone better. Someone worthy of the way you see the world. Of the way you see me.

This is my chance to figure that out. And – as always – my timing is absolute shit.

Our timing is shit.

Love always,
Ren

Ren

The door banged three times on my second swirl of the beef ragu, 'Watermelon Sugar' blasting from my speakers. Peggy cocked her head, listening intently. I thought it must be my mad neighbours in another argument of theirs until Peggy shot up, barking, at the fourth and fifth bang on the door. I huffed, laying down the wooden spoon, and strolled to the door in a leisurely fashion. Banging at my door wouldn't make me rush. It wasn't until I looked through the viewfinder at the blonde head at the door that I stood ramrod-straight, my breath coming short.

TAKE A HIKE!

Lydia had her arms crossed, her face flushed, and sporting her familiar colourful workout gear. Today it was bright green. Something dropped in my stomach, but butterflies quickly took over, lifting whatever had dropped down my throat. Sure, I'd been around her, walking beside her, sleeping near her for days. But now she was at my door for the first time in *years*. I fumbled with the lock on the door, about to ask her in, as she took advantage of the open door and pushed past me into my apartment. She already knew the layout, so she swung left into my kitchen. I pushed down the smile that threatened to appear.

'Lydia. Come in. Make yourself at home,' I said dryly, earning a sharp look that rippled all over my skin.

I missed the curl of her lips, her laugh and her friendship. But, God, did I miss that cutting look more than anything. The look said I was more than the sunshine facade she gave everyone else. It meant she gave me light and dark and everything else in between.

Lydia whirled around. Peggy circled her, her tail wagging, oblivious to the tension in the room.

Lydia's eyes glazed over, travelling down my bare torso and back up again. Light pink dusted her cheeks.

She huffed and raised a palm. 'Can you put some clothes on? God!'

I wanted to chuckle. So this attraction of ours wasn't one-sided. Even if she was less likely to admit it than me.

'You stormed into my flat, Lyds.'

'Don't.' She held up a finger, her eyes sharp. 'Don't open your mouth.'

'Really? Women usually like my—'

'What were you thinking?'

'You'll have to be more specific. Before or after the almost-kiss at the top of Mam Tor? Or the part where you caught me fresh out of the shower? Are you sure you want to know what I was thinking? Or will it make you run again?'

I stepped forward. Her eyes widened, her gaze tracing the tattoos on my chest. Her breath was coming quickly, and I knew she felt this pull between us, even if she denied it.

'Craig.'

Ah. That. I should have known someone in Everly Heath would spill the beans.

'I was thinking,' I said firmly, 'that prick had it coming. That someone needed to do something. That you deserved someone who'd stand up for you.'

'I didn't ask you to do that.' Her eyes flared, cheeks flushed with anger. 'I don't need a white knight charging in to save me.'

'Well, tough. You have one. And I don't regret it. Just like I won't regret it if you want to drive over and tell that arsehole yourself.' I grabbed my car keys. 'I'll go now if you want. You can say whatever you want to say, to his face. I won't say a word. I'll just sit back and watch you eviscerate him.'

'Ren.' She swiped a hand across her forehead. 'You can't do this, Ren. This – this is all so fucking confusing.'

Her voice softened and it broke me. I could take her anger and bear it, but she looked soft and defeated. And I couldn't stand it. It made me want to wrap her up in my clothes, run her a bath and keep her fed.

'I'm sorry. I came on too strong. Come here, sit down.' I nudged her gently towards the bar stools. 'My point is, I'm not going to let some smug, entitled arsehole – who has made your life hell for years, by the way – manipulate you out of a job you love. A job you're brilliant at. Not without consequences.'

She sat stiffly, her eyes on the floor. I tucked a loose strand of hair behind her ear, desperate for her to look at me. But her jaw was set, all quiet defiance.

'What are you doing, Ren?'

I glanced around the kitchen. 'Well, until you stormed in, raring for a fight, I was making dinner. Still warm, if you want some?'

Her eyes flicked to the pot on the stove, then quickly away. 'Not that. This. *Us.* What exactly is your play here?'

I raised a brow, but she barrelled on.

'You say you just want to be my friend. Then you flirt with me. You touch me. And at the top of Mam Tor we—'

Her mouth snapped shut like she could take the words back.

I stepped closer. She didn't move or breathe. And I saw it then. The panic and the ache she was trying to hide under all that fire.

I tilted her chin with my fingers, slowly and gently. 'Look at me.'

Her wild blue eyes met mine.

Home, I thought. These eyes were *home*.

'We almost kissed,' I said, voice low. 'You can say it out loud, Lydia. God knows, I've thought of nothing else since I drove away.'

Her eyes narrowed, smacking away my hand. 'And what if we had kissed, Ren? Would you have disappeared again?'

I rubbed a hand across my mouth. 'No, Lydia. I've told you. I'm here. I'm not going anywhere.'

Her voice cut through me, hard as steel. 'This could never work. And it's not just us, you know. We'd be dragging everyone into it – Mum and Dad. Kat and Liam. Your dad too. If we messed this up again—'

'We don't *have* to mess it up again.'

She shook her head. 'We already did. We ruined the friendship the night we—' she broke off, jaw tightening. A long breath. Then her eyes found mine.

'When you woke up in my bed,' she said quietly, 'and left without a word.'

'I left a note—'

'Oh, fuck your note!' she spat out. 'It didn't say anything, Ren. It was a collection of bloody riddles. I couldn't make head nor tail of it. All I know is you got on a flight. I don't even know where you were. I didn't know who you were with. If you were safe—'

Her voice broke at the last word, and so did my heart. So I took a calculated risk. I stepped forward, cradling her jaw in my hands. And I wagered wrong, because she pulled away like I had scorched her.

'I don't want your sympathy.' She rose from the bar stool, stepping into my space. Did she know she was doing that? 'I want to know what you think will happen once we're *friends*. What is your play?'

'I never said I had a play, Lydia.'

'Then why do you keep *looking* at me?' she snapped, her cheeks pink. Her fiery blue eyes didn't leave mine, and I was transfixed. 'You keep looking at me. Touching me. You're always there, helping, being—' she gestures to me. 'Being you. It's insufferable. I can't stand it.'

'Sounds like I've got under your skin, Lyds.'

She scoffed. I take a step closer, and her face drops.

'Good. Because you're under mine. I tried to escape it. I tried to convince myself I could stay away from you. I tried to convince myself that I could move miles across the globe and not think of you *every single fucking day*. But guess what? I was wrong. So fucking wrong. So if I have to be your friend, then fine. I'll take whatever you give me.' I stepped forward, my eyes blazing up and down her. 'But let's not pretend it's gone. This.' I take her hand, bringing it to my chest so she could feel my heart race for her. 'Let's not pretend that whatever we started that night, whatever has always existed in some way between us, whatever I ran from like a coward, isn't still here. Because it is.'

Her face was angled up, her eyes shifting between mine. Her chest heaved like mine. She wet her lips.

'You have no idea what you do to me. How much I want you.' I said it low, rough with truth, every word peeling off a layer I'd been hiding behind. It felt reckless. It felt *right*. 'When you pull your hair up into a ponytail, I want to wrap my hand around it badly. When you glare at me for being helpful, I want to kiss the look off your face. When you laugh, your face lights up. When you're jealous...' She let out a puff of indignant air. 'Even if you won't admit it. You have no idea how much I *want* – and how much of it is not friendly.'

She sucked in a breath.

'So you're right. We can't be friends. Maybe I lied. To myself, more than anything. I'm not sure I can ever *just* be friends with you, Lydia. But I know that if you rip this cord, this connection between us, I'm not sure I'll survive it. So I'll give whatever morsels you'll give me.'

My gaze dropped to her lips. 'And you should know. All I can think of right now is how much I want to kiss you – and how I know you want to kiss me too.'

Lydia's eyes shifted to my lips and it took everything I had to hold still. Time stretched between us.

'Fuck it!'

And her soft lips met mine.

It took a moment of brain lag to wonder if this was another dream and if I'd wake up frustrated and alone. But then her lips pulled back, and I seized the opportunity, moving forward to meet her lips. She paused, and I pulled back, only to kiss her again, soft and sweet, on the corner of her mouth. Gentle. As if I was trying to temper any panic or thoughts that might follow this kiss. I kissed the other side of her mouth.

Her hands came up into my hair, and she finally pulled me closer; her lips landed on mine. There was no playing this time. And she lit me on fire. The kiss intensified, a battle of our wills and lips, until I had her pressed against the kitchen counter, and my hands palmed the back of her legs, sliding her up on to the counter without breaking our kiss. She gasped as I pulled her flush against me, our bodies aligning as if it was the most natural thing in the world. My cock pressed against the edge of the counter, and I bit back the urge to grind into it – just to feel something, anything, that might take the edge off.

She felt like heaven, and I let my hands roam up the soft material that covered her strong thighs, up to her hips. My hands on her arse, I pulled her towards me, making her gasp into my mouth. In answer, her teeth sank into my bottom lip, and I couldn't hold back the desperate laugh that escaped my lips. Of course, it was a competition.

'God, I've missed you,' I groaned, kissing down her neck, my hands in her hair.

But Lydia stilled. My stomach plummeted.

Don't tell me you've missed me.

I'd done the one thing I'd promised I wouldn't. I wanted to kick myself. Of course I had to ruin this with my big mouth. I couldn't even bring myself to look at her as she pulled herself down from the counter, fixing her ponytail – the one I had messed up.

'Lydia—'

She squeezed her eyes shut. 'Shit! This is so messy. What am I doing?'

'Hey, hey.' My palms grazed her arm, trying to get her to look at me. 'It's okay.'

'This is a mistake, Ren,' she said, softly. She pushed past me, her rose musk lingering in my hallway. I stared after her for a moment, as the door swung shut.

'Well, Peggy,' I said, looking into her warm brown eyes. 'I think I fucked that up.'

Chapter Fourteen

Lydia's Diary, 14 Years Old

Dear Diary,

Soz. I've been MIA for, like, years. But I have something I need to say, and if anyone else ever sees this, I WILL DIE.

This summer, Ren got hot.

Like hot, hot.

It's his fifteenth birthday soon, and I swear it was like BOOM – puberty just smacked him in the face. He's grown a foot since June, his spots are completely gone, and he's actually good at football now instead of falling over his feet.

I mean, usually, I'm the one who's good at football, but he's caught up, and I kind of love it. We push each other, and I don't know why, but it makes me feel... weirdly giddy.

I think it's because it feels a little bit like flirting.

Which is SO stupid. Like, we could never be together. Our families would have a meltdown, and it's not like he actually likes me like that. It's probably just because he's the only guy I hang out with. He's literally my only option.

... Right?

Anyway, I just needed to tell someone.

Love,

Lydia.

Lydia

'Wait. You kissed?' Amy squeaked, nearly dropping her drink.

Two days had passed since the kiss. Two days spent avoiding Ren in Everly Heath. Two days spent trying not to replay the stupid, reckless kiss in his apartment. And now, I was avoiding him in another country – Wales. North Wales, specifically, just at the foot of Snowdon, the largest mountain across both England and Wales.

Gen, Amy, and I sat at the breakfast table of the Red Dragon B&B after a sleepless night. Not because of the beds. The rooms had been perfectly cosy. Mandy had good taste – she never picked a place that wasn't up to scratch. But I hadn't been tossing and turning over thread count. Ren had kissed me. And now, as he sat at another table with Jade and Amara, lazily picking at the bacon and sausage on his plate, my brain was stuck in an endless replay of that kiss.

Scene by scene. His hands, his lips are on mine. The way the playback would slow, stretching every moment to something almost unbearable, only to speed up again – his lips brushing mine, his husky voice in my ear.

You have no idea how much I want you – and how much of it is not friendly.

Pure torture.

I watched as Ren leaned towards Jade to make a comment that had her laughing. I clung to my spoon until it dug into my palm.

'Are you gonna kill someone with that?' Gen asked, her eyebrow raised. ''Cos fine. But you need to warn me so I can get some solid alibis.'

I released the spoon, pushing away the yogurt and berries.

'You should eat,' Claire said as she sat her plate next to us. 'You look a bit peaky, love.'

'I'm okay, but thanks, Claire.' I smiled, but it came out like a grimace. I hated that I was bringing down the energy. I baulked when several of the ladies asked if I was okay this morning, as if sensing my low mood. I needed to pull myself together. I needed to put up a better front than this.

So I pulled the yogurt back towards me and ate a spoonful as Claire smiled. I swallowed, hoping I wouldn't bring it back up.

'So what next?' Amy asked a few moments later, lowering her voice so she wouldn't interrupt Claire and Gen's conversation about our route to Snowdon today – our most challenging hike yet, with steep climbs, scrambles and rough landscapes.

'I don't know. I just left.' I bit my lip. 'I think I should just... ignore him?'

'Ignore him? Can you do that? Can you forget and be friends?'

'I don't know, Amy. I'm not sure we can ever be friends. It would mean rewriting that night. It would mean being happy if another woman came into his life, leaving lipstick smudges on his cheeks and cold cups of tea on his nightstand.'

Amy shot me a sympathetic smile. 'That sounds like you want to be *more* than friends.'

I groaned, 'No. It would never work. We've been there, and we ruined it. I would never want to risk that again.'

'So,' Amy whispered. 'What was the kiss like?'

'Don't make me talk about it, please.'

'Oh, come on.' Amy shot me puppy-dog eyes. 'I'm living vicariously through you here.'

'It was...' I thought about his palm on my jaw, his hands on my waist as he effortlessly lifted me on to the island. My cheeks warmed. 'Something else.'

'Wow. That good, huh?'

'Yes.' I bit my lip. 'But it can't happen again.'

It didn't matter that I'd woken up this morning from a dream where we continued our kiss, feeling his body pressing me into the mattress, him settled between my thighs, and I woke up agitated and confused.

Amy and I glanced over to Ren, but found he was already

looking at me. His gaze was intent, unwavering, eyebrows drawn like I was a puzzle he couldn't quite crack.

I looked away fast as heat rushed to my cheeks.

But when I dared another glance, he winked.

The sheer cheek of it stole my breath. My eyes narrowed. His grin widened.

He knew we were talking about him or, most likely, about the kiss.

'Bastard,' I muttered, stirring the yogurt pot.

'Just ignore him,' Amy said, but it came out like a question.

I needed to get this under control. We needed boundaries. Last night was a moment of weakness and I *wasn't* planning on repeating history.

Hiking was fucking bollocks. I mentally chanted the sentence again and again.

My fist clenched as the wind whipped around us, sparking a cacophony of groans as we made a slow trudge up the path to the top of Snowdon. The mountain looked fearsome and impenetrable in the grey, heavy clouds. At this point, I didn't know who on earth thought it was a good idea to bring together nine strangers and make them hike up through the mud and wind and rain. Rain splattered over me with another gust of wind, whipping my hood from my head, making me gasp.

The skies were grey and rumbling. While Mandy had insisted it was just another rainy day, I wasn't convinced.

The weather felt oppressive.

We'd begun the day by walking to the Cae'r Wyddfa Campsite at the base of Snowdon. It was a popular site with a lot of amenities for hikers. We had set up our tents and eaten snacks before heading to the Walkin Path, the most challenging route up Snowdon.

I tried to stop my nerves from fluttering. This would be a real achievement. Something to tick off.

But it was so much more challenging than I'd expected.

We passed waterfalls and climbed up steep rock scrambles for nine painful miles, and I cursed every single step. The group was silent, apart from the odd groan and Mandy's attempt to cheer up the group with phrases like 'Halfway!' and 'Almost there, team, you're doing so well!' The cloud broke away enough for us to see a distant, blurry view of the lakes that Mandy informed us were Llyn Llydaw and Llyn Glaslyn, which Mandy told us translated into English as Brittany Lake and Blue Lake, respectively.

'Legend has it—' Mandy shouted to us over the wind and rain whipping around us, '—that King Arthur's sword was thrown into Llyn Llydaw, returning it to the lady of the lake, before Arthur was placed on a boat and found his final resting place through the mists to Avalon.' She grinned, her face bright against the storm. 'Easy to imagine on a day like this, isn't it?'

Ren lingered near but didn't speak to me as we walked side by side and began to reach the Snowdon summit, our breaths haggard.

I rolled my ankle on a stone and Ren was there, at my elbow. Those deep brown eyes searched mine, looking for signs of pain. It made me miss Peggy. She would have been a welcome distraction from the vile weather and tension between Ren and me. But Ren had left her with Pat and Steve and their pug, Noodle, after Mandy suggested that some of the ascents might be challenging for her.

'You okay?' Ren asked, voice low and strained. My eyes tracked where his elbow touched my skin.

'Fine.'

He stepped back, dropping his hand and we continued up the well-trodden path.

The last few metres to the summit were slow, as we made our way carefully up the narrow stone steps to a trig point – a large stone table – on a platform. Ren offered his hand as he pulled me up to the platform, standing close to me, so everyone could fit on to the summit. There was a 360° view – although the visibility wasn't great with the weather. Mist clung to the mountains as if they were whispering secrets, curling around the peaks and giving the air a sharp tang of metal. The lakes below were grey and dark. It added to the atmosphere – ethereal, otherworldly.

Around me, the girls hugged each other, laughing, gushing over the achievement.

I stared out at the view, and felt…

Nothing.

What was wrong with me? Why didn't I feel anything? This was a huge achievement. I'd climbed the biggest mountain in Wales, through stormy weather and difficult ascents.

But I felt nothing.

'Hey.' A warm, familiar hand landed on my shoulder. 'Are you okay?'

I looked at Ren, and the words came tumbling out.

'What is wrong with me?'

Ren's eyebrows drew together, 'What do you mean? There is nothing wrong with you—'

'There must be. Who gets to the top of a mountain and just… feels nothing? Who pushes and pushes, through rain and exhaustion and blisters, and still comes up empty? I should feel proud. I should feel *something*. But I don't. I just keep pretending. Smiling when I'm not okay. Making jokes so no one asks questions. Pretending I'm fine with the fact I have no job. No place to live. Pretending I'm okay with the fact I'm almost thirty, the decade when you are supposed to have your shit together, and I'm starting from scratch. And I'm on this hike, thinking it's some sort of *Eat, Pray, Love* expedition that will magically sort everything. Except it's not, is it?' I shook my head, the words speeding up. 'I mean, look at *us*. I'm acting like everything's fine between us. Like what happened didn't matter. Like I don't care what we lost. No one back home even knows why. I haven't told anyone. I can't even say it out loud.'

I looked up at him, throat tight. 'Is that normal?'

Ren sucked in a breath. 'No, Lyds. Probably not. But it doesn't mean there's anything wrong with you. You just process things differently—'

'I know.' I cut him off. 'And I think you were right. About me pushing things down. Avoiding the truth. It needs to change. I need to stop hiding.'

He shifted, turning me gently to face him. 'I couldn't agree more—'

'It's not healthy. I'm tired of pretending.'

His eyes scanned my face, his palms moving up and down on my arms. 'And I'm tired too. I'm tired of pretending—'

'So you win,' I said.

His mouth parted. Eyebrows lifted. 'I win?'

'We can be friends.'

'Friends.' He echoed the word as if it didn't quite land.

There was a beat. His eyes flicked to my mouth, then back to mine.

'Isn't that what you wanted? To be friends again?'

'I thought—' he ran a hand across his face, voice catching. He glanced to the women behind us, and whispered. 'We kissed.'

'The kiss was a mistake. We both know that. We've been there, done that.' I gave a forced laugh. 'And I think we can agree that we don't want to repeat the same mistakes. Mistakes that could mean we don't speak to each other again for years.' I shifted my weight, holding his gaze. 'I'm sick of pretending I didn't miss you, Ren. Because I did. I missed my best friend,' I said, words tumbling now, because if I didn't say them fast, I might choke on them. 'And having you back this week – I just – look, you win. I missed you. I want us to go back. To before. To when it didn't hurt like this.'

But I saw it – that flicker of something raw before he shoved it down again. And suddenly, I felt exposed. Had I read this wrong?

'Unless you aren't comfortable with that—'

'No, no,' he said, eyes a little wide, like he was worried I'd jump off the sheer drop behind us. 'It's not that – I've missed you too. So much.'

He paused, as if he might say something else.

But then he just smiled, softly uttered, 'Friends. Of course.'

Chapter Fifteen

Ren

I'd barely stepped out of the shower block, hair still dripping, when Lydia pounced, and not in the way I would have liked.

'Jesus—' I flinched, clutching my toiletry bag to my chest.

I was fully dressed, thankfully. Or maybe that was a shame — because part of me wouldn't have minded wiping that friendly smile off Lydia's face and replacing it with something more interesting.

She'd been all light and cheerful since we came down from Snowdon yesterday. Like whatever knot had been inside her had finally unravelled. And I loved that. Of course I did. I wanted her happy.

But there was a part of me — a very loud, obnoxious, selfish part of me — that missed that... charge. I wouldn't have minded her catching me shirtless again, like in the Peaks. That glazed expression, the way her eyes had trailed across my tattoos. I swear I could still feel her eyes on me.

Friends, Lawrence.

She's your friend.

Lydia was grinning like a maniac and I knew this look. It used to mean trouble. Like when we were 12 and she convinced me we could build a rope swing across the canal, or when we were 15, when she said we could bribe our way into a sixth-former's party as long as we had the half-drunk bottle of Campari from

Sandra and Brian's garage. Spoiler, we weren't let in. That look was rare. But, God, I'd missed it.

'Relax,' she said, practically vibrating with excitement. She was wearing a bright pink set – leggings and a crop top – and I made a quiet, desperate promise not to look at her arse today. 'I'm not trying to steal your hair wax. We're skiving off today.'

I raised an eyebrow. 'Skiving?'

'Yep,' she said, hitting the 'P' as if it was a punchline. 'Mandy approved it.'

I glanced over her shoulder to where the ladies were gathered around a picnic bench, sipping tea from enamel mugs and pretending not to stare at us. Interesting. Mandy approved it. And now she was watching us as if she was betting on a horse race. I'd bet that she was texting Sandra with updates right now.

'Surprise field trip,' Lydia said, brandishing her keys and heading for the adjacent carpark. 'Come on.'

'My hair's wet,' I said, in a weak little protest.

Because the truth was I felt off balance. I'd made peace with the idea of being just friends at the top of that bloody mountain yesterday. I'd thought I could handle it. Having Lydia as a friend was better than nothing, of course. But being near her again, with her smiling at me like that. Well, it felt as if someone had yanked the ground out from under me.

You know why, you arse.

Lydia rolled her eyes. 'You and your hair. Dry it in the car. We're going to be late!'

She trotted to the car and I had no choice but to follow, dumbfounded, and trying not to notice how peachy her bum looked.

I climbed in, still slightly damp and confused. 'Where are we going?'

'You'll see.'

★

TAKE A HIKE!

About 30 minutes and several winding Snowdonia roads later, the satnav chirped, and Lydia turned down a gravel path marked by a carved slate sign: Glynmere Farm. Despite the isolated location, the path broke into a carpark full of families with SUVs and couples strolling hand in hand. She pulled into the carpark and came to a stop.

She turned to me, an expectant smile on her face. 'I wanted to show you that your idea for Everly Heath Farm isn't mad. Places are making this work, and Glynmere Farm is just one of them. We're meeting Bethan and Gareth, the couple who've run this place for thirty years.'

I followed her eyeline to find a couple waiting at the entrance. A woman in a yellow fleece and wellies, and a tall man with grey-streaked hair, wearing a gilet.

I looked around at the bustling farm, busy with families and couples, even on a weekday. I was... speechless.

'You're making me nervous.' Lydia gave a stuttered laugh.

I stared at her. 'You did this... for me?'

The words barely made it past my throat. Not even my own brother believed in me – not really. Yet this woman sitting in front of me – who could barely say my name a couple of weeks ago – went out of her way to bring me here. To a shining, beautiful, and *real* example of what I wanted to make happen. A farm converted into a bustling, lively place full of people, laughter, and food and drink. I hadn't felt this seen by someone... well, ever.

And now I was speechless, like some fumbling idiot, trying to form the words of what this meant to me – and, of course, coming up blank.

Lydia rambled, 'If it's too much, we can go. But I thought maybe, maybe, you needed a reminder. And someone to speak to who has actually done it, you know? If you don't want to, we can go. But... we have a tour booked and they're waiting.'

I squeezed my eyes shut, trying to hold back the bright, shining feeling spilling from my chest straight towards the woman beside me. If I looked at her right now, I might say something I couldn't take back. Something that didn't belong in the little friendship-shaped box we had agreed on.

Finally, I met her gaze. 'No one's ever done anything like this for me. No one's ever taken the time to help me dream bigger. To... believe in me.'

She shrugged, her blue eyes shining, 'Well, their loss.'

I didn't know what to say to that, so I followed her towards the couple, my heart pounding.

'Now, it's not easy, you know. It's hard work, especially at the beginning,' Gareth said, his voice low and melodic as we walked through the busy farm, dodging kids with candyfloss. 'Days like today can take their toll. It's market day.'

'But we take Mondays off.' Bethan chided her husband. 'Stop scaring the boy, Gareth. We're here to help.'

Gareth had greeted us with a firm handshake and an assessing look, while Bethan's face was smile-lined as she hugged Lydia like an old friend and welcomed us to the farm. We followed them under the wooden archway and Gareth led us down a gravel path to the left with the determination of someone who has toiled the earth all his life. The path opened into a walled courtyard flanked by food huts and market stalls, all buzzing with energy. The scent of roasting meat, sweet waffles, and something floral hung thick in the air.

'Market days are Wednesdays and Sundays,' Bethan said. 'We bring in local vendors from across the valley.'

Families wove past us – toddlers with ice cream, couples holding paper cups of cider. A group of teens hovered near a hut selling Welsh rarebit toasties.

Gareth led us down the main stretch with the determination of someone who'd done this walk a thousand times. He nodded at every other person we passed. Bethan explained how they rotated stalls, partnered with small producers, and occasionally hosted themed weekends and a midsummer cider festival that apparently got 'a bit lively' last year. I could believe it. The place had that kind of buzz – somewhere between wholesome and slightly chaotic.

Helpful wooden signs pointed to places to visit. *FARM SHOP & CAFE*, *HORSE STABLES*, *PLAY AREA*. The list went on and on.

Everywhere we walked was full of energy – food, drink, laughter.

'This place is alive,' I muttered without meaning to.

Lydia nudged me. 'Exactly.'

I gazed at the rolling fields stretched out ahead of the farm, dotted with sheep grazing on the dewy grass, their thick coats making them look like fluffy clouds settled on the hillside. Beyond the pastures, a dense cluster of ancient oak and pine trees framed the land, leading up to the rolling hills in the distance.

Gareth brought us to a stop before a wooden gate.

'This is the heart of Glynmere. Started as a working sheep farm but we had to adapt. Land alone doesn't pay the bills these days. So my brilliant wife decided we should open the farm to the public. Twenty-nine years ago now.'

'He thought I was mad when I suggested it. But he came around eventually. With some persuading.' Bethan smiled, gazing at her husband, who glanced down.

Lydia nudged my elbow.

'He's blushing,' she whispered under her breath, making me chuckle.

'The Farm Shop started first, using the products from the sheep and bees and sourcing from other farms who were interested.'

'Are those yours then?' I asked, nodding to the sheep grazing in the field.

'Yes,' Gareth replied. 'I'll always have sheep on this farm until I die. It was what my father did and his before that. As much as the diversifying of the business was needed, we think it's best to stick to our roots.'

Ren faltered now. 'I'd be buying a derelict farm. It's not a family tradition or anything.'

Gareth clapped a hand on his shoulder. 'Then you create your own roots.'

We moved on, towards the cafe and farm shop – a converted stone barn, softened with ivy and hanging flower baskets.

'Right,' Gareth grunted. 'Let's get this over with before Bethan forces you to taste-test everything in the bleeding shop.'

'Hey,' Bethan nudged her husband. 'This shop paid for your new tractor. So shut it.'

Bethan came alive when we walked into the shop, pointing out all the relationships she had built with local farms and vendors. Inside, the air was warm and rich with the smell of coffee and freshly baked bread.

'Everything here's either made on site or comes from someone we know by name,' Bethan said proudly. 'The honey's ours, the jam's from my neighbour Rhian, and the mead's brewed just up the road.'

She opened up jars, giving us tastes of the preserves – strawberry, raspberry, and lemon. All of the tastes danced on my tongue, tart and sweet.

I loaded up my basket, earning a small smile from Bethan. We squeezed past a display with red dragons and alpacas.

'The tourists love these,' Bethan said. 'Even if they are a little overpriced.'

I grabbed two and shoved them into my basket, earning a giggle from Lydia.

'What?' I said innocently. 'Abi will love this.'

Abi was probably a little old for toys but, if she didn't want them, then I'd keep them myself. To remember today.

'Softie,' Lydia muttered, as I paid for my basket, after waving off Bethan who tried to give us complimentary jars of preserves.

They toiled to make these themselves, so I wouldn't accept anything other than full price. Working in hospitality for over a decade gave you a respect for how much effort goes into making things by hand and, as a business owner, I knew how fine profit margins can be.

We made our way out of the shop, one hundred pounds lighter, to find Gareth's smug smile.

'She's done it to you too, lad?' Gareth shook his head, smiling. 'Alpacas and all.'

Gareth and I walked ahead, rounding the corner near the stream, where the wooden cabins overlooked fields for miles and miles. The path was edged with raised flower beds and little solar lights that probably looked magical at night. He was mid-sentence about occupancy rates and seasonal demand for the cabins when I heard it – Lydia's voice, soft but clear, drifting from just behind us.

'I can't thank you enough,' she was saying to Bethan. 'He was... discouraged by his business partner. His brother. Liam reminds me a bit of your Gareth, actually. Strong, silent type.'

Bethan gave a low laugh. 'I wish Gareth was silent. I'd get a bit more peace around here. So this Liam – he doesn't want to run the farm?'

'No. But I think he's wrong. I think he's scared. And risk-averse. And it would be Ren's baby really. He would champion it.'

'Understandable to be apprehensive,' Bethan replied. 'Gareth is right, it isn't easy, starting something like this. Both of you would have to move on site. Really live it. Early starts, late nights.'

There was a pause.

Then Lydia said, 'Oh – I mean – we're not... I wouldn't be living *with* Ren. We're just friends.'

My stomach twisted.

I stopped beside a signpost marked **CABINS** and nodded towards the nearest one, making some vague comment about the view.

Behind me, Bethan chuckled. 'Friends. I've heard that one before.'

Lydia laughed, just a touch too high-pitched. 'No, genuinely, we are. But I'll help him as much as I can.'

Bethan didn't let it go. 'Cariad, I'm not daft. I see the way he looks at you – and you at him. You might believe you're just friends now, but give it time.'

I swallowed hard, every part of me resisting the urge to glance back at Lydia. One look and I'd give myself away.

'I've said enough, haven't I? But just think about it. Life's too short to waste time, love. It's precious. And he'll need all the help he can get.' A pause. Then, 'What is it you do? I'm sorry, I never asked.'

'Oh—' Lydia hesitated, then said firmly, 'I'm a personal trainer. But I'm between jobs doing a bit of soul-searching at the moment.'

Bethan didn't miss a beat. 'Well, it seems pretty clear to me. You should open a gym onsite at this farm. It'd be a brilliant offer for the hotel guests. You could run retreats. Fitness and nature go hand in hand.'

It was like something short-circuited in my brain and, in an instant, I could see it.

The gym in the old stone barn. A glass-walled studio looking out over the north field. Yoga mats rolled out at sunrise. Weekend retreats. Then it shifted to *us*. Lazy mornings watching the sunrise from our bedroom. Hosting our friends and family on a huge oak table we'd move to the orchard. Lydia walking barefoot through wet grass, coffee in one hand, Peggy snuffling around our feet.

Shit!

Lydia had brought me here for inspiration – for the farm, for *my* dream. She had no idea she'd just become part of it. My heart sank and I squeezed an eye shut, trying to push away the images stuck in my brain.

We're friends. Just friends.

That word tasted like ash in my mouth now.

'Meddling,' Gareth muttered beside me. I blinked and turned to find him watching me, a knowing look in his eye.

'My wife likes to meddle,' he said, wearing the ghost of a smile.

'Yeah,' I tried to laugh, but it caught in my throat. 'She's good at it.'

We said our goodbyes to Bethan and Gareth, and then we were alone. Just the two of us, next to her car, carrying all of this – this adoration for her.

Lydia smiled at me – the kind of bright smile that made me want to squint like she was the sun.

'That was so much *fun*.'

Fun didn't cover it. It meant so much to me, I wasn't sure I could put it into words. Surely doing this – going out of her way to help me – meant her feelings had changed?

God, she was so gorgeous when her eyes were like this – bright and excited. She was almost rocking on her heels, like she couldn't contain herself. There was a smudge of red jam at the corner of her mouth.

'Yeah. Fun,' I murmured, stepping closer to brush it away before I could think better of it. I licked it off my thumb without breaking eye contact.

Lydia's lips parted. A flush bloomed high on her cheeks. For a moment, I wondered if she was thinking what I was – that we could step forward right now, close the space between us. I would kill to press my lips against hers, to show my gratitude with a swipe of my tongue. But she stepped back and my delusion reared its ugly head.

'Right. We should head back.' Her voice full of cheer. She

pointed to the sky. 'Looks like it's about to piss it down any second.'

The moment was gone, and I was left feeling empty, hollow, and so fucking stupid.

She doesn't feel that way about you, you twat. This didn't mean anything. Lydia would bend over backwards to help a stranger. You aren't special. She is.

So I climbed into the car, the sky thick with rain clouds, and felt the same heaviness slide over me.

Chapter Sixteen

Lydia

The silence was killing me. The sun was setting as we drove back to the campsite and Ren hadn't uttered a word. I turned up the radio, but the inane chatter didn't help. The rain pelted across the windscreen. I glanced at Ren and found his face neutral, his jaw locked.

'This rain is horrendous,' I said, my eyes flicking to Ren. 'God, I hope it isn't like this all night.'

A hum.

I turned down the narrow country road, gravel cracking under the tyres. I pushed on the full beam, as the light was slowly being drained from the sky.

'I hope Mandy isn't worried. I said we'd be back by now.'

'I've texted her,' he said, his voice low. 'Don't worry.'

'Oh. Thank you.'

The rain came down harder. The people-pleaser inside was banging at my chest, begging to be let out. I needed to ask what was wrong. Was he pissed off with me? I wanted to ask if the farm was too much, too overwhelming. I know if someone had taken me to a state-of-the-art gym, pointed and said, 'Do this', I would have run a mile. Maybe this was a mistake. Maybe all I'd done is show him what he can't have – and he wants this *desperately*. I could tell by the way he looked at me before we got into the car. He was so full of energy, it was like he was lit up from within. It was infectious.

Maybe it was my fault. My brain had stuttered the moment he swiped away the jam on my face. I'd stared at the thumb in his mouth way too long for friends. I'd pictured the way his tongue would have swiped across the pad of his thumb, and I hate that my brain imagined that feeling... elsewhere. It was stupid, reckless.

'I love this song,' I said, leaning across to turn it up. I didn't love the song. It was some indie band I'd heard on the radio a few times.

More silence. My teeth were on edge.

What's wrong? I wanted to scream. I wanted to climb into his head and read his thoughts. Did he like the farm? Was he inspired? Could I help him persuade Liam to take the leap?

No, Lydia. Other people's emotions are not your problem.

I'd promised myself on top of Snowdon that I wouldn't shrink myself just because someone else sighed or stared out of the window a bit too hard. If Ren wants to talk about something that is wrong, he will have to say it out loud.

Finally, we pulled into the campsite carpark, the windscreen wipers were going like the clappers, barely keeping up with the downpour. I turned off the engine, throwing us into darkness. Ren was still quiet, although I could see the steady rise and fall of his chest out of the corner of my eye. Anxiety clamped down on my chest. I couldn't breathe in the car. I needed to say something or I was going to explode.

'Look,' I began, voice thick. I pushed it into a light, airy sound. 'If it pushed you too hard, or freaked you out, I get it. I mean, if someone took me to a random gym and told me I could open one, I'd probably have a meltdown too. I just wanted you to see that it was possible. That it wasn't a crazy idea. But if you'd prefer, we can just forget it. We don't have to mention it again.' I spotted a light by the campsite. 'Oh – I think Mandy is waiting up for us.'

TAKE A HIKE!

I pushed out the door, the rain hitting me full in the face. The wind and rain whipped around us, and I could hear the sound of the tarp of the tents in the wind.

'Lydia. Wait!' A hand came to my elbow, stilling me. Ren was in front of me, rain hit our faces, but he didn't seem to care. 'What are you on about?'

I licked the rain from my lips. I was grateful for the dark, so Ren couldn't see my cheeks flushing in embarrassment. 'You haven't said a word in the car. I read between the lines. The visit to the farm freaked you out. It's fine! I'd be exactly the same.'

I turned, pacing across the campsite, lit only by the glow of half-asleep tents.

'You have it so wrong, Lydia,' Ren called back. 'Will you just stop, so I can talk to you?'

'It's fine!' My voice broke. 'We don't need to talk about it.'

'Clearly we do, because you've got the wrong end of the stick completely.'

I turned to face him. 'Then why were you so quiet? Why were you so miserable in the car? You know how things like that make me feel. I can't stand the silent treatment, Ren.'

Ren huffed. 'That's rich—'

Ren stopped himself, closed his eyes, but it was too late. Anger burned through my chest.

'That is not the same thing,' I snapped.

He rubbed a hand across his forehead. 'I'm sorry. It was a stupid comment. You know I don't think before I speak.'

My eyes burned. God, I hated that I always cried when I argued.

'Hey, hey!' Ren stepped closer. 'I'm sorry I was quiet in the car. I just had a lot on my mind. And it was *nothing* to do with the farm.'

He said it in this low, knowing voice, like it was supposed to be obvious.

'Then what does it have to do with, Ren?'

I'm sick of his bullshit. I'm tired of the lack of communication.

Ren stepped forward, his face fierce. 'It's to do with the fact I was trying to figure out how the fuck I can be your friend – *just* your friend – when you did something like that for me.'

My heart raced as he took another step closer, rain dripping from his lashes and his mouth, and I couldn't help but imagine tracing those raindrops with my mouth. I should be opening my mouth to disagree with him – to tell him we would never be anything but friends, but I couldn't, especially when Ren said the next words.

'I was trying to keep myself from kissing you senseless.' My lips parted at his words, and his eyes followed the movement. 'I was trying to forget that I know the way you taste. The way you moan. I was trying to forget the fact that I remember every *second* of that night, even if you're busy trying to burn it from your memory. I was trying to convince myself that having you in my life is more important than the fantasy of having *all* of you.' He said those words like a caress. I shivered. 'I was trying to remind myself that having you in my life – as a friend – is better than not having you at all. I was trying to remember that I should be grateful you even talk to me. Grateful you are so kind, so thoughtful, that you'd take me to that farm and show me my dream up close. The whole way home I was trying to remind myself that I had my chance, and I completely, utterly, fucked it. And that I *deserve* to feel the twist in my chest every time you say the word "friend".'

He spat the last word.

'So no.' Those dark eyes shifted all over my face. 'I wasn't overwhelmed. Or suffocated. I'm—' he dragged in a breath. He gave a huffed laugh that sounded a little hysterical. Like he'd gone mad. 'I want you, Lydia. I want you as more than a friend. And it's killing me.'

Our breathing was ragged as we faced off.

His words eddied around my brain. While I had been spiralling in the car, Ren had spent the entire journey thinking all of that. Thinking about kissing me. About making me moan.

'So yes, I guess you could say I was "freaking out". But it certainly wasn't about the farm. It was about what I would do if you ever looked at me like *this* again.' His hand trailed across my jaw. 'Just like this. A little wild.' His thumb ran across my lips. 'And a little like you'd like me to mess you up.'

Desire bloomed low in my belly, just as Ren's eyes dropped to my mouth. Mine followed like a reflex. The rain slid down his cheeks, tangled in his lashes. Every muscle in my body tightened. Every instinct in my body screamed *yes*. Lean in, let go, forget everything other than his words and how they made me feel soft and achey and languid.

And I couldn't fight this any more.

A beam of light shone across Ren's face.

'Lydia? Ren? There you are!' Mandy's voice sounded across the campsite. 'I've been trying to call you!'

I stepped back, out of Ren's arms' way. Mandy strode across the camp, her short, dark hair soaked, her eyes shifting between Ren and me, eyes more than a little curious.

'Lydia, your tent is flooded, love. I'm sorry. Bloody rain came in sideways in the past hour, and with the rain yesterday too.' She put her hands on her hips. 'Well, the ground couldn't soak it all up.'

'I told you to camp nearer me,' Ren said under his breath. 'You were on the lowest ground.'

I blinked. 'Sorry, I think I heard you wrong. You said my tent is flooded.'

'Completely. I couldn't even recover the pyjamas you'd left. And the book you'd left out – *Savaged by the Sea Lord*, was it? It's completely soaked.'

My face turned pink, and I heard Ren's exhalation of surprise.

'Desired effect, by the sounds of it,' Ren said, his voice low and dry.

'Shut it,' I elbowed Ren before turning to Mandy, plastering on a smile. 'I'll share with Amy.'

Mandy's smile turned to a grimace. 'Amy and Gen are sharing and they've headed to sleep already. They tried to stay up, but they were so tired after the walk today.'

My eyes shifted to Amy and Gen's tent. Their lamp was on. My eyes narrowed.

I cleared my throat. 'I'm sure they wouldn't mind me waking them up in this circumstance.'

Mandy glanced behind her, to Amy and Gen's tent. She hummed. 'Their tent is small for three people.'

Shit! It was a small tent, one that was low to the ground, too. Panic began to set in. Problem solving began to kick in.

'My tent can't be that bad,' I laughed, making my way over to my tent. I unzipped it to find three inches of water. 'No, no, no. This can't be happening.'

I stood up, needing to pace. 'This can't be happening.'

'It's okay. I've thought of a solution while you were gone.' Mandy turned to Ren, 'Ren, I don't suppose you would mind sharing with Lydia? Your tent is bone-dry and you're old friends, right? So it won't be a problem for one night.'

My heart lurched. Share a tent with Ren – after he'd said all of those things. I could almost feel his thumb tracing across my lips. My eyes shot to him. He had an artfully schooled expression.

'Of course,' he said, his voice low.

'No.'

Ren shot me a warning look. *Be reasonable*, it said.

'We'll manage,' Ren said to Mandy, who nodded and headed back to her tent. He turned to me, guiding me by the elbow towards his tent. I resisted.

'No, no chance,' I said. 'This is a serious inconvenience. I'll sleep in my car!'

Ren didn't stop, didn't hesitate. He just kept moving, chivvying me along by my elbow as we approached his blue tent. It was further away from the other tents, and on slightly higher ground.

'Lydia,' he said in my ear. 'It's one night. We can dry your tent out, and it will be as good as new tomorrow. You can share with me.' He lowered his voice. 'No funny business. We don't—' he squeezed his eyes shut. 'We can just forget what I said.'

'Forget,' I repeated.

'If it helps,' he said, strained. 'One night. I can keep my hands to myself.' He smiled softly. 'Just like old times.'

My pulse jumped.

'Fine. But we're doing the pillow wall.'

'Lydia.' Ren's voice was low, and knowing, 'You and I both know those pillow walls never worked. You'd wake up wrapped around me in the morning anyway.'

Pink stained my cheeks.

'That's what I'm afraid of,' I muttered to myself.

Chapter Seventeen

Lydia's Diary, 15 Years Old

Dear Diary,
 I think maybe I like girls as well as boys... maybe. Probably.
 Last week I caught myself staring at Bella in PE when she was tying her hair up. She has that really soft brown hair that does that swoosh thing. It made my stomach flip, same way it does with Ren sometimes. So I told Ren, just to see what he'd say. We were lying on his bedroom floor, listening to one of his stupid indie bands. He was sketching something and I just said it.
 Something like 'I think I like girls as well as boys'.
 He didn't even look up.
 He just said 'Yeah?'
 He asked if there was someone I liked, so I told him about Bella. And he just nodded and said, 'She's pretty.' Then he went back to his sketch. It was so anticlimactic that I almost laughed. They make a big deal about it on *Glee*.
 But it didn't feel like a big deal telling Ren.
 He knows everything about me anyway.
 Love,
 Lydia

I must have done something really sick and twisted in another life. That's the only explanation – because right now, Lydia was peeling off her soaking clothes beside me, while I stared rigidly at the panel of the tent as if my life depended on it.

Hell.

I was in hell.

I'd laid everything bare in the rain. I'd told her exactly how I felt and now — every thought, every feeling I'd had since this hike started — and now I was expected to spend a whole night with her, surrounded by the smell of that shampoo she loves to use. Hearing her breaths. Feeling the warmth of her body next to me.

I just needed to get through this with some dignity intact. But firstly, I needed to make sure she was comfortable. Shit. She must be freezing in those clothes. Why hadn't I offered her anything yet? *Idiot.*

'Here,' I held out the grey T-shirt between us, a peace offering of sorts. 'You can wear it. If you need it.'

I wished I hadn't turned around.

She had stripped off her leggings, and her long legs, toned and athletic, were exposed. Her soft skin — and memories of them wrapped around my waist — hit me like a truck.

'Sorry.' I glanced away quickly.

'It's fine.'

Nothing about this was fine.

'I'll turn around. So you know.'

'Oh,' she said again. Her cheeks flushed. 'Thanks.'

The whole thing was painful.

I busied myself with the sleeping bag, turning back to the nylon wall while she changed. But it was impossible not to hear the soft rustle of her clothes, or imagine the slow drag of fabric over her skin.

'I didn't realise you still had this.'

I almost jumped out of my skin. I turned and my breath caught.

Lydia was in my shirt, my Manila Times gig tee, faded and baggy. Her legs were bare and, fuck me, how was she hotter in *more* clothes? My eyes dragged down her thighs before I could stop them.

I forced myself to look away, running a hand through my hair.

'I couldn't get rid of it,' I said, keeping my voice even. 'It was our first and only date.'

She blinked. 'Date?'

I locked eyes with her.

'Yes. Date.'

'Ren,' she said slowly, almost lethally. 'What are you on about?'

'It was a date. I asked you out. I bought the tickets. It was just us.'

She looked so confused it almost made me laugh. Or cry. I wasn't sure which.

'We've hung out, just us, for years. What was so different about that night?' she said, a little defensive.

'Yeah, we did,' I agreed. 'At family stuff. Or when we were kids. But that night… it was different. Or at least I thought so.'

It was the summer after we'd finished our A-levels, and I'd had a tough year. I'd had my first really bad bout of depression. It had hit me like a truck. I couldn't get out of bed. My teachers were concerned I wouldn't pass any of my exams. My dad and Liam were trying to be as supportive as possible, but I knew I was being a burden by the way they would talk in hushed tones when they thought I wasn't listening. Or when Liam would talk over me at the doctor's.

But Lydia had been my saving grace. She hadn't put pressure on me to be better or make plans with her. She was there if I needed a late-night phone call or a quiet walk around the park. And it was more than that, something I couldn't put words to. It was like I didn't feel heavy when I was around her. She never drained me or made it worse. If anything, she made it better. A solid, calming presence, like the soft glow of a lamp as the sun began to set.

And I knew I was starting to feel... more for her. But I also wasn't in the right headspace for a relationship with someone who always gave so much for other people. I didn't want to take advantage.

So I held back.

But, by summer, I'd finally got on some medication and was feeling a lot more stable.

And Lydia was more gorgeous than ever. My heart skipped when she walked into a room. She had grown out her hair, and she had started wearing these jeans that hugged her curves. She was more confident, and I loved hearing about her plans to train as a PT, because she would just come alive. Don't get me wrong, she'd always been beautiful, I couldn't deny it, even when we were in our awkward, the-opposite-sex-is-disgusting phase. But there was something about that summer – we were newly minted adults with no responsibilities, no exams, and no teachers. It was charged with possibilities.

I had thought, without my lows, that maybe I could be good for her. Worthy of her.

So, I'd bought the gig tickets, and we'd woven our way through the crowd, my hand wrapped around hers. I remember glancing back at her, just to check she was real. She was here with me.

In the crowd, I leaned down to whisper in her ear.

'You look really beautiful tonight.'

She turned to me, brows quizzical, like she couldn't hear me.

Then a squeal. Pale arms wrapped around my neck. I turned to see Lindsey Matthews and my stomach dropped.

'Lindsey Matthews was there.' Lydia snapped me back into the present. 'You danced with her.'

I winced. 'She was drunk. And clingy. I'd made it clear we

went to the prom just as friends, but she latched on that night. I didn't want her there, Lyd. I wanted it to be us. But you wouldn't even look at me after she showed up.'

Once Lindsey had turned up, Lydia avoided me like the plague, and then the gig started, and there were what felt like a million sweaty bodies around us, keeping us apart.

She stared at me like I'd just told her I wanted to join the circus.

'You can't just rewrite history, Ren.' Her voice shook. 'And why didn't you just tell me?'

I sighed, rubbing the back of my neck. 'I was eighteen and scared. Worried you'd say no. Or everyone in Everly Heath would jump on it. You know what they're like. We'd have this pressure on us before we even started. I was hoping you'd guess it was a date.'

'Guess?' she repeated incredulously.

'Yeah, I know. Dumb,' I muttered. 'I've made a lot of mistakes, Lydia. But I'm trying not to make them any more. I wish I'd just grabbed you and kissed you that night, instead of taking another ten years to do it.'

Lydia's eyes widened, her eyes darting to my mouth, then she pulled herself together. 'It wouldn't have mattered. We're—' she stuttered. 'All of this has been a mistake. You have to admit—'

'I won't admit it,' I said. 'I won't admit that any time I spend with you – kissing or not – is a mistake.'

Lydia sucked in a breath. 'Ren—'

'Are you not over Casey?' I asked quickly, like I was trying to rip off a plaster. 'Is that it?'

I dreaded the answer. The idea of Lydia choking up over someone else – after that kiss in my apartment, after every moment pulling us closer again – sat in my gut like a punch.

'What?' she asked, her brow furrowed.

'Casey,' I repeated. 'Are you not over her?'

Is that why you're pushing me away?

Her expression softened, as if she realised it had been gnawing at me.

'I'm over Casey.' Her gaze dropped, thumb picking at her nail. 'Don't get me wrong, I was gutted when she left. But I don't think...' She paused, and I hung on every word. 'I don't think I was honest – with her or myself. I don't think I was as invested in that relationship as I could have been.'

Was that because of me? The thought flared – arrogant and a little tempting. I didn't ask because, if I pushed, she'd bolt. But part of me hoped.

And then there was the way she kept dodging my gaze... only for her eyes to flick, almost involuntarily, to my arms, my chest. Yeah, I caught that. She knew I did, from the way her cheeks blushed.

'Ren, we said we were just going to be friends.' She kept her voice even. 'I know you think we can be more—'

'Look, I'm not going to force you to see it my way. Particularly because it would be borderline creepy when we're sharing a tent and you are just in a T-shirt. But let's say this—' my voice lowered. 'We can play it your way. But, Lydia, that means that next time you want me to kiss you – you're going to have to ask me.'

'That's not going to happen,' she said. But her voice was softer now, like even she didn't quite believe it.

I shrugged. 'We'll see. In the meantime...' I patted the sleeping bag, 'Let's go to sleep.'

I lay down, and she did the same, and I could tell she was holding herself stiff so we didn't touch. I draped the sleeping bag over both of us, like a duvet.

Then her legs touched mine and she bolted upright.

'We don't have to share. I'll be fine without.'

'Lydia,' I said gently. 'I told you. We're just sleeping. And you're not wearing anything on your legs. And as torturous as it is to know you're only wearing my T-shirt and one of those tiny thongs – don't interrupt me – I don't want you to be cold. So let's just… accept our fate, share the bloody sleeping bag, and sleep. We can both pretend this never happened in the morning.'

Something in my voice cracked at the end, a quiet ache I didn't mean to let out.

'Okay?' I asked.

'Okay.'

She curled in beside me, and I felt her breathing slowly. The rain outside softened and the silence inside thickened – comfortable, for once. Like an old rhythm, remembered.

I lay there, and wondered how many near misses with Lydia I'd have to endure.

Chapter Eighteen

Lydia's Diary, 16 Years Old

Ren asked Lindsey Matthews to prom today.

And I hate how much it bothered me.

We've been spending more time together at school this year because we're both taking GCSE PE. I swear, I'll glance at him in class, and he's already looking at me. Then there's the little things — he sometimes carries my PE kit when he knows my English books are already weighing me down.

And then there's the nights.

This year's been hard for him. Pressure from school, missing his mum more than usual. Especially when he's stressed. So every Friday he texts me. *Can I come round?*

At first, it was just chilling in the lounge with Mum and Dad. But then, the texts started coming later at night — his messages sounding heavier, sadder.

And I always say yes.

I tell him to come in the side door to keep it quiet from Mum and Dad. They'd go ballistic if they knew. At first he promised he'd stay until the film's end and then sneak out. But the third time? The fourth? He fell asleep. We both did. I'd insist on a pillow wall between us, but somehow I'd wake up in the middle of the night, my head on his chest.

He's taking Lindsey Matthews to prom.

But he sleeps in my bed.
That's weird, right?

Lydia

At some point during the night, I'd stripped off the sleeping bag. The cool draught of the morning air hit my bare legs. Legs that were resting on top of something stronger, harder. Warmer. Something heavy sat on my stomach, but I liked it. It was soothing, like a weighted blanket. The soft rhythm of breath, in and out, had been the soothing score to my sleep.

Open your eyes, my brain demanded. So I did.

A dark mop of hair was buried in my neck, my throat. It was the steadiness of their breath I could feel now.

Ren.

Ren was wrapped around me like a vine, his arm draped over my chest, my leg tangled with his. We were angled towards each other as if this was mutual – like both of our subconscious minds wanted this. God, he felt so good. Just the smell of him. That smell had so many memories wrapped up in it. It was enough to make me want to sigh. I couldn't help but feel how my body lit up like fireworks just to have him near me.

No, this was wrong.

He was asleep. He didn't even know what he was doing. I squeezed my eyes shut. *Stupid, stupid, Lydia,* my brain shouted, *getting set to get her heart broken all over again.*

I shifted, but Ren gripped tighter and made a sound in his throat as if he was waking from a deep dream and wanted to go back to sleep just to find out what happened next.

'Lyd,' he murmured.

Was he dreaming? His hand moved, skating over the exposed skin on my stomach, where Ren's band t-shirt had ridden up. My back arched. His palms were large and warm, and I remembered, distantly, the way they had made me feel once upon a time.

TAKE A HIKE!

Ren paused at the arch of my back. He was awake. I was sure of that now. And I was sure we were back here again, balancing on that line between whatever we were now and *more*.

'Lydia,' Ren's lips moved against my neck at the words. 'I need you to move away from me right now.'

My breath caught at the sound of the gravelly desire in his voice. I could feel him, hard, against my leg. I felt like the last bit of chocolate melting slowly into the fondue. Softening, molten, malleable.

'Lydia. Please.' Ren groaned, the noise shot low within me.

I was sick of this ache. I was sick of hating myself for wanting him. I was sick of not being able to do anything about it. I'd been staring at him all week. Wherever I was, he was there. He was walking ahead of me, handing me precisely what I needed whenever I needed it. He was helping the ladies with every whim, carrying Amy's bags or making Jade and Claire laugh, that charming, boyish grin on his face. He'd even won over Gen, who gave him a begrudging smile when he shared funny stories from our childhood. And our talk last night had softened something in me. Something I'd been stubbornly clinging to for the last year. Ren's words, murmured in the dark of the tent, echoed through my head.

Anything. Anything you want.

And boy, did I *want*.

So it was his own fault when one of my legs snaked down to lock with his. I shoved him on to his back, my face inches away from him. His eyes widened as they scanned my face.

His hand came up to my hair, tucking it behind my ear. His face was tender and tentative. As if he didn't want to scare me off. As if he'd already pictured this scenario a hundred times and lost each time.

'So that's how it is, huh?' he murmured. 'Trying to kill me?'

'Maybe you deserve it,' I murmured back.

'Oh, I do not deserve this.' He leaned in to drag his lip across my neck. 'I've never deserved you.'

'Ren.'

'Lydia.'

'If you don't kiss me in the next three seconds, I'm leaving. I'll go and find another tent and—'

He pulled my hair into his hand, causing me to gasp, as he angled my lips directly to his.

'If you leave me, I'll drag you back in front of everyone. By your ankles.'

A laugh bubbled out of me, at the same time as desire burned through me at what Ren *could* do with my ankles, or my wrists, if we had time, much more time, to play.

'What an image! The girls would be scandalised.'

'I'm serious.'

'I'm sure you are.'

'Ask me again, Lydia.' He gave a small, playful bite to my neck. 'I said you'd have to ask, didn't I?'

'Kiss me.'

'In a minute. I'm roaming.'

'Roaming.' My breath hitched as his hands drifted up my legs, across my bum, which he gave a squeeze before pulling it closer to him so I could feel how hard I'd made him.

'You drive me crazy,' he said. 'You've always driven me crazy. But now it's a different kind of crazy.'

'What kind of crazy is it now?' I gasped as he arched up, pressing into me.

'The kind that is going to grind against you just to feel you. I know what it feels like not to have you, so I'll take anything you give me.'

'Ren—' My eyes stung at that admission.

'No, no pity. You know I don't deserve it.' He pulled back, his familiar brown eyes burning. 'Will you let me make you feel good?' His hands drifted lower towards my bare legs. 'Please?'

'Okay,' I said. 'But after—'

'We don't have to worry about after right now.' He kissed me. 'Just let me make you feel good.'

'Okay.'

He shifted us so that I was on my back, and his shaking hands drifted up my legs. His eyes tracked every movement, as if he was trying to take it all in, as if he was trying to memorise every moment.

'You look so good in my T-shirt. I thought I was going to pass out when I saw you in it last night,' he said, wrapping it in his fist. 'You look like you've just finished a class.'

'Yeah?' I asked, as his hand caressed up my calf slowly. 'That tickles.'

'Sorry,' he mumbled but carried on, fascinated. 'I always liked that look on you. After your classes. Pink cheeks. Slightly out of breath. I just thought I liked it when you enjoyed yourself. But now I've realised it might have been for a different reason.'

I gasped as he made his way up to my inner thighs.

'Yep.' He smiled. 'Definitely a different reason.'

'Stop messing.'

'Shush,' he said, 'or I'll find a more creative way to keep you quiet.'

My eyes widened. 'What if they hear—'

'They won't. I pitched this tent far enough away.' His eye glittered with a challenge, 'So you'll just have to keep as quiet as you can. Can you do that?'

Ren was done with teasing as he lowered a kiss to my thigh and then the other one, kissing further and further up. I gasped as he pulled at the lace of my thong, pulling it down and hard. For most men, they probably couldn't have pulled that off, but somehow Ren managed it successfully, pulling my thong from my legs with ease.

'You've done that before.'

'Jealous?' he said, his breath on my sex, making me wriggle.

He was teasing me again, but I managed to bite out, 'In your dreams.'

'Every single fucking one,' he said as he lowered his mouth to me, swiping his tongue across my clit. I gasped again and threw my head back as pleasure flooded my body. Ren hummed, the feeling intensifying the pleasure. I moaned, needing to move, needing more friction than this. But he was taking his time, savouring me, building me up. Ren's hand travelled up my body, squeezing my breasts. I met his gaze, and he hummed against me, like this was a fantasy playing out in real life. He pulled the tops of my thighs hard, moving them closer to him.

'You taste like I remembered.' His eyes met mine. 'Pure sunshine.'

'Stop playing, Hunter.'

He laughed and lowered his mouth again; he didn't play this time. It was embarrassing how loud my moans were. Ren rewarded each of them with a hum, bringing his fingers to me and pressing one, then two, inside me.

I tugged Ren's hair hard and he let out a low hum that vibrated through me, his fingers sliding between my legs – one, then two. My back arched, a moan escaping around my palm, and I couldn't stop the fluttering pulse in my core, as I saw Ren's hips shifting, as if he was desperate to get some relief himself. I met his eyes, and the sight stole the breath from my lungs – eyes full of hunger, hair messy from my grip, cheeks flushed. He looked ruined, wrecked. Perfect. And he was loving every second of it. His pace quickened, dragging me higher, teasing me right to the brink.

Then he slowed.

Then he stopped.

The whimper I made wasn't dignified, but I didn't care. I gasped, letting my head thump back on to the pillow. A moment later, he started again – more slowly, more softly this time, as if he was savouring it. As if I was dessert.

I climbed towards the edge again, and again he pulled away.

'Ren, please.' My voice broke on the word, my whole body shaking. 'Please.'

'Begging already?' he murmured, kissing the inside of my thigh. 'I thought I had more time to play.'

I glared down at him, breathless and half-feral, and he just grinned, wicked and smug, as he buried his tongue back into me. I moved against him, desperate for friction, no longer able to control my body. I knew how I must look, unhinged and needy, and it only made me wetter. There was something dark and greedy in his gaze, like he wanted to collect every version of me – especially the wild ones.

He pulled back again, shifting so he was beside me, not between my legs, and I blinked at him in disbelief.

'What—' I began, but he just smiled, stretched out beside me, looking sinful. I reached for the waistband of his boxers, intent on returning the favour, but he caught my hand and held it away.

He gave a dark chuckle, 'Oh, I'm not finished. Ride my face, Sunshine,' he said, pressing a kiss to my mouth. 'I wanna see you come on my face.'

My brain stalled. Stuttered. I blinked, too dazed to speak.

But then I saw the look in his eyes, determined and *very* much into this, and heat rolled. *Yes*, my body screamed.

We moved, shifting awkwardly in the cramped tent until I was straddling him. He reached for my thighs, guiding me down and, when his mouth found me again, I cried out. I couldn't help it. His hands roamed over my skin – my thighs, my arse – and I moved above him, riding his face with a slow, desperate rhythm.

When he pressed two fingers inside me again, I lost it.

I clenched around him, head thrown back, one hand clamped over my mouth to muffle the moan that tore through me. The pleasure crested like a wave, unstoppable and shattering.

When I collapsed beside him, panting, he looked unbearably smug. I could barely catch my breath but my eyes found his, then trailed down his chest to his arms, and finally to the bulge in his boxers that had been there the whole time.

'Your turn,' I said, licking my lips.

He shook his head and said, 'We don't do turns, Lydia.'

I groaned as he pulled me against him, laughing at my pout as if he hadn't just destroyed me.

'I'm serious,' he smiled. 'That was for you.'

'You don't want anything in return?' I asked, studying him. 'Most men I've slept with are reciprocal. With women, it's less like that—'

'I want a lot of things,' he said, brushing my hair back gently. 'But we can wait. There's no rush.'

'I feel bad,' I admitted, staring at his collarbone.

'That's your people-pleasing talking,' he hummed. 'And we're not bringing that into the bedroom.' He glanced around. 'Or the tent. Come here.'

We lay there in silence, curled up in the hush of the woods. I glanced up at Ren, his eyes were closed, a light smile on his face, as if he was blissfully happy, despite the fact he'd given me the orgasm, not the other way around.

Then, as if the universe wanted to send me a message, a warning, Ren's phone vibrated. I sat up, and caught the message out of the corner of my eye.

LEXI MEXICO

Can I call or are you still with her?

Chapter Nineteen

Ren

Lydia wasn't speaking to me.

It was two days since we shared a tent, and not a *word*.

I'd fallen back asleep that morning, with her in my arms, safe and sound, but by the time I came around, I was alone. I stumbled out, half-expecting a smile, a look, something. But she was by the campfire, eating a granola bar, laughing with Amy and Claire, carefully avoiding my gaze. As we did the final hike back to the Red Dragon, she wove in and out of the other hikers, avoiding me at all costs. When we reached the B&B, I tried to hang back, to find a moment to talk about what had happened between us, but she climbed straight into her car and drove off.

No goodbye, no glance, nothing.

I spent the drive home reliving every conversation, every touch, my palms sweating. I texted her when I got home. No reply. Every time my phone vibrated, my heart pounded, praying it was her. But no luck. I didn't understand how we'd gone from her curled in my arms to this suffocating distance.

But guilt gnawed at me all the same. This is how she must have felt when I left. Confused and hollowed out. Alone.

You deserve this, the familiar voice said, *you deserve this pain*.

I'd headed out on a walk, needing to clear my head, when I found myself at the steps of my brother's house, a renovated 1930s semi, with hanging baskets and a newly painted yellow front door, painstakingly painted by Kat when she had felt like a colour change. I rapped my knuckles against the door, the porch light flickering on.

The door opened, my brother crowding it.

'Ren?' he said, his voice low and a little tired. He was in a T-shirt and a pair of long striped pyjama bottoms.

'Shit! Were you asleep?' I checked my watch and recoiled. Jesus, it was only 7 o'clock at night. Were all blissfully happy couples looking like something out of a Dickens novel at this time of night?

Liam's eyes flickered across me, like he was scanning for injuries.

'Sorry,' I rubbed a hand across my mouth, feeling stupid. 'I'll leave you to it—'

Liam grabbed my shoulder and pulled me into the house. 'Get your arse in here.'

My brother had a weird way of showing affection.

'Who is it?' Kat's voice echoed down the hallway.

'Ren.'

'Oh,' Kat said, appearing at the end of the hallway, also dressed in a pyjama set that looked worrying similar to my brothers.

Matching pyjamas, too? Maybe I was happy single.

Then again, I'd wear a clown suit down Everly Heath High Street if it meant Lydia would speak to me.

Kat's eyes were curious. 'Ren. This is a surprise. Do you want a drink? Liam made a bolognese.'

She led us into the kitchen, the soft pink cabinets lit by the counter lights. The patio doors were dark, but I could just about make out the garden studio Liam had built for Kat for her interior-design business. Liam's hands reached across Kat, grabbing a Coke Zero for himself, before turning to me.

'Beer?'

'Please.' I accepted the can from Liam. 'Thanks.'

I pulled up a bar stool, sitting at their kitchen counter, taking a long sip of the beer. I glanced up to find Kat and Liam staring at me, with mixed expressions of worry and bemusement.

'What?'

'You look...'

'Terrible,' Liam concluded.

Kat swatted at Liam's arm. 'Don't say that!'

'What?' Liam said, gesturing a hand to me. 'He does! He looks like he hasn't slept in days. I mean, his lovesick arse did decide to go on a hiking trip and sleep in tents for weeks, so I guess it's his own fault.'

'It's romantic,' Kat said in a low voice, between her teeth.

'So come on then,' Liam said, folding his arms. 'What's up?'

'I'm fine, I'm fine. I was just out for a walk. And before I knew it, I was here.'

More silence.

'Okay, okay,' I sighed. 'I'm not fine.'

Kat took a seat. Liam moved closer.

'Okay,' Kat said, nodding. 'Shoot.'

I told them about the last day or so – keeping it PG – and finished with the fact that Lydia hadn't answered any of my calls or texts and I was near a breakdown. Well, I didn't actually say it like that, but I was pretty sure they could tell from the strain in my voice. And the expression on my face. When I was finished, they were both frowning.

'So...' Kat bit her lip. 'Let me get this straight. You two share a tent...'

I held up a hand. 'I'm not getting into the details with you.'

Liam grimaced. 'Please don't.'

'I think we can use our imagination.'

'Nope,' Liam said, hands in front of his face. 'My mind is blank.'

Kat continued, undeterred, 'And you woke up. Everything fine. But now she's ghosting you?'

'Bingo.'

'Right. Okay.' Kat tapped her fingers on the counter top. 'We need to think about what would've triggered that.'

'Maybe she came to her senses,' Liam said dryly.

I stood up, pushing the bar stool back. 'Right. I'll be off then.'

Kat shot out a hand to stop me, then swivelled to her fiancé, raising a single, deadly finger.

'Liam.'

His eyes widened, even as his eyes flickered across Kat's face, a little fascinated.

'Your brother is having a crisis. You will *not* take the piss. You will listen, and you will give him sage, big-brotherly advice. Now, I'm going back to watch *Love Island* so you two can talk.' Her eyes narrowed on Liam. 'Understood?'

Liam raised both hands in surrender, a little satisfied smile on his face. 'Sufficiently threatened, Red.'

More like sufficiently turned on. *Yuck*.

Kat gave me a pat on the back and a sympathetic smile, and made her way back to the front room. Once she was gone, Liam looked at me expectantly.

'Right.' Liam came around the island to sit next to me. 'Let's go over this again.'

I sighed. 'I told you everything I know. I've not got a clue why she won't speak to me. As usual, I've done something wrong. I'm sure you're ecstatic that I've fucked up this grand-gesture plan of yours,' I mumbled. 'You can rub it in now.'

I hated the petulant tone to my voice. Liam always looked for the worst in me, and now I was proving him right.

'I'm not going to rub it in, Ren,' Liam said softly.

I shrugged like a grumpy child. 'I wouldn't blame you.'

'This is my fault.' Liam sighed.

I frowned, glancing up to find Liam rubbing his forehead. 'What, because you encouraged me to go? I mean, Sandra would have killed me if I hadn't—'

'No, not that,' Liam said, looking at me. 'Look. I'm jealous of you.'

My eyes widened. Then I chuckled.

'Jealous of me?'

Liam nodded. 'I've always been a little jealous of you, Ren. I'm not too proud to admit it. When Mum died – you got to keep being a kid. And I felt like I had to step up, and be like her – a person everyone relied on. I felt like I needed to be a replacement parent to you.' Liam placed a hand on my shoulder. 'But at some point I let that turn into resentment and I shouldn't have done that. I shouldn't have put that on you. I let our relationship turn from brothers to parent-and-child and it's not healthy for any of us. And I'm sorry.'

My mouth was agape as I stared at my brother. He'd never admit any faults to me – he'd always been this untouchable, perfect son.

'You – you're sorry.' I shook my head, my world view shifting on its axis. 'You're jealous of me? What—' I stuttered. 'What do you have to be jealous of?'

'You don't see it, do you?' Liam smiled ruefully. 'You're everyone's favourite. You come into the room and no one else wants to talk to me, the boring, morose one. You're the fun one, the magnetic one. It's something you and Lydia have in common really, when I think about it.'

Liam smiled and I was desperately trying to let the words sink in, but they didn't make sense.

My voice croaked. 'I don't have a life – not like yours, Liam. I mean, I have no life apart from Lily's.'

'And, by the way – I vastly underestimated your role at Lily's, as I've realised since you've been gone the last few weeks.' Liam shook his head. 'We ran out of the Vinho Verde. I didn't know which supplier we sourced it from. And I need you to order some more of those cocktail napkins, because I ordered some plain ones and Kat hates them. Apparently, they are too big for cocktails and look like something you'd give out at a barbecue, not a restaurant.'

Something like pride burst in my chest. It felt foreign and indulgent, so I laughed it off.

I held up my hands. 'It's not our fault you have shit taste in napkins.'

Liam doesn't laugh, as if he sees through my attempt to lighten the mood. 'And it's not just that – it's the energy around the place. The staff are lower when you aren't there. The regulars have been asking where you've been. I'm just stuck in the kitchen, no one cares about me. It's you they come for.' Liam slaps his thighs. 'So I've been meaning to talk to you about the farm.'

My heart sinks. I want to stay in this bubble, not hear how the farm is a bad idea, yet again.

'We don't have to bring this up, Liam.'

'I'm in,' he says. 'I've spoken to Kat, and we're willing to put some of the money from when I sold my house. And we might have to put this house up for collateral too.' Liam sucks in a breath. 'Kat says she will. And we'll need Dad's and Jack's help, of course, for the renovation, but I'm sure we can figure something out. We can make it work. I can call Bert tomorrow—'

I clenched my fists. He had a determined edge to his jaw. Liam's face was… determined. Hopeful. As if he'd really thought about this, and wanted to figure out a way – any way – to make it work. He was trying to be the superman, the untouchable problem solver for everyone else's problems. But after what he had just told me about shouldering the burden of losing Mum, I couldn't do that to him.

'Liam,' I said softly. 'There is no way I'm getting you to risk this house – the house that means so much to you and Kat.' I shook my head. 'I could never do that.'

Liam frowned. 'But you want to do this – I can tell. I've been worried about you – you seem lost. It's partly why I encouraged you to go on this mad hiking trip. Not just for Lydia, but because you didn't seem yourself.' Liam paused. 'I thought the farm might have something to do with it. I shut you down quickly, and I've been thinking about it – and it was a mistake.'

'Well,' I shrugged. 'Maybe that's true. But we can't take huge risks. Things are going well, but now is the time to think through the next step. Not rush into it.'

It was Liam's turn to look shocked.

'I never thought it would be you lecturing me on rushing into things.'

I chuckled. 'First time for everything.'

'Okay.' Liam nodded after a second. 'If you're sure. We can look elsewhere.'

I thought about Bert's farm, the smell of the grass and the expanse of blue sky all around. I thought about Bethan and Gareth and their bustling farm, full of life and laughter.

And then I let it go.

'So, what are you going to do about Lydia?' Liam said softly. 'Have you tried calling her?'

My heart swooped at the mention of her name.

'She won't pick up the phone.'

'Have you thought about speaking to her in real life?'

'I—' I hesitated.

Sure I had. I'd thought about going over to her apartment the minute I got back. I would ask her what was wrong. I would make it right. I'd convince her I was happy just to be her friend. I wouldn't push like I had that night in the rain. I wouldn't flirt and tease her, just to get a blush on her cheeks and proof she felt this too.

Because she's won.

I needed her in my life. Full stop. So somehow I'd shrink that part of my soul that wanted more from her, if it meant she would answer her fucking phone. But going over to her house and saying all that meant accepting defeat. And I wasn't sure I was ready for that yet.

'We know Lydia,' Liam said evenly. 'She doesn't do things randomly. If she pulled away, something set it off. She's probably spiralling right now, same as you.' Liam pulled out his phone. 'She added me to this app thing. She can see where I am and I can see her. I don't really understand how it works.'

I rolled my eyes. He was so bad with technology, he was worse than Dad.

'God, you're thirty-three—'

'Thirty-two,' he grumbled.

'Give it here,' I said, taking the phone from his hand and finding Find My Friends. My heart pounded when I saw Lydia's smiling face on the phone.

Liam hummed, leaning over the screen. 'Ah yes. She's at the social club. They have a singles night.'

My eye snapped up to Liam. 'A singles night?'

'Kat,' Liam shouted. 'Did you say there was a singles night at the club?'

'Yes.' Kat poked her head around the door. 'Some plot of Pat's, I think. Sandra is helping out too.'

My eyes narrowed. 'A fucking singles night.'

Liam's eyes shifted around, which only made me feel worse. Kat padded into the kitchen.

'Don't stress, Ren,' she said, shrugging. 'It's probably just some name badges and warm Prosecco.'

'And a room full of single people.'

Liam grimaced. Kat looked sheepish. 'Well, yeah. I suppose so.'

My hands fell into my head. I didn't want to be an irrational, alpha dickhead but the green monster couldn't help but take hold – she could be flirting with someone right now, thinking about how much easier it is with them than with me.

'Ren,' Liam said, his voice firm. 'If you want her, you should fight for her.'

'Of course I want to fight for her. But we've had so many

near misses over the years. So many times we were almost there, only for something to pull us apart. What if this is another one of those times?' I glanced up. 'I'm not sure I could take it again.'

I ran a hand through my hair, a little breathless, as I confessed, 'I – I'm in love with her. I love her so much it terrifies me. It actually hurts in my chest. And I want this – *us* – so badly I can't afford to fuck it up again.'

My heart raced, and I felt a little lightheaded. But there was something expanding in my chest – something like relief, blended with determination. After keeping it down for so long, keeping this love, this total adoration for Lydia under wraps, it was finally out.

But the room was silent. I glanced up to see Kat, her mouth parted, her eyes shining.

'Wow!' Kat said softly.

Liam's face broke into a broad smile. 'Well, took you long enough. I'm happy for you.'

Kat smiled, something fierce and fond in it. 'What are you still doing here? Go. Go and get her. She could be talking to anyone right now!'

'Kat's right.' Liam shot me a brotherly look. 'You've kept her waiting long enough. It's fair game.'

'Not helping,' I said, downing the rest of my beer and heading for the door.

Kat and Liam followed me to the door with an air of energy and excitement.

'Wish me luck,' I said, as I pulled open the door.

'No,' Kat said, smiling. 'You won't need it.'

'Yes, he does,' Liam replied in that droll voice of his. 'Good luck!'

My lips twitched. Liam and I might have had some kind of breakthrough tonight, but it was oddly comforting to know some things never change.

Chapter Twenty

Lydia's Diary, 16 Years Old

Prom was shit.

I hated my dress, the DJ was awful, and the whole thing felt like a waste of time. But then Ren and I ended up outside the hotel, just the two of us, talking for ages. Making stupid jokes about which teachers were definitely shagging and how Pete Jones looked constipated when he danced.

'He goes so red and puffs out his cheeks,' Ren said, flicking ash on to the pavement.

Yeah. He was smoking like an idiot. I blame the flask I'd been sipping from because I asked him why he was out here instead of with Lindsey. He shrugged and asked me the same thing – why wasn't I with Tim?

I didn't know what he meant. Tim asked. And I turned him down.

Ren went quiet, staring at the ground as he tapped his cigarette. Finally, he said something like, 'Lindsey told me you were going with him.'

Before I could stop myself, I snorted and said, 'Well, Lindsey was wrong. She probably just wanted you all for herself.'

Ren's head tilted slightly, and he gave me this strange look. Like he was studying me, trying to work something out. Then he flicked his stupid cigarette away, shoved his hands in his pockets, and said, 'I wish I'd asked you instead.'

And then it was my turn to go quiet. I always wondered if we'd ever cross the line between friends and... something else. I think I've already crossed it. And I'm ready to admit it. But he won't.

So I just laughed it off and said, 'Yeah, well. You didn't.'

Lydia

'So, do you do *massages*?' James wiggled his eyebrows.

My phone vibrated, making my heart lurch into my throat. Ren had called and texted a few times since we got back from Wales. I couldn't bring myself to answer. I was confused, shaken. I didn't know where we stood. We hadn't just kissed this time – he'd made me unravel in ways I'd been trying to forget for years – and I had no idea how I was supposed to forget that a second time around.

I glanced at my phone. It wasn't Ren. It was that damn NO CALLER ID again. I hit the red button and returned to the infinitely dull man in front of me who was chattering on, oblivious to the fact I was barely listening.

James had latched himself on to me since the beginning of the singles night, when his mate nudged him and angled his head towards me. He shrugged and wandered over.

Pure romance.

I took a gulp of Prosecco and grimaced. It was warm and flat.

The social club was heaving, packed with a mixture of people between 25 and 35, the age range outlined in the guidelines Pat had typed up on the Eventbrite page. Cheesy noughties music played over the speakers and, as James droned on, I stared at the back of Amy's head, as she chatted away to a hippy with baggy trousers and a man bun. Amy's cropped pink hair glowed under the bar lights. I wished that we could ditch and have a proper girls' night. But Amy had been looking forward to it, and I had committed to the night when I was newly single.

At the time I'd thought, Why not? What did I have to lose?

Well, nothing. Because at this point I was repeatedly banging my head against rock bottom. I still had no job, no flat, and the icing on the cake? I was stupid enough to sleep with my best friend. *Again*. What made it worse was I was trying and failing *not* to think about said best friend, the memory of coming apart on his lips, and the fact that he was texting a woman called Lexi. A woman he had never mentioned before.

My mouth tasted bitter, and suspiciously like jealousy. It was pathetic. I was, yet again, at the mercy of how Ren made me feel.

'What about a sports massage?' James asked, those eyebrows going again. His breath smelled like stale lager. 'I've got a terrible pain in my shoulder. And I wouldn't mind a rub down.'

'I'm a personal trainer. Not a masseuse,' I said flatly.

I refused to make this man more comfortable by laughing off his shit joke.

James worked in finance, wore a quarter-zip, and when I asked if he lived in Everly Heath, he said, 'Oh, God, no! I could never live anywhere like this. I live in the city centre. I'm from High Wycombe, originally. But London was so expensive, you know? So I bought a flat in Manchester. You know the one right above Gail's?' He took a sip of his drink. 'I'm only out here 'cos my mate thought it would be a good laugh. Get to know some of the locals.'

He said 'locals' as if we were zoo animals. If it wasn't already over, it was over then, but I hadn't had a chance to shake him off yet.

'Do you do discounted rates for mates?' James wiggled his brows again.

I took another sip of the Prosecco, hoping it would knock me out.

James launched into a monologue about cryptocurrency, and I nodded every now and then. Across the room, Amy caught my eye, winced, and mouthed *Sorry!* over the man bun's shoulder. James was on to NFTs when I heard a voice.

TAKE A HIKE!

A deep, familiar voice.

My stomach did a flip.

'Mind if I cut in?'

My head snapped up and there he was.

Ren stood there, name badge crooked on his chest. His eyes locked on mine. I hadn't clocked that James was short. Not that there's anything wrong with that. But next to Ren – who was looking tall, broad, and a little intimidating right now – well, James just looked... puny.

Ren's gaze pinned me in place.

James spluttered, 'We were just talking—'

'*You* were talking,' he said, voice calm. '*She* was falling asleep.'

My lips parted. James's eyebrows went up into his soon-to-be-receding hairline.

Ren finally looked at James. 'Look, mate, I'm going to offer you some advice. Women – or anyone, really – don't want to hear you drone on about your investments in little pictures, okay?'

James frowned. 'They're *digital assets*—'

Ren leaned down, voice low. 'And we all know they're worth fuck all.'

James opened his mouth, then closed it again. Like a fish. God, I almost felt bad for the guy. Then I remembered the massage comment and pulled myself together.

'Ren.' I caught his sleeve, fingers wrapping around his biceps. The smug bastard flexed it under my hand.

His eyes met mine, fiery and intense.

'Am I wrong, Lydia?'

Silence.

Then I realised it wasn't just me that was silent. I glanced behind me. Every single eye in the social club was on us. My mum, Pat, Amy. Even Peter, who was a miserable curmudgeon at the best of times and couldn't give a toss about anyone else's drama.

They were *all* watching.

I grabbed Ren by the arm, pulling him away from James towards a quiet corner of the social club by the loos.

I rounded on him and jabbed my finger at his chest. 'What the hell was that?'

His eyes flared as he looked down to where I touched him, then back to me.

'I know. He was a prick.'

'No. *You*. What are you doing here?'

He folded his arms across his chest. 'You've been dodging my texts. And calls.'

My cheeks flushed with heat. He was right. I was avoiding him. After I saw the message from a LEXI MEXICO, it was like something cracked open. All these deep-seated insecurities I'd carefully packed away came tumbling out. Things I thought I'd buried. Things I didn't want to admit.

I was jealous.

And I hated it. Hated the way it made me feel. I hated that my first instinct was to snap *'Who the fuck is Lexi?'* at him. It was immature. Childish. And a sign that I wasn't feeling secure. Not in this, us or even myself.

'Can we talk?' Ren said, his voice low, his hands reaching out to touch me, but I dodged him. I knew I would crack if I let his hands on me again.

'This isn't the time or place to have this discussion, Ren.'

'Lydia.' Ren's voice was low, and strained. He took a step forward. I took a step back. I hit the cool wall behind me. Ren's eyes tracked me, my eyes, my lips. The scent of him surrounded me.

'I'm not leaving until you tell me what's wrong. You won't even look at me. And after everything that happened that night, in the tent—'

It was far too public to have this conversation.

I turned on my heel, heading for the exit, knowing that he was right behind me. Outside, the balmy air hit my face. The

TAKE A HIKE!

high street was quiet, the deli, butcher's and hardware shop were all closed for the night.

'There is nothing wrong,' I lied. I crossed my arms, facing him, doing my best at looking defiant.

Ren's eyes narrowed and he called my bluff. He stepped closer, chest brushing my shoulder. The heat of him sank into me and I flushed even at that tiny contact.

Ren's voice was low, sultry. 'Fine. Then you won't mind me talking about that night. When I made you come apart with my fingers and—'

My hand shot over his mouth, even as my body flared with heat. His chuckle rumbled against my skin. He caught my wrist, turned it, pressing a soft kiss to my pulse.

Jesus, he shouldn't be allowed to be this lethal.

'Talk to me, Lyd,' Ren said softly. 'Did I hurt you?'

I pulled my hand back. 'No, of course not.'

'Then what is it?' He reached for me again, but I stepped away.

'You don't get to do this,' I said, hands fisted at my side. 'You don't get to come in here, all guns blazing. All jealous—'

'Of course I'm jealous!' His hands went to his hair. 'I'm jealous of anyone who gets to speak to you when you're icing me out. I'm jealous of the way you laugh so freely with your friends, because I can see the way you hold back around me. I'm jealous of the fact that you are more than comfortable enough to come to a singles night, while I'm at home losing my mind wondering why you won't answer my calls.'

Losing his mind? He's losing his mind about the fact I won't text him back, when *he* has some random woman trying to call him in the early hours of the morning.

I couldn't keep a lid on my temper any more.

The words came out, harsh and forceful, like a full stop.

'Who is Lexi?'

Ren's eyebrows furrowed, his eyes shifted.

'Lexi? Why—'

'She texted you. I saw it on your phone that night we shared the tent.'

Realisation dawned on his face, slowly, like the sunrise. Then, hope cracked over it.

'So I'm not the only one who is jealous.'

I recoiled, embarrassment burning in my cheeks.

'Oh, fuck you!'

'Lydia—'

'I hate this.' I flattened my palm against my forehead. 'I hate the way you make me crazy. You make me feel weak. Vulnerable.'

'I make you *feel*, Lydia,' he shot back, stepping closer.

I snapped. 'I don't want to feel! You *left* me. I didn't even believe the letter. I thought it was some dumb joke. I went over to your dad's house, stood on his doorstep. And he looked at me like I was some wounded puppy.' I shook my head, my eyes burning. 'He told me it was true. You'd boarded that flight without a word. After that night. You started it, Ren. You finally saw me that night. And you changed everything—'

Ren's voice turned dark. 'It wasn't just me, Lydia, and you know it.'

I ignored him. 'You turned around and left me. Do you know how embarrassing—'

'Lydia.' His voice cut through mine. 'Before that night, I'd thought about you for years.'

My breath caught. 'Years?'

'Yes. Years. But you were my best friend – the person I trusted with everything. And I was scared. Scared I'd ruin it. Scared I'd lose you. So scared I ended up doing exactly that.' His eyes shut. 'And I've regretted leaving you every day since—'

'Good!' My voice broke. I wanted to sound angry, but I just sounded broken. 'Do you know how pathetic I felt? How embarrassing it was? How people would ask me at the club how you were doing, because as far as they were concerned, we were just Lydia and Ren – childhood friends. Little did they know that I was broken. And the funny thing was, before we slept together, I told myself I was over you.' My laugh came out high and sharp. 'Naive eighteen-year-old Lydia from that gig was gone. I'd accepted that you never saw me that way. I was happy to have whatever morsel you'd give me – pathetic, by the way.'

I drew in a tight breath. 'And then that night... I thought maybe I'd been wrong. Maybe you did feel the same. Maybe I wasn't imagining it.'

Ren's hands hovered like he was aching to touch me. 'You weren't imagining it.'

I gave a bitter laugh. 'I must have been. You made me hope. And then suddenly travelling the world was more important than I was—'

Ren gave a frustrated growl. 'I wasn't travelling, Lydia.'

I scoffed. 'What the hell are you on about?'

Ren took a deep breath. 'I didn't leave to hurt you. I left because I thought I'd lost everything here. Liam had pulled the rug from underneath me. I'd already resigned at work. And a job came up – no, not just a job. The best job someone like me could get. At Nocturne in Mexico City.'

My mind reeled. Ren used to wax lyrical about that place – Nocturne. I'd never been, obviously, but I'd heard him go on about it enough times to picture the whole thing: a black marble bar that looked like it belonged in a Bond film, low amber lighting, cocktails delivered perfectly, but with that calm ease that said they did it a million times a day. It came up often, back when I used to tag along to his Sunday-night pub crawls with the team – half of whom spoke about Nocturne reverently, with a sort of glassy-eyed awe.

'They're going to win it again,' Gareth, Ren's old boss, had said once, while we were sitting in the smoking area of the old, crooked pub in town. 'A mate of mine went last month. Said it was perfect. Sophisticated but not snobby – unlike half the bars in London and New York.'

Ren continued, snapping me back into the present. 'I could be a bartender for the best bar in the world or I could get another dead-end job in town. Apart from you, it was simple. If I couldn't have my own bar, I'd work for the very best. But I couldn't bring myself to tell you. I couldn't bring myself to see your face.'

My throat constricted, and I pictured another version of our lives. A version where he had told me. I would have been proud – gutted at first, yes – but I would have smiled and made him a playlist for the flight. We could have talked, and figured something out. We'd been friends since we were six – what were a few more months, a few thousand miles? I would have visited.

I pictured myself walking down busy streets, crossing bustling squares, eating in intimate restaurants Ren couldn't wait to show me.

But he'd taken that choice away from us. He hadn't even given us a chance. And that – more than him leaving – was what hurt the most.

'You should've told me.' My voice came out hoarse. 'I would've been happy for you. So happy for you.'

'You would have hated me.'

'Would I have been gutted? Maybe a little.' My voice dropped. 'But you seriously underestimate my feelings for you if you think this would've ruined us, Ren.' I opened my arms wide. 'And guess what? I ended up hating that you left, anyway. So you got your wish. Congrats.'

'Lydia.'

'You know what I hated the most? That you could leave me.' I glanced down. 'I've been ignoring you these past few days to prove to myself that I can do the same.'

His mouth opened, then closed. His shoulders lowered in defeat. 'I deserve that.'

My chest heaved, my eyes heavy. 'How are we supposed to do this, Ren? When I feel like this? When it hurts this much?' I shook my head. 'It shouldn't be this hard.'

His hand lifted to my cheek.

'Don't,' I whispered.

My phone buzzed, and I picked it up to find a familiar NO CALLER ID ringing. This fucker. They'd been calling me for weeks now, at all times of the day. Well, this was the perfect excuse to leave this conversation with Ren, whose soft, devastated expression was killing me.

'I need to take this,' I said, turning around, and swiped to answer. 'You know what? I probably *do* owe you money for some shitty, overpriced utilities, but I've lost my job and I'm really fucking angry tonight, so—'

'Lydia?' A lilting Irish voice – familiar and deep – sounded over the phone.

I froze.

'Is that you? God, woman, you're impossible to get a hold of, I'll tell you that. I've been trying for, God, it's got to be two weeks now. That fella of yours, well, he wouldn't stop calling me. And I don't blame him. I fired that fecker when I found out.'

'Niall?'

'I owe you an apology, Lydia,' Niall said, his voice grave. 'Craig told you he had permission to fire you, but let me tell you, he didn't. He pulled the wool over my eyes – he told me you'd left the business. He told me it had been your choice. And I was happy for you. I didn't realise, until your lad called—'

He sighed.

'Ren?' I whispered.

'That's the one. Ren. He was relentless. Wouldn't let it lie. And I don't blame him. I'd have done the same. Now, listen. I've got an opening at Momentum in Everly Heath. If you're willing to come back...'

The rest of Niall's voice faded, swallowed by the rush in my ears.

Ren had called him. Ren had hounded him and made him listen. Ren had done what I was too scared to do.

I turned around, but he was gone.

Chapter Twenty-One

Ren

The text came through as I pulled into the carpark of Glenhaven Lodge. My stomach fizzed, and my shaking hand swiped at the notification.

A pin. Just 500 feet from the carpark. Just 500 feet from Lydia.

I'd spent most of the beautiful drive up to the Highlands of Scotland wondering if I was making a mistake coming here. Lydia clearly wanted space. But when I pictured missing out on the final trip – not feeling Gen's eyes narrow when I opened my mouth, not seeing Amy beam with pride after finishing her final challenge, or not eating one of Claire's homemade flapjacks, still warm from her backpack – I felt something tighten in my chest. I realised I'd started these trips with Lydia in mind, but slowly, quietly, they'd become something for me too.

And if anything could soothe my bruised heart right now, it was Scotland.

Because, fuck me, it was beautiful.

The kind of beauty you couldn't imagine from pictures or videos. You had to see it. The roads, winding and rural, revealed a new, breathtaking beauty at each turn. Mountains pierced the clouds, casting scattered patches of sunlight over the land below. It was so beautiful that it looked like those pristine screensavers from the 90s.

By the time I pulled up to the wood-cladded hotel the sun was setting. Mandy had mentioned it was a bit of an institution with hikers and climbers in the region. The hotel was only two storeys high and nestled down a remote road, surrounded by mountains and a picturesque loch. Mandy said that we would travel to Ben Nevis on the first day to tackle the most challenging ascent. Then we'd come back here and spend the rest of the trip walking more manageable summits and walks around Glencoe and Ballachulish.

But now, as I stared at my phone, I wasn't thinking of the hike tomorrow.

I was thinking about the fact we hadn't spoken since our argument at the social club. I'd received a fair few sad, sympathetic glances from locals as I'd walked down the high street yesterday to get some last-minute supplies from Ravi's hardware store. I had accepted that when she answered that phone call, I was essentially dismissed, and wanted to give her the space she clearly needed. I spent the rest of my evening regretting listening to Kat and Liam's advice. It was bogus. Just because they were sickeningly in love, didn't mean they knew shit.

But now Lydia had sent me a pinned location. No message, no explanation. Just a pin about 500 feet from the carpark. I unpacked, checked in, and dumped my bag in my modest, tartan-patterned room, then jogged through a gate, eyes on my phone, following the flickering blue dot that told me where she was. Past some trees, into a clearing, then down a grassy path that opened on to a small loch. And there she was – a blonde head by the water, her knees pulled tight to her chest, staring out at the view. It was dead quiet, no one but us and the sounds of the water gently lapping against the loch's bank.

I sat next to her. We stayed silent for a moment before she opened her mouth first.

'I don't think I've seen anything more beautiful.'

She was partly right – as the sun was setting, the sky of oranges and pinks reflected on the water below, bracketed in by the dark, broody mountains.

'I have,' I said, eyes on her instead of the view. 'Seen something more beautiful, that is.'

She turned, finally looking at me, her head resting on her knees. She gave me a soft, shy smile that I wasn't sure I'd earned.

'I—'

'Ren—'

I chuckled. 'You go.'

Lydia took a breath in, and began, 'I'm not going to apologise for what I said the other night. It was a long time coming and it felt good getting all that off my chest. I'd been keeping it locked up for so long. So I'm not going to apologise. Even if it was public and messy and not usually how I do things. I feel lighter for it.'

I nodded. 'Fair enough. All I've ever wanted was for you to be honest. And to be yourself. Your true self, underneath all the smiles and people-pleasing. And I hurt you, so you should tell me how you feel. Shout at me. Whatever you want, Lyds.'

'But I don't want to hurt you too.'

'You didn't say anything I didn't already know, Sunshine. And about Lexi—'

Her shoulder tensed. A telling sign that she was still thinking about this.

'Lexi is married.' I pulled out my phone, showing the smiling faces of a couple – Lexi, with her platinum-blonde, poker-straight hair, and next to her a man with a wild, dark mullet – 'That is Lexi and Tim. Odd couple, but it works. She's a posh Londoner, he's a typical Aussie. They met travelling a couple of years ago, eloped in Peru. Now they have a place in Mexico City, but travel all around the world. I met them on my first day at Nocturne. They ordered my favourite drink and we hit it off.'

I put away my phone and glanced at Lydia, her face unreadable.

'Lexi was texting about you. Yes. Because she knows about you – I confessed it all drunk one night. That I had a best friend I had hurt and I missed her so much.' I chuckled, remembering the way Lexi had recoiled when I told her what I did and who I left at home. 'She smacked me on the arm. Girl code, she called it. Then, after a few weeks, she said I had a sadness in my eyes. She made me realise I wasn't happy. Then, she suggested I come home and make it up to you.'

Lydia exhaled. 'Well, I feel fucking stupid.'

I ran a hand down her ponytail. 'You're not stupid. If I'd read that on your phone, from Casey or someone – I would have thought the same.' I clasped her chin, making her look at me. 'But there is no one else, Lydia. No one but you. And I know it doesn't erase the fact that I left in the first place, but I was in the airport, boarding a flight back to you when Liam called and asked if I would come back.'

Lydia inhaled sharply.

'I came home for *you*. Not for Liam. Not for Lily's. I would have got a job at a drive-thru if it meant I could be with you.'

Lydia's eyes caught on my lips, then she stood and held out a hand for me to follow. Then she kicked off her trainers and socks and pulled her baggy gym tee over her head. Heat and desire rocketed right through me. Followed shortly by confusion.

'What are you doing?'

She pulled down her leggings, slowly, like I've imagined doing again and again since our night in that tent.

'What do you think?' She smiled mischievously. 'Skinny-dipping.'

A laugh stuttered out of me. 'Lyds, this is Scotland. It's going to be—' my voice died when she pulled her bra off, then her thong and she was standing naked before me. Blood rushed to my cock as I stared at the defined lines of her stomach, and her strong legs, up to her breasts, that were small, but perfectly shaped, her dusky pink nipples hardening as the spring breeze caressed her. God, she was a goddess. I wanted to trace the dusting of freckles on her thighs with my tongue. I wanted to sink my fingers into her soft hips. I wanted to make her *mine*.

'Come on, Ren,' she said, humour in her voice, even as I could hear the gravelly desire there too. She turned towards the water, then shot me a sexy smirk over her shoulder. 'Don't go mute on me now. You said you were so good with that mouth.'

I choked a laugh. God, I wanted to wipe that smugness off her face with my mouth. But all I could do was stare at her beautiful, round arse as she walked into the loch, her shoulders tensing as the cold hit her legs. She didn't hesitate, only gave a graceful dive before coming up, and smoothing her wet hair off her face.

I stared in awe, as she grinned at me, looking all the part of a water nymph or siren, destined to drag me to a watery grave.

'Ren.' God, her voice was... seductive. 'We don't have all night.'

In a flurry, I pulled off my jumper and jeans, followed by socks and boxers, leaving them in a dishevelled pile next to Lydia's, and made my way into the water, half hard. Although, I was sure the cold water would do something about that.

I watched Lydia eye me as I stepped into the loch, her blue eyes fiery and intense. I did my best not to show how chilly the water was. The sun was gone now, and the water was a dark blue, and surprisingly clear.

I swam closer to Lydia, as she treaded water.

'You should have told me about Nocturne.'

'I know.'

'What was it like? Living out there? Working there? I always wanted to ask your dad or Liam how you were doing, but I chickened out. I was worried you were blissfully happy, travelling the globe. I wish you'd told me about the job. It's really impressive, Ren.'

I swam closer, and our legs grazed. I wanted to grab her, and wrap those legs around mine. But I wanted to let Lydia lead.

'I was miserable. The owner, Andrea, had approached me at the Worlds.'

The competition brought together all the best bartenders in the world, to compete for the world title. As I had won the UK title, I competed and lost. But Andrea had seen my cocktail and the recipe, and had been impressed.

'She asked if I wanted a job. At the time, I'd said no, because Liam and I were already planning to open Lily's. She accepted, but then I called her again once I could see Liam was wavering. She set me up in a little apartment in Mexico City. It was beautiful. It was chaos and colour all at once, like a living mural. It was loud and bright and alive... but in the best way.' I hesitated. 'I'd – I'd love to take you one day, if you wanted.'

Lydia gave me a soft smile. 'I'd love to. I'd love to see where you were building this life, making friends—'

'It wasn't a life, Lydia,' I said, floating closer to her.

My hand grazed her waist. I allowed myself that little touch. Her eyes heated.

'It was great to pretend I was someone else for a while. But it didn't fill me up. Nocturne was just a bar. Mexico City was just another place. And all I could think about was you. I wished you were there with me. I missed you. God, I missed you. I thought of you every day. Wondering what you were doing, how you felt about me. I'd spin nightmares, imagining how much you hated me. Convinced myself you had moved on, and probably found better than me. Andrea,' I chuckled. 'Well, it was so bad Andrea sat me down and said that while I was doing the job fine, I didn't seem right. She was right. I was just going through the motions.'

Lydia nodded, her hand coming to my wrist. She pulled me closer, and I almost wept when she wrapped her hands around my neck. Her blue eyes tracked me.

I almost groaned, 'Lydia. What are we—' I squeezed my eyes shut. 'If this isn't going anywhere, I – I don't think we should be doing this. I'm not sure I could take it. Having you here, naked, and then having to pretend we're nothing—'

She answered with a kiss to the corner of my mouth.

'I know about Niall. The calls you made. He called me after our fight and offered me Craig's job. To manage the gym myself.'

My eyes widened, and I let myself tug her into my arms and spin her around. She giggled.

'Are you serious?' I pulled back my hands in her hair. 'Are you going to take it?'

She sobered. 'I'm not sure. After this trip – well, it's got me thinking more about doing something for myself, you know? I'm wondering if it's worth the risk, if it means it's mine. If it means no one can take it away from me again. I put ten years into Momentum and Niall didn't know about what Craig did – but it still happened, you know? My job, gone, poof.'

I nodded, pulling her legs to wrap around mine. I held her up, keeping her away from my growing erection. I didn't need a distraction... right now at least.

'I think that's amazing, Lydia.' It was my turn to kiss the side of her mouth. Slowly, like she might pull away. She let me, so I kissed her cheek, then her forehead and her neck. Small, little kisses that I hoped conveyed how much I loved her, even if she wasn't ready to hear the words yet.

'I want to say thank you,' Lydia murmured as I peppered kisses. 'No one has ever done anything like that for me. Taken matters into their own hands, you know?'

I pulled back, running my thumb over her cheek.

'I would do anything for you. No, I'm serious, Lydia. If I haven't made this abundantly clear – I'm in this. I'm ready for us. Properly this time. No more false starts. No more keeping our feelings locked away out of fear of losing each other. Because you aren't going to lose me, okay?'

I kissed her softly, our tongues barely grazing, then I placed my forehead against hers.

'I'm glad Niall came to his senses and fired that arsehole.'

Lydia hummed. 'Just a shame I didn't get to have it out with him.'

My mind whirled with plans to correct exactly that.

'I'll find his home address and drive you there. When we back—'

Lydia laughed, 'Ren. We don't need to do that.'

We, we, we. We were a we.

Lydia's smile was terrifying. 'Besides, I may have had my own Lydia brand of revenge…'

I stilled and cocked my head. 'What did you do?'

'Let's just say I heard through Niall that Craig has somehow managed to get a new job. And I may have sent him a little present in the mail…' Lydia's laugh was melodic. 'It's just a little glitter bomb. Special delivery for when he runs his HIIT classes. Let's make him clean the gym this time. I have a friend of mine who works there. She's going to send me the video.'

I kissed her, hard. 'Brilliant. Evil, but brilliant.'

She shrugged. 'He had it coming. And I couldn't let you have all the fun.'

My hands slid lower, bolder now, finding her gorgeous arse and squeezing until she gasped. She looped her arms tighter around my neck and shifted so we were aligned, her soft against my hard.

'Lydia,' I moaned into her hair. 'Careful.'

'Why so careful now?' she whispered, her lips brushing my jaw. 'You worried I'll break you?'

'No,' I hissed as she gave a gentle bite to my neck. 'I don't want to push you. A few nights ago, you hated my guts—'

'I didn't hate you, Ren,' she said softly, but her hips rolled, teasing, and even in the cold water, I felt like I was on fire. 'I wanted to hate you, but you're impossible to hate. And I want you, Ren. I've wanted you for a long time, but I couldn't let myself be hurt again. But I'm tired of being scared. I'm ready to be fearless. With you.'

There was something in the soft, but certain way she admitted that she was ready – ready to explore this. *Us.* Maybe she wasn't as ready as me. I wanted to burrow her away in my flat for months, keep her fed and watered and make her come. I wanted her to wear my clothes and smell like me. I wanted to give her a diamond ring and make her mine. Like I was hers.

But that would all come in good time.

Because she felt ready in my arms.

I pulled her closer, grinding her over me. I wanted to bottle the sound of her soft gasp. My hands gripped her arse, shifting her against me, knowing it would stoke some of the ache between her legs and mine.

She whimpered, rocking harder, chasing friction with no shame. Perfect.

'How much do you ache, Sunshine?' I rasped. 'As much as me? Because you've been keeping me on a knife edge these past few weeks. Tortured by those looks you gave me. Are you sure you're ready for me?'

'Say it. Say you want me. All of me.'

'I want all of you, Ren.'

Chapter Twenty-Two

Lydia's Diary, 18 Years Old

Dear Diary,
 I left school today – just like that. Done.
 I start my personal training apprenticeship in a few weeks, but right now, I just feel... weird. Ren left too, and everyone's freaking out over what he's going to do. Liam's already working for his dad at HBC, so no one questions him. But with Ren? It's like they expect nothing from him. It makes me so angry how much they underestimate him. He got the highest art grade in the whole year. He's so talented. And not just that – he's driven. If he wanted to, he could do something extraordinary. Something creative. But even if he doesn't, that's fine, too.
 Ren says he wants to work in a restaurant, save money, and travel. Everyone acts like it's typical Ren – like he's just avoiding responsibility – but I don't see it that way. He knows what he wants and he's actually going for it. I wish I could do something adventurous like that, but... I'm too much of a homebody. Or maybe that's just an excuse.
 Sometimes, I wonder if I hold myself back because I'm scared of doing anything out of the box. Mum's always worried about things that feel risky, and maybe I've just inherited that.
 We've got a few weeks just to chill, and he asked if I wanted to see a gig with him on Saturday – just us. And I thought,

maybe now school is over... maybe we'd become more than friends.

But maybe I'm reading too much into it.

Lydia

We tugged dry clothes over our wet legs, and I giggled when Ren hopped around on one foot, wrestling his jeans back on.

'Turn around,' he laughed, breathless. 'This is not part of the sexy show I promised.'

'I like seeing behind the scenes,' I shot back, grinning. The comment earned me a playful pinch on my bum.

Once we were dressed enough not to give the other guests a heart attack, we hurried back towards the hotel, Ren's hand squeezing mine. A giggle bubbled up in my throat. Something about it felt stupidly exhilarating – childish, reckless. Like sneaking out when we were grounded, as if we were getting away with something we shouldn't. We slipped down the path, under the canopy, past door after door, my pulse beating in my ears. Ren grinned as we headed towards his room.

I'd decided, after the call with Niall – and after saying every messy thing I'd kept locked up – that I was done waiting. I was done holding back from him.

We came to a stop outside Room 401, Ren's room. And he turned to me, suddenly looking like a younger, more unsure version of himself. A version I'd seen years before. I pushed away a wet strand of his hair, and he leaned into my palm.

He started, voice low, careful. 'I know I said all of that in the loch. But it's a big day tomorrow, so I understand if—'

I ran my hand along his jaw, fingers trailing over the stubble before gripping it firmly, tilting his face towards mine. The way his breath hitched sent a thrill through me. I had his full attention.

Good.

I let my thumb brush over his bottom lip, teasing, before leaning in to whisper, 'I'm done waiting, Lawrence. So tell me. Are you going to let me go back to my room, where I can take care of myself, or are you going to invite me in and fuck me senseless, like you promised?'

Ren's breath hitched, his eyes darkening as they flicked to my lips.

I turned, as if I was going to walk away. 'Or the pub at the hotel is busy, so I'm sure I could find someone to help me out—'

Ren was on me in an instant, pressing me against the wall. 'You don't need to look for someone else to solve a problem I created, Lydia,' Ren whispered and I shivered. 'I can take care of the ache. What would happen if I touched your pussy right now? Right out here where anyone could see us. Would I find you wet for me?'

'Ren—' I smiled, sounding breathy.

I loved that I could get a rise out of him like this. Our friendship had been light and fun. But this felt charged and competitive. As if we both wanted to make the other suffer with ache.

'Yeah, I bet I'd find you soaking for me. I bet I'd only need a few touches to get you there.' He kissed my throat and whispered into my skin, 'God, you are so fucking sexy.'

I took the keys out of his hands and opened the door, stepping inside, the heat of Ren's body following me. The room was dark, but I could see a small double bed, then another door leading to an en suite. Blue and yellow tartan accents were littered on the cushions and curtains. It was homey and lived in. As soon as Ren shut the door and locked it, I reached for the hem of my pink long-sleeved T-shirt and peeled it off, letting it drop to the floor. I still wore my underwear, a white bra and thong, but the air hit my skin anyway, cool against the warmth of the room, against the heat of his gaze.

And even though he had already seen me completely naked this evening, that didn't stop Ren's eyes dragging over me, slowly, lingering on my breasts, still a little damp from the loch. He was memorising every inch.

His throat bobbed. 'God, you're perfect.'

I stepped closer, feeling the heat roll off him. I tilted my chin up to meet his dark brown eyes.

'Then don't waste any more time.'

Then he was on me.

His hand in my hair, his lips on mine, firm at first, then softening as his tongue grazed my lower lip, making my stomach flip over. I wrapped his T-shirt in my fist, pulling him towards me until the back of my thighs hit the edge of the bed. Ren didn't push me on to it yet. No, he took his time kissing his way down my neck, giving a light bite to my collarbone, and lower. I arched as his tongue swirled on the edge of my breast, agonisingly teasing, which was so Ren.

I went to lie on the bed behind me, but he stopped me with a hand around my waist.

'Ah, ah.' He clicked his tongue. 'When I want you on the bed, you'll be there. Laid out for me. Like my perfect feast.'

'Ren,' I groaned. 'Too slow.'

'It's been two years since I've had you all to myself.' He smiled, a glint in his eyes that told me he would make me suffer in the most delicious way. 'I can wait a little longer. Can you?'

He gently pulled the strap to my bra, kissing the little red mark it left and then lower and lower. He pulled the bra down, but instead of licking, biting, and kissing, he blew a puff of air, making me wriggle.

'Ren,' I moaned.

He was playing. I was like a piece of chocolate melting on his tongue. I hated it. I loved it.

'That's it.' He gave a wicked smile. 'I want to hear those moans, Sunshine.'

His tongue swirled across my breasts finally, and I arched into his mouth, my head thrown back. It was the most delicious, infuriating sensation, doubled by the graze of his teeth. Ren finally unclipped my bra and drew one nipple into his mouth while he palmed the other. It was impossible, almost painful, how desperate I was for him.

I clawed at his clothes. 'Off.'

'Yes, ma'am.'

Ren grabbed the hem of his T-shirt and pulled it off in one motion. My hands traced the tattoos – the sun and moon that represented us. I placed a kiss there, and my hand drifted over his abs. He tensed and flexed. And I don't know how I hadn't noticed it before, when I'd seen him outside the showers, or that night in the tent. His stomach was defined, more muscular than I'd noticed then.

My eyes narrowed. 'Have you been working out? Where? With who?'

Ren laughed, a lovely, low sound. 'Are you jealous of my gym buddy, Lydia?'

He took a step closer, pulling us flush together. My breasts pressed into his chest. Ren's lips grazed my ear, his palms across my waist.

'I'll only go to the gym with you from now on, love. Happy?'

Ren grinned as he tucked a strand of hair behind my ear. The gym was my love language, and he knew it.

'Maybe.'

'Can I make you even happier now, please?'

'Yes.'

Ren's eyes grazed over me again, 'Struggling to know where to start.'

'Well, I can help with that.'

I shifted us around and pushed Ren on to the bed, feeling empowered by his gaze and the way he looked at me like I was a goddess. He leaned back on his elbows, stomach flexing and dark hair ruffled from where I'd pulled at it. His eyes were molten and kept tracking my movements as if he couldn't – wouldn't –

miss anything. He looked like a god of debauchery and sex.

I undid the button on his jeans. Ren cocked an eyebrow when I shrugged them off him with ease.

'You're good at that.'

'Jealous?' I raised an eyebrow, quoting him.

'Always.'

I pulled back Ren's black boxers, exposing his hard cock. I slid my hand up his thick thighs to tease him, running my hands near, but nowhere near enough. His cock twitched, desperate for attention. I laid a kiss there.

'Lydia.' He breathed.

'Now who's the tease?' I smiled before pulling him out and giving him a single, hard stroke.

A noise reverberated through Ren's throat. It was desperate and needy. I smiled and shifted so I was on my knees between his legs. I leaned down and kept my eyes on Ren as I opened my mouth and swiped a tongue over the head of his cock.

'Fuck, Lydia.' He groaned.

I swirled my tongue again, making Ren's eyes roll back, and I sucked a bit harder this time. Then, once he got used to that teasing, and watched me in rapture, I took him deeper, humming as he swore again, and wrapped his fist around my ponytail.

'Fuck. That feels so good. You feel so good.' Ren groaned, and I took him deeper. 'Look at you. Taking my cock deep in your mouth. God!'

As if he couldn't take it any more, his head rolled back, his Adam's apple bobbing. I sucked him harder. His eyes rolled back in his head. I bobbed again, but took him deeper this time.

'Nope. No.' He shifted away from my mouth. 'If you keep doing that, I'm going to embarrass myself.' He ran a thumb over my swollen lips. 'And I need to touch you.'

Ren guided me up the bed, kissing me. His erection pressed

into me right where I needed him, and I gasped. Ren smirked as he shifted us and timed his tongue with the pressure of his hard cock on my clit. He kissed down my neck, and I wriggled, needing more.

'So impatient.' Ren tutted as his hands drifted lower. He toyed with the lace of my thong.

'Stop playing.'

I stared at his smug smirk as he pulled the lace aside and ran two fingers over my clit, deliciously delicate.

'I was right, Lydia. You're so wet.' He tutted, and I hated how much I liked the tone. 'All of this for me, huh?'

'Yes.'

His dark eyes met mine. 'You're such a good girl.'

Ugh. Did I have an undiagnosed praise kink?

'Yes,' he murmured in my ear. 'Such a beautiful, wet pussy. I can't wait to make you come apart on my cock, Lydia. You're going to take me so well, aren't you?'

I moaned, as he moved his fingers quicker over my clit. Still light, but just enough to feel my orgasm build. His voice was helping.

'Tell me you're going to take me so well.'

'I'm – I'm,' I gasped as he pushed two fingers inside me. 'I'm going to take you so well.'

He gave a dark chuckle. 'Tell me you're going to come all over my cock.'

'I'm going to come all over your cock.'

'Good girl. I can't wait to see the mess you make.'

It was all too much. I could feel his body on top of me, his fingers inside me, his breath at my neck and his words in my ear. Everything was building, I was so close. I desperately wanted to throw myself over that edge and feel some relief. We'd been playing around this – this tension – for days, maybe weeks, if I was honest with myself. And I needed release.

Now.

And, of course, Ren pulled back, slowing down. I groaned into his neck.

'Ren.' He pressed his fingers against my clit again, like he liked the sound of his name. 'If you don't make me come in the next thirty seconds, I'm going to kill you.'

He gave a low chuckle. 'I'm at your command.'

He moved quickly, shifting us and lowering himself down my body. He pulled my thong roughly aside, and I felt his warm breath on my sex. Ren sucked on my clit hard and pushed his fingers inside me. Oh. Oh.

'Play with your tits for me. I want to watch.'

I did as he said, and I glanced down. His eyes rolled back in his head at the sight of me playing with my nipples.

I gasped as he sucked harder, then soothed with slower sensual strokes of his tongue. My back arched as the orgasm built again. It took me less than ten seconds to come, stars exploding. The rest of the world disappeared until I came back down to earth, heart racing and breathless. Ren kissed my thighs, gliding his rough hands in soothing circles across my legs and up my chest. He grazed my nipples, and I arched again, feeling both sensitive and ready for him again.

Ren's voice was strained. 'That was so hot. I could come just from you clenching around my fingers.'

'Come here,' I said, my voice hoarse. 'I need you.'

Ren smirked, moving towards me without hesitation. 'If I heard you say that every day, I think I'd die a happy man.'

Ren kissed me, and I could taste myself on his lips. Above me, Ren rolled his hips, his hardness hitting my softness, making me gasp.

'Please, Ren.'

'I love hearing you beg.' He murmured into my hair, 'What do you want? I want to hear it.'

I grabbed a handful of his arse, pulling him closer to me.

'Please fuck me, Ren.'

TAKE A HIKE!

'God.' Ren shuddered. 'Yes. *Yes.*'

Then suddenly he froze, his body tensing. 'Shit. I don't have any condoms.'

'I'm on the pill,' I said quickly, searching his face. 'And I got tested after Casey.'

Ren's eyes flicked up to mine, his voice steady, certain. 'I got tested before I left, but it wouldn't matter because I haven't been with anyone else since...'

Since you.

I stilled, processing his words. My brow furrowed. 'You haven't been with anyone in two years?'

'I meant it when I said I was miserable without you, Lydia.' His voice dropped lower. 'I didn't want to be with anyone else. I don't want to be with anyone else.'

My heart hammered. God, when he said things like that – well, it made me feel... alight. Like I was floating. Like I wanted to blurt out the words I hadn't heard from his mouth yet.

But it was too soon, so I answered by pressing my mouth to his. Then I pulled back to look down at us, at where our bodies aligned. His skin against mine. I marvelled at Ren's flexing biceps as he held himself above me. I leaned down and touched his cock, giving it a stroke that had him gasping, then brought him closer to my centre, not wanting to wait any longer.

Ren took over, pressing his cock into me, slowly. There was a pressure. Delicious and firm.

He rasped in my ear. 'So tight.'

I bit my lip to keep the moan from escaping as Ren pressed into me, stretching. He was big, but it felt so good after I just came – the perfect friction. I gasped as Ren pushed deeper, his hips rolling against mine.

'Are you okay?'

'Yes. Yes, I'm perfect.'

He glanced down, eyes wide, panting a little, like he was

fascinated by watching himself fill me. He pulled back out and then pushed back, slowly, too slowly.

'Harder,' I moaned. 'Please.'

'More demands, baby?'

Ren had the cheek to smirk at me as I was sweating and desperate. His confidence was hot, even if I'd never admit it. But he did what I asked – pulling back and slamming home, making us both groan. He kept at that pace for a while before he lifted my legs higher, hitting even deeper. My leg kept going until it was by my ears.

'Flexible, huh?' Ren's voice was laced with wicked amusement as his hands traced over my calf. 'That's gonna be fun... seeing how far I can bend you.' He rolled his cock into me, chuckling. 'Over the back of the sofa. On my kitchen counter. In the back of your car.'

I groaned as he tucked my other leg over his shoulder, taking me deeper. Wet kisses landed on my cheeks and neck, and Ren rocked against me. I couldn't help but arch. Ren's fingers came between us, stroking my clit, making stars shine behind my eyes. I clenched and Ren moaned, and he kept thrusting and retreating, picking up the rhythm.

'Ren,' I panted. 'I'm close again.'

'Come for me. Be a good girl and come all over my cock.'

Yep. I definitely had a praise kink.

He sped up the movement of his fingers and slowed down the pounding of his cock, the combination sending me hurtling over the edge for the second time. He murmured praise as the orgasm crashed over me, *just like that, you're perfect, I missed this so much*. The caresses between my legs didn't let up – he kept his hand there, stroking more gently, as he captured my mouth again, his tongue and talented fingers working in tandem.

And suddenly, I was near the edge again. I clamped down on his cock again, but this time, it was met with a rough groan as Ren spilt into me a few seconds after.

TAKE A HIKE!

We were panting, a sweaty mess, as Ren pulled out of me. Another groan escaped his lips, along with a muttered *so perfect* that made me smile. I had that stretched-out, spent feeling that I got after a good workout. The air was already cooling the sweat on my skin. I loved feeling my muscles ache, knowing where Ren had gripped me, filled me.

'If you're smiling like that, I must have done something right.'

I turned my head to see Ren staring at me with a matching, soft, satisfied smile.

He lifted his arm, 'C'm'ere.' I tucked into his side and Ren pulled up the sheet to cover us from the growing chill.

'I'll clean you up in a minute.' He gave me a rough kiss to the temple. 'Just want to feel you first.'

So I let myself be held, let the warmth of him soak into my bones, and drifted to sleep to the hush of the room, and the rhythm of his heartbeat under my cheek.

Chapter Twenty-Three

Lydia's Diary, 18 Years Old

Ren and I went to the gig yesterday. Lindsey Matthews was there.
Ren smiled at her.
I want to die. Actually, die.
I don't know why I thought this could be something. It's not.
Ren and I just aren't meant to be.

Ren

I woke to the warmth of sunlight spilling across my face and Lydia wrapped around me like a vine, her legs tangled with mine, her greedy hands splayed across my chest. I smiled at the curtains we'd forgotten to close in our desperation to get naked as quickly as physically possible. I glanced down to see that we were still naked. Looking at Lydia's peaceful face and eyelids fluttering, I knew she was still in deep sleep. She could always sleep like the dead.

When we'd have our sleepovers as kids, I'd always sneak out before she – or, more importantly, her parents – knew I was there. I'd slowly move her head from my shoulder, flinching if her breath hitched. Even on my heaviest days, when I'd been unreachable by Dad and Liam, I wanted Lydia to stay asleep, safe and warm. I did the same now, tucking from under her, and heard that familiar breath hitch, but she didn't wake, just tucked her hands under her head, a perfect picture of peace. God, she was beautiful. Her messy blonde hair spilt over the pillow, her lips puffy from kissing.

I wouldn't wake her again, even if I wanted to roll her over and kiss down her back, and bite into that gorgeous arse. I'd woken her up once already. In the middle of the night, I had been half-awake and needy for her, rubbing my hands up and down her curves until she turned to me, giving me open-mouthed kisses. I'd pushed inside her from behind, her breathy moans becoming the noise I always wanted to wake me up. She came first, with my hands at her clit, and I followed after.

Jesus. I was so gone for her.

Last night had altered me, just like it had done two years ago, but I wasn't a coward now. I was ready to be everything I could be for her – anything she'd want from me. I checked the clock. Five-thirty and the sun was only just coming up. We'd be setting off on our penultimate hike – the toughest ascent we'd tackled yet.

Ben Nevis.

At just under 1,400 metres high, it was the highest peak in the United Kingdom. And I'd seriously depleted my girl's energy last night. So there was only one thing for it – coffee and croissants. That would keep her happy until she inevitably got hangry on the way up the mountain. Even though they were disgusting, I made a mental note to stop at the shops and get some of those high-protein energy bars she liked. I dressed, trying to be as quiet as possible, my hand hitting the door handle, when I realised she might wake up and I wouldn't be there.

I was not in the market to repeat my dumb mistakes.

'Hey.' I pushed back some of her hair, kissing her forehead. She moaned and I tried not to react. *It wasn't a sexual moan, idiot.* 'I'm going to get some coffee, okay? I'll be back in half an hour.'

We'd passed a bakery around the corner called Stiff Peaks that looked incredible. Lydia shifted, one eye cracking open like the little dragon she was in the morning. God, she was adorable.

'I'll come with,' she whispered, but closed her eyes again.

I kissed her forehead. 'No, you stay here. I'll bring you pastries, okay?'

'Mhm.'

When I returned to the hotel carpark, the scent of coffee filled the car, and I practically bounced up the stairs. I pushed open the door to find Lydia sitting up, sheets tangled around her waist, her hair a wild mess, eyes still heavy with sleep.

'Morning, Sunshine,' I teased, crossing the room with slow, deliberate steps, holding the coffee just out of reach.

She stretched her arms towards it, fingers flexing like a greedy child.

'You are too chipper in the morning,' she grumbled.

I finally handed her the cup, watching as she wrapped both hands around it, bringing it to her lips as if it was the only thing keeping her alive.

'Oh, come on, you get up early for a living.' I sat on the edge of the bed, flipping open the box of croissants.

'I'm out of practice. Plus, you kept me up last night.'

I shot Lydia a smirk over the rim of my cup. 'Oh, I'm sorry. Did you not appreciate the multiple orgasms?'

She hummed, and I knew from her sly smile it was the opposite.

I kicked off my shoes and slid back into bed beside her. She was warm, and I couldn't help myself. I pulled her close, breathing her in, my fingers splaying over the small of her back. I needed her close. I'd thought about this too many times – these small, domestic moments that meant she was mine.

She sipped her coffee, shooting me a curious look. 'Why do you call me Sunshine? You know it's funny.' She huffed. 'When Mum plotted to get me out of my funk, she called it Operation

Sunshine. Weird.' She leaned over to put her coffee down, and then lay on my chest, her hand splayed across it, like she owned me. I liked that a little too much.

'Well.' She shifted, laying her head on her hand, as she looked up at me. My throat thickened. 'I call you Sunshine because when I was feeling my lowest, you never left. You didn't ask anything of me. You just stayed. A therapist once said that we can always depend on some things. That the earth will keep spinning. The tides will come in. And the sun will always rise in the morning. At my lowest, I clung to that idea. No matter what my brain was putting me through, the sun would rise. Just like I could depend that you'd be there, too.'

'Can,' she said, blinking. 'You can depend that I'm there.'

'I know,' I said, smiling. 'And it was called Operation Sunshine because I named it.'

Her lips parted in surprise, her eyes shifting between mine like she was trying to understand what I was saying.

'When I texted your mum to check you were okay, we got to scheming.'

'You booked the spa?'

'Well, she wanted to get you out of your funk. And before I knew it, I'd sent the link. I knew the combination of Pilates *and* award-winning coffee would get you.' I smiled down at Lydia. Her eyes were a little glassy. 'I'd also suggested they take you to Formby 'cos it's your favourite beach. And then, I said they had to take you to the Green Plate for their Burrito Bowl, but it had to be followed by a trip to Sugar and Spice on Manchester Road for the waffles or you'd crash.' I paused. 'But they didn't take all of my suggestions. Which pissed me off a bit.'

I'd wanted to be there so badly. I'd wanted to bring her coffee and drive her around and make her laugh. But instead I was on the outside, only able to make pathetic suggestions by text.

Lydia shifted, sitting up. 'Ren – I had no idea.'

'I know,' I said, running a hand down her hair. 'I preferred it that way. I didn't want you to know. I just wanted you to feel good. You deserve that.'

'How did you know exactly what to do?'

'How did you know that I'd need the visit to Glynmere Farm?' I shrugged. 'We know each other, Lyds. One of the many benefits of being friends for so long. Even if it's probably also why it's taken us longer to be able to do this—'

I pulled her into a kiss, soft and languid. *I love you*, I tried to say. *So much*, I followed with the swipe of my tongue, making her moan.

Lydia pulled back, taking my coffee from my hands, placing it on the side table, and then straddled me, and all the blood left my head. She smiled triumphantly, and I reached up to tuck a strand of hair behind her ear. God, she was so gorgeous!

'I should find a way to thank you.' She grinned, with a slight roll of her hips that made me groan. Then her hands were exploring my chest, her lips were on my throat.

'As much as I very much want tha – Lydia,' I groaned, as she bit my earlobe. 'Love.'

That word seemed to make things worse – or much better – because she rolled her hips, making my cock twitch. Brain, brain, come on. Something was important.

'Lydia.'

'Ren.'

'Time. The time.'

Finally, Lydia's head shot up, and I angled mine to check the digital clock, flashing green. I was still trapped under her body, and not at all mad about it.

Lydia groaned, running her hand through her hair. 'Shit. It's seven. We leave in half an hour.'

My head flopped back on to the pillow. I was basically panting. Lydia shifted.

'Mercy, please.' I groaned into a laugh.

Lydia chuckled, and leaned down to whisper in my ear, 'It's

okay, I can make it up to you in the shower. Much quicker.'

I huffed a laugh. 'That will not make things quicker, and you know it.'

'I know.' She winked. I was picturing the creative ways I could use Lydia's considerable flexibility, and torture her with pleasure in the shower. 'But it will make it more fun.'

Lydia

Everyone seemed to be in good spirits as we headed up the path towards Ben Nevis. Ren and I had decided to keep our distance, so we weren't that obnoxious couple that were all over each other in public, but I spotted him eyeing me every now and then. *Stop it*, I mouthed to him as we stomped on the gravel path, the crunch of boots our soundtrack. Ren continued his perusal of me, his eyes slowly undressing me as they skirted over my curves, my hips, then he punctuated it with a wink that heated my cheeks.

I shook my head, trying not to trip down the gravel path that looked deceptively easy right now. A slow ascent past stone walls and fields of grazing sheep. My legs were sore, and so was the delicious ache between my legs.

This morning had been something I'd usually wake up from in the middle of the night, disappointed. But it wasn't a dream. Ren had woken up beside me, brought me coffee and pastries. His hands didn't leave my arms, my waist, like he couldn't stand not to be touching me. And when he told me it had been him behind Operation Sunshine, tears had burned in my eyes. I couldn't believe that, even when I wasn't speaking to him, when I had been avoiding him at all costs, he still made sure I was looked after. He had known exactly how to get me out of that funk, that low point.

I blushed when I thought about what we'd done afterwards, in the shower. Ren had got very creative with my legs – lifting them, so my feet were by his ears. He curled my leg over his forearm, his biceps flexing as he pinned me against the tiles and fucked me, hard and steady, never breaking eye contact. We'd been late to join the group, and they'd been waiting for us on the grass outside Ren's room. I'd frozen when I spotted them.

Busted.

'You look sweaty,' Gen said, making me jump.

'Oh, my God!' My palm hit my chest.

'I've been walking next to you for ten minutes.' Gen's lips twitched.

Claire wrapped a hand around my shoulders, peering at me from behind. 'Do those pink cheeks have something to do with you coming out of Ren's room this morning?'

Gen smirked, and Claire waggled her eyebrows. As if smelling gossip, Amy turned to glance at us, her eyes brightening.

'Are we talking about the vibes between Ren and Lydia?' she whispered, far too loud.

I shushed her. 'You're all gossips.'

Gen pointed. 'She hasn't denied it.'

'Come on.' Amy jumped up and down. 'You know I love love. Are you two together now? Are you going to get married and have loads of cute babies?' Amy gasped, and whisper-shouted, 'Have you said the L-word yet?'

'Lesbian?' Gen said dryly. 'She's bisexual.'

Amy rolled her eyes. 'No. *Love*. Duh! Have you said it yet?'

Ren's head turned as if by instinct, his eyes landing on mine, lighting little fires across my skin.

I grabbed Amy around her shoulder, covering her mouth with my palm. 'Amy! Inside voice.'

Ren arched an eyebrow at the scene, a smile curling at the corner of his mouth. Then he gave me another wink before resuming his walk. Butterflies erupted low in my belly. Well, clearly he hadn't been freaked out by talk of the L-word.

Which was good, because I was one hundred per cent in love

with him. I'd realised it this morning, when he'd told me it was him behind Operation Sunshine, but I was keeping that fact close to my chest until we were away from the gaggle of women who were using Ren and me like a juicy episode of *Love Island* with walking boots and flasks of tea.

'Whoa!' Amy said once I let her go, her eyes wide. 'I didn't realise men could do that.'

'What? Be sexy from a distance?' Gen asked.

'Trouble,' Claire added, but there was a smile on her face. 'He's trouble, that boy.'

'He's always been trouble.' I smiled quietly. 'I just think it's the good kind now.'

The rest of the hike was done mostly in silence, apart from Mandy's occasional chat and guidance around the steep ascents. Luckily, as Mandy had said, we had beautiful weather, not too hot or too cold. The sky was clear, a gorgeous pale blue with the occasional puff of white cloud. We had a 360° view of some of the most cinematic landscapes on the trip yet. If I'd thought the drive up was beautiful, this was incredible. There were endless rolling glens and brooding mountains, with perfect views of the reflective, shining lochs below.

But then we hit 1,000 metres and the picture changed.

Once a steady ascent, the path turned into a relentless climb over jagged rocks and loose scree. Every step required effort. The wind, which had been gentle lower down, now howled around us, tugging at our jackets and pushing against our bodies as if trying to force us back down. Mandy had warned us about the false summits, but knowing about them didn't make them any less demoralising. Every time we thought we'd made it, another rise appeared in the distance, steeper and crueller than the last.

Some of the group struggled. Claire, usually one of the strongest hikers, had slowed, her breath coming in sharp gasps. Jade had stopped talking, her usual easy-going energy replaced with quiet determination. Amara, the quieter member of the group, was now silent. Even Mandy looked serious, her usual bright encouragement replaced by short, sharp instructions – where to step, how to balance on the loose ground, and when to take a break. Gen and I kept an eye on Amy, not wanting to patronise her or presume she was weaker, but just to keep an eye on her breathing. But she kept going, and I was so incredibly proud of her. At one point, I paused as she laced up her boots. When she rose, she gave me a tired smile.

'I'm so proud of you, Amy. You know that, right?' I pulled her into a quick hug. 'You are incredible.'

Amy's smile widened. 'Thanks, Lydia.'

My heart wanted to burst as we joined the group, Amy keeping up with them easily, and it struck me that I'd had something to do with it – I'd given her the tools to become stronger, fiercer.

Maybe I could do that with my own gym?

Ren and I pressed on, our legs burning, our boots scraping against the rock. My lungs ached with the effort, and I could feel sweat cooling against my back despite the chill in the air.

I glanced at Ren. He was tired, too. I could see it in the tight set of his jaw, the way he kept rolling his shoulders as if trying to shake out the ache from his back. But there was something else too. That stubbornness, the quiet perseverance that was always there, was buried beneath his usual nonchalance.

The last few feet were the hardest. The air was thinner up there and every breath felt like trying to sip through a straw. My legs felt leaden, my steps slow and deliberate as we climbed the final rise.

Then, suddenly, we were there.

The summit.

A rugged plateau of stone, a small cairn marking the highest point in the UK. And beyond that, nothing but the sky.

Ren turned to me, hazy mist behind him at this height, a wide smile on his face.

'You did it.' He pulled me close as if he couldn't hold himself back.

I tilted my head to glance at him, as we faced the view before us — a blend of white mist, blue skies, and green below. It was breathtaking, even more so with Ren's arm wrapped around my shoulder.

'We did it.'

Three weeks of aching muscles, sleepless nights, blisters, and self-doubt had led to this. Tomorrow would be a leisurely walk around Glencoe, but this? This was the showstopper.

And then, all at once, the weight of everything hit me.

The last year. The fights. Losing my job. Losing Ren. The slow, exhausting climb — not just up this mountain, but back to myself. I knew exactly where I'd be if I hadn't taken this trip. I'd still be in bed or back working for someone like Craig again, bending over backwards to please a manager who made my life miserable — still playing it safe, scared to take risks, terrified to rock the boat. I would have been stuck coasting through life, smiling when I was supposed to, nodding along, and making sure I never made things too difficult for anyone.

But this trip had dragged me out of my comfort zone, kicking and screaming. It had forced me through blisters and nights in cold tents, aching muscles and muddy fields, and long stretches of silence where I had no choice but to sit with myself. It had shown me I was stronger than I ever gave myself credit for. And without it, I would never have found my way back to Ren.

I looked at him then, standing in front of me. The sun lit him, breaking through in soft, golden streaks. If I hadn't done this, if I hadn't taken that first step, I might never have realised he wasn't lost to me. And that I had been too afraid to reach for him.

The weight of it hit me all at once. My throat tightened, my eyes burned, and before I could stop them, tears slipped down my cheeks.

Ren's face softened. He pulled back just enough to see me properly, his thumb brushing my cheek.

'Hey, what's this about, huh?' His face grew more grave. 'Why are you crying? Did you hurt yourself?'

'No, no!' I let out a shaky laugh, 'They aren't bad tears. I – I just realised. This trip hasn't just been about being lost or confused. It wasn't about Casey or Craig. It was about finding myself again. And it was about finding you too. Falling for you again.' Tears rolled down my face, 'I love you, Ren. And I want to spend the rest of my life with you. I want to wake up next to you every day. I want to walk Peggy to the park and make shopping lists of things we need. I want to buy a house and get Kat to decorate it, because you know neither of us has a clue. I want to watch you open Everly Heath Farm and make it a success, because you will.' I laughed, tears streaming. 'I'm sorry if I've dragged my feet and put you through the wringer. But I'm here now. I love you.'

The words felt green – after all, I'd never said them to anyone else before. They made my heart hammer against my ribs and my legs felt a bit like jelly. But the love beamed from my chest was steady and sure. Ren's eyes searched mine, as if he was trying to tell if this was real, then his face broke into the most beautiful, heart-stopping grin. And then my face was in his palms, and he was kissing me.

Somewhere behind us, someone whooped. Then another. I turned to see and then the whole group was cheering and clapping alongside some other hikers, who looked bemused. I turned back to Ren, whose eyes hadn't left me.

'I love you so much, Lydia,' he said, laughing softly, emotion catching in his throat. 'You have no idea how many times I've wanted to tell you – I almost blurted it out at the social club the other night. I mean, Kat and Liam already know because once I'd admitted it to myself, I had to tell someone.'

I laughed, my eyes wet. 'So everyone in Everly Heath knows at this rate.'

TAKE A HIKE!

Liam and Kat were discreet, but I'd bet someone would weasel it out of them with some choice questions.

Ren gave me a rueful look. 'Sunshine. They knew anyway. They just have to look at how I look at you and realise it.' He kissed my cheeks, then my eyelids, until I was laughing again. 'If you give me the chance, I won't mess this up again. I promise you that. I'll spend every day showing you just how much I love you. You can count on that.'

'Count?' I mock-pouted. 'Bit insensitive given my track record with numbers.'

Ren groaned, 'Stop ruining my grand gesture with maths jokes.'

I gasped. 'Excuse me, this was *my* grand gesture.'

'Yeah, yeah.' He grinned. 'You can argue with me when I'm done kissing you, Sunshine.'

Ren didn't waste any time bringing his soft lips to mine. He smelled of sweat and citrus and *him*.

At the top of Ben Nevis, with everyone cheering, Ren kissed me as if we were on top of the world.

Chapter Twenty-Four

Ren

'Lydia,' I whispered, keeping my voice down so I didn't wake the other campers. 'Lydia. Wakey, wakey.'

It had been three days since Ben Nevis. Three days of wandering the Highlands – kayaking across Loch Leven, lazy pub lunches in Glencoe, Lydia squealing over Highland cows with that soft, gooey look I was kind of jealous of. We'd steal moments on the paths, her back against a tree as I pressed her close, kissing her until she moaned into my mouth. I'd catch her by the loos when no one was watching, my hand up her shirt, her laugh muffled against my neck. She'd walk away flushed and breathless, that dazed expression I wanted to bottle.

I didn't know I could be this happy – especially somewhere this breathtaking.

So, on our final night in the Highlands, I was determined to make it count. And I wanted her all to myself.

Lydia's eyes fluttered open, her brow furrowing. She sat up out of her sleeping bag, hair sticking up at all angles, adorably dishevelled. For tonight's sleep, we all set up camp in a wild field overlooking Loch Leven, where dragonflies darted around the pools at the edge of the loch and the smell of sweet vanilla was in the air. Mandy explained Scotland allowed wild camping, meaning you could pitch up anywhere within reason, so long as you left no trace and avoided farmland. This was easily the most stunning spot but they had no facilities, no frills.

But tonight, I fancied a bit of luxury.

So, when everyone turned in early, worn out from the hike, I took one look at how shattered Lydia was – even if I did like the way she curled herself around me in the tiny tent – and started plotting.

'Come on,' I whispered. 'Bring some of your stuff. We're going on an adventure.'

Her eyes brightened with curiosity. 'What kind of adventure?'

I grinned. 'You'll have to wait and see.'

The others had left their stuff at the hikers' hotel or at the base of Ben Nevis, but I'd volunteered to stash mine closer to the campsite with extra supplies – just in case we needed more water or ran out of dry socks.

'Wait, Ren.' Lydia turned, frowning. 'They'll worry if we're not here—'

I booped her nose. 'I've got it covered. I told Mandy I was stealing you away for the night. But don't worry – we'll come back and say goodbye to everyone tomorrow.'

Lydia planted a finger on my cheek. 'Sneaky.'

I caught her fingertip between my teeth. 'Always. Come on.'

I led her back to my car, loaded our things in the boot, and made the 30-minute drive to our destination. My heart thrummed with anticipation as we drove through huge, austere gates and down a long, gravelled driveway fit for nobility.

'What have you got planned?' Lydia said, her eyes narrowed, but she had a smile on her lips.

'You'll just have to be patient and you'll find out.'

We passed a sign that read THE GLENCAIRN ESTATE as we kept travelling down the long driveway, with trees and woodland on one side and vast open fields on the other. Eventually, the manor house came into view, and Lydia's breath hitched.

'Oh, my God!' she breathed, leaning forward in her seat.

Lydia marvelled at the huge estate, with ivy climbing the pale stonework. The sheer awe in her voice sent a rush of satisfaction through me. I pulled up in front of the enormous doorway, with sliding glass doors displaying the Glencairn coat of arms. Standing before them was a tall, broad-chested man dressed in a navy-blue suit with a dark green tartan waistcoat. His dark red hair was swept back from his face, and his usual beard was gone, replaced by a clean-shaven look. I jumped out of the car, travelling round the side to open Lydia's door before she could pick her jaw up from the ground.

I chuckled. Her blue eyes were comically big as she stepped out of the car.

'Where on earth are we, Ren?' she whispered. 'Do I need a bleeding gown?'

I laughed. 'It's a hotel, Sunshine. No gown needed. I figured we could use some luxury after three weeks of sleeping in tents. Plus, I fancied treating you now that you'll let me.'

Her eyes flickered, something unreadable there before she smirked. 'This is kind of sexy.'

I winked. 'I know.'

Lydia rolled her eyes as I took her hand and led her up the steps. She was still in awe, but the squeeze of her fingers told me she wasn't mad about it.

Waiting at the entrance was Duncan, exactly as I remembered him from the last time we had seen each other in London for the British Bar Awards a few years ago.

'Lawrence.' Duncan threw his arms open and pulled me into a bone-crushing hug, clapping me on the back hard enough to rattle my ribs. He had a very soft Scottish lilt to his voice. 'I'll tell you what, I never expected this call. And at six in the evening too. Thought you'd gone soft.'

His eyes shifted to Lydia and he extended a hand. 'And you must be Lydia. He wouldn't shut up about you on the phone.

I had to tell him to stop waffling and get to the bleeding point.'

Lydia raised a brow at me, then shook Duncan's hand firmly. 'What can I say? He's obsessed with me.'

Duncan barked a laugh. 'Now I can see why.'

I sighed, pinching the bridge of my nose. 'I should've known this was a mistake.'

Lydia gave me an innocent smile. 'Oh, come on. You love it when I tell everyone how much you adore me.'

Duncan grinned, arms crossed over his broad chest. 'And here I thought you were the cocky one, Lawrence. Looks like you've met your match.'

'Oh, he's been trying to keep up for years,' Lydia said, flicking her eyes up and down me with a slow, smug grin that set my blood pounding. 'Bless him.'

Duncan let out another booming laugh. 'I like her.'

I rolled my eyes, fighting a smile. 'Yeah, yeah. Me too.'

Duncan nodded towards the door. 'Do you two fancy a whisky? I kept the bar open. Got some cracking new bottles in.'

I turned to Lydia, running a hand down her ponytail. 'Fancy a nightcap?'

Lydia nodded with a faint smile. 'Sure.'

'Crackin'.' Duncan clapped. 'Leave the car. I'll ask Brian to bring your bags up to your room. We're quiet tonight, so I've put you in the Glencairn Suite. You'll be very comfortable.'

Duncan winked and then led the way through the glass doors. The stone flags looked hundreds of years old, and the vaulted ceilings gave the space a grand, yet inviting, feel. Upholstered in the same deep green tartan as Duncan's waistcoat, grand armchairs sat around a roaring fireplace. I ran my hand down Lydia's arm, clasping her hand.

'If this is what I'll be getting used to being Ren Hunter's girlfriend, sign me up,' Lydia muttered.

I laughed and squeezed her hand, grinning as warmth bloomed in my chest. Girlfriend. That word sounded bloody good coming from her lips.

'Get used to it, Sunshine.'

After a few whiskies with Duncan, his raucous laugh and stories started to wear on me and, typically, I could chat with him until the 'wee' hours of the morning. But right now? I wanted to be alone in a massive hotel suite with Lydia, preferably naked, underneath me. All I could focus on was the iron-like grip of Lydia's fingers on my thigh, teasing, creeping higher than was strictly appropriate in polite company. Every accidental brush of our legs sent my blood pounding south, making it nearly impossible to concentrate on Duncan's latest tale about his niece's pet rabbit.

I turned slightly, catching the smug little smirk on her lips as she sipped her whisky. She was playing with me, testing my patience. Seeing how long I'd last before I snapped.

I exhaled slowly, gripping my thigh just to stop myself from grabbing her. Get it together, Hunter. But when Lydia shifted in her seat, crossing her legs, I knew she was trying to relieve some of the tension building between them.

Enough.

I downed the rest of my drink, feeling the heat slide down my throat before placing the tumbler down with a quiet thud. 'Mate, this has been great. I really appreciate it. But we've been sleeping in tents for the last three weeks, so we're going to hit the hay.'

'The very expensive, luxury hay,' Lydia added huskily, her lips curled at the corner. She was enjoying this way too much.

Duncan raised his glass. 'Aye, fair enough. The Glencairn Suite should more than make up for it.'

'Thanks, mate.' I got up, reaching for Lydia's hand. I was one minute away from throwing her over my shoulder like some caveman. She made me pathetic. She let me pull her to her feet, her fingers lacing through mine.

'Lawrence,' Duncan called, and I turned, cocking my head.

'Try not to break the furniture, aye?' Duncan's laugh echoed through the quiet bar, empty apart from us.

I shook my head, and Lydia's replying giggle made me want to do just that. We stared at each other in the lift up to the suite. I was near panting, watching Lydia's chest rise and fall, her pupils dilated. She bit her lower lip and I couldn't stop lifting a finger, dragging it out, and rubbing my thumb against it. I wanted to kiss her right there, but the lift doors opened. We went down to the end of the hallway, where a door was marked as the Glencairn Suite. I pushed the card against the pad, relieved when the door gave way, and pulled Lydia in behind me.

I didn't waste time. I pushed her up against the door, making sure to cushion her head with my palm. I kissed her hard, unable to hold back, but she answered with a moan into my mouth and wrapped her legs around me, and I ground us into the door.

'Ren,' she rasped, her voice sounding raw. She swivelled her hips, pushing into mine. My palms glided over her hips and arse. I grazed a thumb over her nipples, making her arch for me. It was as if every moment spent hiking, talking, and just existing that day had been wasted time. Time I hadn't been inside her, time I hadn't heard her moans.

'God, you're so beautiful,' I murmured into her neck. 'You drove me insane today – bending over to tie your boots like that, knowing damn well I was right behind you.' I gave a gentle bite to her neck. 'I wanted to drag you behind that stone church and have my way with you.'

She gasped, then chuckled. 'Blasphemous. Bed,' she panted. 'Now.'

I obliged, carrying her through a small sitting room into the main bedroom.

'Later, we'll talk about how insane this suite is.' She laughed breathily. 'But right now, I need you.'

I grinned as I pressed her into the bed and stepped back, pulling my T-shirt over my head. I went to climb on the bed, eager to feel Lydia's lips on me again, but she planted a palm on my chest.

'Jeans too.'

I smiled, shaking my head and unbuttoning my jeans. 'You have no idea how hot you are.'

She cocked an eyebrow. 'How do you know I don't?'

She peeled off her own top, revealing a bright pink lace bra, making my nails dig into my palms.

'Are they a matching set, Lydia?' My voice was low, teasing, as I took in the sight of her. I was down to my boxers now, so my hands slid to the waistband of her jeans, undoing the button, dragging them down her legs – just enough to see the matching pink thong underneath.

Fuck.

I planted a slow, deliberate kiss over the thin fabric covering her, feeling her body twitch under me.

'Did you wear these for me?'

'Maybe,' she breathed, shifting under my touch.

I kissed lower, right over the lace, swiping my tongue just enough to make her gasp.

'Ren.' She huffed, wriggling to kick off her jeans. 'Stop playing.'

I smirked against her, my hands sliding up to her bra straps, pulling them down just enough to palm her breasts, my thumbs flicking over her hardened nipples.

'Tell me you wore them for me,' I murmured against her heat, pressing down with my tongue again. 'Say it and I'll take them off.'

Her blue eyes flashed – a challenge. I grinned. She loved this game as much as I did. Another slow lick, another stuttered breath. She held out for a little longer, grinding herself into my face until she couldn't take any more.

'Fine.' Her voice was breathless, desperate. 'Yes. I bought them for you. I wore them for you.'

Triumph burned hot in my chest. I stepped back just enough to take her in, my grin slow and satisfied.

I helped her shuck off her jeans, throwing them to the corner of the room, and I lay on the bed, pulling her on top of me. We kissed for a little while longer, until the roll of Lydia's hips was too much to bear, and she took me out of my boxers, tugging me until I grabbed her wrist. It was too much, and she knew from one glance.

'I don't need any foreplay,' she said huskily. 'I want you now.'

I watched as she pulled down my boxers and straddled me, and I watched in lust-addled fascination as she pulled her thong to the side and guided me to her entrance. My fist came to my mouth, the other dug into her hip as she lowered herself on to me, making both of us moan. I let her lead when she was fully seated, rolling her hips. She felt so tight, so warm. I undid her bra and palmed her breasts, her head falling back.

'That's it. Ride me,' I said as I raised my hips to meet each move in her hips. 'God, you feel like heaven.'

'Ren,' she panted as I circled her clit, making her movements choppy. 'I think I'm close.'

A few moments later, she clenched around me.

'Come for me, gorgeous girl.'

I kept my pressure on her clit, until she fell forward, coming, and I thrust upwards through the waves of her orgasm. She clenched around me, and I couldn't take it any more. I shifted us so that I was on top, so that I could see her beautiful face. Our mouths met, wet and messy. I came deep inside her, jerking and moaning. I was still panting when I shifted us on to our sides, so that I was not weighing her down but was still touching her. I touched her face, kissed her cheeks and neck.

'I can't get enough of you, I swear,' I murmured into her skin.

I pressed a kiss to her temple, my heart pounding stupidly fast. The words slipped out before I could stop them.

'We should do it, you know.'

She shifted to meet my gaze, sleepy but curious. 'Do what?'

'Everly Heath Farm,' I said into her hair. 'We could go to Liam and see if he could be persuaded. We could renovate the site together – find a little nook or apartment for ourselves. Or there's that cottage tucked away down the bottom of the farm. It's probably a bit too far away to convert it for visitors anyway. It's overgrown, but it's got good bones.'

I felt her breath hitch against my chest and, for a second, the world felt terrifying and perfect all at once. So I kept going.

'And you could open up a gym with private studios for Pilates or yoga. Eventually we could add sauna pods, make it really fancy. Momentum wouldn't know what hit it.'

She was quiet, and for some reason, I couldn't shut the fuck up.

'I mean, Bethan and Gareth seemed happy enough. Thirty-odd years together. That could be us maybe. Not that I need marriage or anything like that—' I squeezed one eye shut as the cringe wracked through me. 'We haven't even talked about that. Although I'd like that. I mean, just forget I said that. It's too early. What I'm trying to say is I could see it, Lydia. I could see us running Everly Heath Farm. You'd be incredible running your own gym—'

'Ren.' Her voice was thick and unreadable, and suddenly I wished I hadn't said anything at all. I thought she was about to tell me it was too much, too soon. But when I glanced at her, there was something soft in her eyes I couldn't quite name. Pity? Worry?

Brilliant. I'd only just got her back and here I was, already pushing for more. Like buying, fixing up, and running a giant money pit of a farm was standard *second-day-of-being-official* behaviour. God, I'm an idiot.

I squeezed her to my chest. 'Just think about it. You don't have to say anything now.'

'Okay,' she said, a smile in her voice. 'I love you.'

Those could be the only words I'd hear forever, and I'd be happy.

'I love you too.'

As I drifted off, a tiny corner of my mind caught the sound of Lydia's voice, low, serious, like she's talking to someone. Part of me wanted to wake up and pull her back into me, but the exhaustion won. So I let her words slip under the tide, and sleep carried me away.

Chapter Twenty-Five

Ren

A bang on the door jolted me out of sleep. Instinctively, I shifted, my hands searching for Lydia, only to find the sheets peeled open, cold to the touch. I frowned, sitting up, rubbing a hand over my face. Swinging my legs over the side of the bed, I pulled on a pair of trousers before heading towards the bathroom.

'Lydia?' I called towards the en suite. No answer.

A prickle of unease crept up my spine as I moved through the living room, my brow furrowed. Something was off. I felt it in my bones.

I pulled open the door to find Amy and Gen standing in the hallway. Gen had her arms crossed, dressed head to toe in her usual all-black hiking gear, her expression unimpressed, as ever. Amy, on the other hand, looked like Lydia had dressed her herself, decked out in bright pink leggings, matching top, hair dyed to the same pastel shade.

'Morning, Ren,' Amy squeaked, an awkward smile on her kind face.

Gen's eyes flicked down to my chest, pouting, she nodded, 'Fair play, Lydia.'

'What the fuck is happening? Where is Lydia?'

'About that—' Amy cringed. 'She had some business to attend to. We've been sworn to secrecy—'

'—but she didn't want her pookie abandoned.' Gen pinched

my cheeks. 'So we're here to drive you back to Everly Heath.'

'Drive me—' I took a deep breath, calming myself. 'Where the fuck is my girlfriend?'

'Don't worry, she's fine.' Amy smiled, but it was strained. 'She's back in Everly Heath. She'll explain everything when we get back.'

'Come on – let's go.'

As I silently packed my things, my mind wouldn't stop spiralling. Had I pushed her too far yesterday with all that talk about the farm? Shit, I'd mentioned getting married. I'd practically proposed. Who does that when you haven't even had a proper first date yet? Maybe she was freaking out about going back to Everly Heath with me, so got a head start and had gone on her own. Maybe she was worried about her parents, the gossip, all of it.

My brain clawed at any reason, any excuse, for why she'd get up and leave my bed in the middle of the night, and why I'd woken up alone. Defeated, I climbed into Gen's car and let them drive me home – desperately hoping it was towards my future, not my past.

I jolted awake hours later, with Amy's cheerful 'We're here!'

'What—' I frowned, seeing we were parked in a gravel courtyard, overgrown with weeds and flanked by crumbling outbuildings. A dilapidated farmhouse loomed before us – broken window panes with overgrown ivy crawling through them and stonework that needed repointing.

Everly Heath Farm. As I got my bearings, my mind couldn't help but tease me with the architectural plans I had drawn up – the orangery we could have built on the side to extend covers. The rundown barns and outhouses we would convert and repurpose. The courtyard where I imagined we would host markets similar to the ones Gareth and Bethan did at Glynmere Farm.

Then, I saw her.

Lydia was leaning against the driver's side of my car, which she'd nicked. We were absolutely going to be having words about that. But relief pounded through me when I saw she was smiling, completely absorbed in conversation with a man who looked as if he was in his early forties. He was tall, with salt-and-pepper hair at his temples, and he returned her smile easily, gesturing animatedly as he spoke.

'Who's that?' Amy asked, curious.

'No idea,' Gen replied.

A flicker of something sharp and stupid twisted in my chest. Irrational, I knew. But after waking up to an empty bed, finding her here, laughing, so at ease with some stranger, sent a pang through me.

Who the hell was he?

I forced a breath through my nose, steadying myself, said my goodbyes to Gen and Amy and strode across the courtyard.

The confusion, the slight tinge of jealousy, vanished the second she turned to me, a wide, radiant smile lighting up her face.

'Ren.'

Without thinking, I cupped her face in my hands, cradling it, and gave her a slow, claiming kiss on her lips. I felt the shock ripple through her, and when she melted into the kiss, I let her go, pulling back to give her a look.

'Please tell me there's a good reason you drove six hours, alone, before sunrise.'

'Hey,' she said, a little breathless.

'Hey.'

'You made it.'

'I did. What plan are you hatching? You've been slowly torturing me for six hours, Sunshine. You haven't replied to my messages—'

She brought a hand up to my cheek. 'I know, I'm sorry. It's

nothing bad, I swear. I just wanted to be one hundred per cent sure before I told you. I didn't want to get your hopes up.'

She turned to me, beaming. 'Niall, this is Ren.'

Niall was standing there, watching our interaction with a cocked eyebrow, and looking as if he'd quite like some popcorn right now.

'Quite the show, you two. Guess I don't have to worry about you breaking up halfway through the renovations. Maybe we'll put some curtains up first, though, huh?'

Niall grinned. He had a soft Irish accent – sounded like somewhere near Dublin.

'Renovations.' I frowned, turning to Lydia, who wore that sly, mischievous smile she'd had when she'd dragged me skinny-dipping in Glencoe.

I mean, I had no complaints about how that turned out.

'Niall has agreed to invest in the farm,' Lydia said, practically glowing. 'He said he owed me after everything that happened—'

'Didn't expect it to be this expensive a favour,' Niall added dryly, hands up when Lydia shot him a look.

'I called him after our chat last night, because after what you said, well, I couldn't get it out of my head. Bethan had mentioned something about me opening a gym here and I guess it was just... lying dormant. Then I couldn't stop thinking about it. So I called Niall and he agreed to come and see the site, but only if I could meet him here early this morning.'

Niall checked his watch. 'Speaking of – I need to go to the airport. The wife is going to kill me if I'm not back in Dublin by this evening. That's my cab.'

He angled his head towards the black cab pulling up. Then he reached into his messenger bag and pulled out a bright red binder, handing it to Lydia, who tucked it into her side.

My red binder. How—

I didn't have time to ask. Niall extended a hand to Lydia, who shook it firmly. 'We'll chat next week, talk numbers.'

Lydia's smile faltered. I squeezed her hand. 'We'll be there. Both of us.'

Niall smiled. 'Good. Let's make this happen.'

Once Niall had climbed into the cab, I turned to Lydia slowly. 'What – what just happened?'

Lydia gave me a sly smile. 'We just bought a farm, baby.'

Emotions surged in my body, ramming against each other – shock, gratitude, excitement. A healthy dose of fear about the challenge we were about to face. Lydia had just secured us a whole bloody farm. A farm she was planning on being a part of. I couldn't believe it.

All I could say, mouth agape, was, 'I've been working on this for six months, and it takes you one phone call and you've got an investor in twenty-four hours?'

'More like six, actually,' she teased, running a hand through my hair and tugging me closer by the roots.

'Overachiever,' I murmured against her lips before kissing her, softly but deeply. 'But don't leave my bed like that again, Sunshine.'

'Pot, kettle,' she snorted.

'Oh, so it's like that is it? I thought you'd forgiven me. Was this all some perverted revenge?'

She giggled. 'No, but I'll show you perverted later.'

'That better be a promise.' I lean into her ear. 'Looking forward to showing you exactly the reason you should never leave my bed again, Lydia.'

She shivered, eyes dark with heat, and I couldn't wait to make good on that particular promise. But then I saw it.

That damn red binder.

I tapped it. 'How did you find it? I chucked it out.'

'I gave it to her.'

A deep voice cut through the air behind me, and I turned to find Liam and Kat crossing the courtyard. Peggy was barely held back from excitement, her front legs running towards me, as

Liam tried to keep her under control. Eventually, he just let her go and I crouched down, letting her jump up and lick my face.

'Hey, girlie,' I murmured into her fur. 'Did you miss me? I think you missed me.'

Kat chuckled. 'Is any bond stronger than a man and the dog they didn't want? Hey, Cuz.'

She pulled Lydia in for a hug. Their height difference meant Kat's head tucked perfectly under Lydia's chin.

'Ren,' Liam said, pulling me into a back-slapping hug. 'So we're doing this huh?'

'I'm so excited.' Kat beamed, clapping her hands together. 'I have a new project.'

Lydia laughed, and I met my brother's eyes.

'So you're up for this?' I asked Liam, whose stoic expression revealed nothing. 'You're sure?'

Liam held my gaze, making me wait. When he finally nodded, I almost sighed with relief. He might be a pain in my arse most of the time, but I needed his backing – and his talents – to make this work.

A fizz of energy shot through me when I caught the smile tugging at his mouth. Liam wasn't just in – he was sold. He was as excited about this as I was. He showed it in his Liam ways, of course. But all that mattered was that he was rooting for this – rooting for me.

'Well, with Niall's investment, we won't have to sign the house over if it all goes tits-up.' He clapped my shoulder. 'Don't look so surprised. I told you the other night, at ours – I like the idea. It's a brilliant chance to invest in a bit of Everly Heath history.'

His expression softened, and I knew he was thinking about Mum, about all the memories we'd had on this farm. My eyes stung.

'We can't pass on that. Especially now we've got an investor to spread the risk—'

'Risk this, risk that,' Kat cut in. 'Do you see what I have to put up with?'

Liam smirked, slipping an arm around her shoulders, '—and you've solved that issue, so consider me shut up.'

'Lydia solved it,' I said, glancing at her. Gratitude rolled through me. 'She's the one who convinced Niall.'

Liam nodded. 'Well, we're a team now – the four of us. And Niall. Although with the way Kat chewed his ear off about the design budget...'

'Hey!' Kat pouted.

'It's going to be hard work, but if this is what you want, I'm in. And I'm sorry if I ever made you feel I didn't back you. I do. I'm just—'

'Grumpy and cantankerous?' Kat supplied.

Liam clamped a hand over her mouth. 'I am grumpy. And a realist. But I shouldn't have let that bleed into our work – or our relationship. So I'm sorry. We'll go in as business partners. Equals.'

He held out his hand. I stared at it. Really, it was all I'd wanted – his approval. Now I had it, and I didn't know what to say.

'You shake it,' Lydia murmured, amusement in her tone.

I took his hand, snapping out of my daze.

'Good.' Liam's smile deepened. 'Now that's done, this one will probably start designing the second we get home.'

Kat lit up. 'Oh, you have no idea.'

They turned towards the car and we followed. My brain was still catching up, dazed.

'I have a new hyperfocus,' Kat went on. 'You're not going to see me for weeks.'

Lydia nudged me. 'Is it okay? That I asked Liam too? Niall's putting in a fair chunk, but you'll need to go in together for the business loans—'

I pulled her in by the back of her head and kissed her hard.

'Thank you,' I said, my voice thick. 'You don't know what

this means. And it's *we* now, Sunshine. Not you. Not me. Us. Okay?'

'Okay,' she breathed.

A whistle cut through the air. Kat was grinning; Liam just raised a sardonic eyebrow.

'Took you long enough,' he said.

'Yes!' Kat clapped again, practically bouncing. 'We can officially double-date now. This is fantastic.' Kat hooked arms with Lydia. 'Right – about the gym space. Are we thinking the biggest barn for the functional training area?'

Lydia's reply – full of plans and possibilities – was the soundtrack as I looked around the farm in quiet awe.

Ours.

It was ours.

I thought of all those visits with Mum. The birthdays in the cafe. The memories Bert and Mabel had built here with their family. It felt like a gift now, a duty, to build more memories, as many as I could.

With Lydia. Kat and Liam. Abigail. Everly Heath and all its mad occupants. Weddings, parties, celebrations – but also the quiet magic of daily life. Waking up next to Lydia. Walking Peggy. Greeting hotel guests.

Liam's hand clapped my shoulder. 'You ready for this?'

I turned to him, grinning. 'Yeah, I'm ready.'

Chapter Twenty-Six

Lydia's Diary, 29 Years Old

To my younger self,

I found this old diary shoved in the back of the wardrobe today. Mum asked me to clear my stuff out now that Ren and I are moving into his flat. Yes, you heard that right. We're about to live with Ren Hunter.

And we've bought a huge farm. We're going to fix it up together, bit by bit.

Mad, right?

I'm just writing to tell you – it's all going to be okay. Your disability, those bloody numbers, don't define you. You'll love who you love, girls and boys. It'll be fine. You'll find a career you love (so much). And you'll fall for your best friend.

No, it's not all plain sailing to get there.

But all that matters is that when you get there, you take in the view.

Love,
Lydia

Lydia

'Right,' I said, as we climbed into Ren's car in the farm courtyard, 'Do you want the good news or the bad news?'

We'd spent the last few hours with Liam and Kat on the farm,

TAKE A HIKE!

fleshing out the plans Ren had drafted in his red folder. Kat was full of big ideas, and I threw in my two cents on gym design and what to avoid. Like questionable strip lighting that really ruined my gym selfies and how nobody ever put in enough plug sockets. Kat promised some sketches and Liam was already muttering about structural plans, promising that Jack would be over soon to start knocking down plaster.

We were hitting the ground running and I couldn't wait to see it come to life.

Ren groaned, 'I'm not sure I can take any more surprises today.'

'Well, too bad,' I winced, 'Mum and Dad are throwing us a party.'

'A party?'

'Yup. At theirs. It started as a "yay you climbed Snowdon" thing, but then Mandy let the cat out of the bag. About us.'

Ren shook his head, a rueful smile on his face, 'Meddling.'

'I know.'

He scratched the back of his neck, eyes darting away. 'Suppose I should tell you something in case your mum mentions it...'

My stomach dropped. 'What?'

'Your mum's the reason I knew about the hiking trip. She bought my ticket. Told me to go. Basically threatened me.'

I stared at him. 'You're joking.'

My eyes widened.

'I could've said no, but once she planted the idea in my head, it didn't seem like the craziest idea.' He softened his gaze. 'You know, to spend time with you.'

'Don't give me those puppy dog eyes, Ren.'

He hid his smile in his palm.

I shook my head. 'Of course she did. That meddling witch. I'm going to kill her.' I jabbed a finger at him. 'Why didn't you tell me?'

Ren let out a short, manic laugh. 'I'm terrified. Or turned on. Could be both.'

'Ren!'

'Lydia!'

'Why didn't you tell me before now?'

'Because it's your mum,' he said, pouting like he was eight years old again, 'If I'd grassed her up, we wouldn't be having this conversation. I'd be six feet under. I'm only telling you now because, well... she was right in the end. We did make up.' He raised an eyebrow, counting on his fingers. 'In my tent—'

'Ren!' I barked, half laughing.

'—and then at that hotel in Glencoe. And then I really made it up to you at—'

I slapped a hand over his mouth, even as joy bubbled up in my chest at the sight of his triumphant grin. He pulled my hand away, pressing a kiss into my palm.

'And I fully intend to make up again tonight.'

I blushed, heat crawling up my neck, distracting me from the fact my mother was a conniving, nosy so-and-so. But she was also right.

'Give her a gentle telling-off if you must,' Ren said, eyes dancing. 'But she was right.'

I groaned. 'This party is going to be so much worse than I thought. I hate it when she's right. She's so smug!'

Ren shrugged, and said, softly, too softly, 'A mum's prerogative.'

'Hey,' my palm covered the steering wheel. 'Where did you just go?'

'Mum would've loved this. The farm. You. Us. You're lucky that your mum gets to be there, for all of our firsts, you know? Even if she is a bit full-on sometimes.'

My throat thickened, 'Ren, I'm sor—'

Then I saw it – the twitch at the corner of his mouth.

'You—' I narrowed my eyes. 'You're playing me.'

His grin split wide. 'What?'

'You just dropped the dead mum card to get out of trouble!'

Ren held up his hands. 'I wasn't lying, it's true! But you can't blame a guy for playing the dead mum card if it gets him out of trouble.'

I glared at him, lips twitching. 'Let's go face the music.'

'Full-blown orchestra?'

'Trumpets. Drums. Dot's piano. The lot.'

Ren leaned over, pressing a kiss to my temple. 'Nothing we can't handle, Sunshine.'

Music and chatter spilt from my parents' house and it felt suspiciously like déjà vu, except Ren wasn't inside waiting for me this time. I wasn't running late. And he wasn't my best friend any more. He was right beside me, his hand clasped around mine, as we both stared at the door, willing it to open of its own accord.

'Ready?' he asked

'One more minute.'

Ren nodded, squeezing my hand.

A familiar face popped up at the window – Liam's daughter, Abigail, hair curled from the curlers Kat bought her for her twelfth birthday. Ren and I locked eyes, horror shining there.

'Abi, don't—'

It was too late.

'They're out here!' she yelled. 'Standing on the step. Like weirdos.'

My eyes squeezed shut as I could hear shuffling and shushing echoing behind the door.

'Here we go,' I muttered.

Ren kissed my forehead, a soft laugh rumbling against my hair. 'It's not a trial, Lyd. We've got this.'

The door swung open. Mum stood beaming, with half of Everly Heath stacked behind her – Dad, Pat, Mary and Nigel from the deli, John the butcher, Ravi from the hardware shop. Jack hovered by Kevin, Ren's dad. Even Amy, Gen and Claire peeked out from the back, all bright eyes and sly grins.

They took one look at us – looking at the way Ren was turned in to me, my hand tight in his – and the chorus began: gasps, sighs, Dot, the old piano teacher yelled, *'What a handsome couple!'*

Ren tucked me closer, warm and protective. 'Want me to take this one, Sunshine? You've done enough today.'

I leaned in, and whispered, 'Give 'em hell.'

Ren turned, his voice clear and commanding. God, someone get me a fan.

'Right. I'm going to say this once, then that's the end to all the rumours flying about, all right?'

There were open-mouthed nods and mutters of approval.

'Yes, we both climbed a load of mountains together, and yes, it was amazing. Yes, we shared a tent. No further questions.'

My shoulders shook with silent laughter.

'Yes, we're buying Everly Heath Farm, and we're fixing up the cottage and living there. Together. The farm will be converted into a hotel, restaurant, and bar – and the best gym you'll find for miles. Run by the best trainer you'll find, too.'

He glanced at me, eyes warm. I couldn't help but beam.

'No, you can't have freebies. Support local businesses. It's going to cost us an arm and a leg.'

I snorted. God, he sounded like Liam.

He glanced down at me, brushing a kiss over my temple.

'Best for last, Sunshine,' he murmured. Then, louder, 'Yes, we are together. Yes, we got together on the hiking trip. Yes, it took us so long because I royally fucked up. Again, no further questions. But I've loved Lydia Williams since we were kids.'

Ren glanced down at me, his eyes shining with…love.

'And half of you already knew how gone I was for her, so this won't be a surprise.'

There was a chorus of murmurs affirming. Ren turned back to them, his tone serious.

'So, that's it. The juicy details. Now, get us a drink, will you? We just bought a bloody derelict farm, for God's sake. I think we deserve one.'

I laughed, blinking back tears, as Ren glanced down at me, an expectant expression on his smiling face.

'Did I miss anything, Sunshine?'

I laughed, tears stinging my eyes. 'No. You did perfect.'

And then we were pulled into my childhood home, arms wrapping around us, kisses planted on cheeks and surrounded by warmth and noise and a whole lot of love.

Epilogue

Lydia

18 Months Later

The groan was music to my ears. I shifted forward, arching into the delicious stretch, breath catching as my body lengthened just right. My hands gripped the solid frame beneath me.

'That's it,' I murmured, voice low. 'Push into it.'

Another groan joined mine. Then another. Until a full chorus of deep, masculine groans echoed behind me – 11 voices in perfect harmony.

The Lancaster Vale men's first team were lined up on reformer machines, looking like a sexy calendar shoot gone rogue. Shaking limbs jutted out at odd angles. Some shirtless and sweaty. All absolutely hating every second of Pilates.

'Really, lads,' I tutted. 'You haven't been doing your stretches. The gaffer will be hearing about this.'

Cue a chorus of *Lydia, please* and *We'll do extra this week*.

'Fine. But I want box seats next season.' I pointed at Thiago Blundell, Lancaster's star striker, who held up his hands in defence.

'You're the best, Lydia,' added Nico van Haaren, the Dutch-Argentine keeper with hands like dinner plates.

The studio door swung open, sunlight flooding the room in golden beams. A familiar silhouette leaned against the frame, arms crossed in a cocky display. My face broke into a grin, my stomach still flipping with butterflies, even now.

'You'd think I'd be intimidated,' Ren drawled, 'knowing my girlfriend trains eleven professional athletes every Friday. But after the performance you lot gave last week? I'm feeling pretty confident I don't have to worry.'

'Oh, piss off, Hunter,' shot back Robbie McNair, though his lips twitched. Robbie was in Liam's year at Everly Heath High and had known of Ren long before Pilates became part of his pay-cheque-sanctioned weekly torment. 'Like you could do any better.'

'At this rate, they should let me have a go.' Ren sauntered into the room, heading for my reformer.

He leaned over, where I was still stretching out my hamstrings, and cupped my cheeks in his hands. His lips met mine in a long, lingering kiss, slow and unhurried, only pulling back when my tongue grazed his and his chest rumbled in quiet satisfaction.

The 11 giant babies burst into a chorus of 'Eww!', save for Nico, the eternal softie, who let out an 'Aww!'

Ren ignored the lot of them, totally unfazed, and pressed a kiss to the tip of my nose.

'Hey, Sunshine!'

I beamed. 'Hey! What are you doing here? Aren't you supposed to be unloading the wine for the wedding?'

'All in the cellar.' His eyes flashed with excitement. 'It's here. Dad just delivered it. I came straight here to tell you.'

'Oh, my God!' I squealed, pulling myself off the reformer in the most elegant way I could – spoiler: not very. 'Are you serious?'

'Jesus, Lydia!' Heath McKinnon, the Aussie right back, winced. 'Pretty sure they heard you in Blackpool.'

'Right. Class is over!' I announced. 'If you leave now, I won't tell the boss man you've been skipping your stretches.'

The team didn't need to be told twice. They scrambled off the reformers, groaning as they sauntered out of the studio, some rubbing their legs and arms.

I chuckled. 'Honestly, they run flat out for ninety minutes every week against the best of the best. But get them stretching and they turn into big babies.'

'Those are some of the richest athletes in the Northwest, Lydia,' Ren said, eyes crinkling. 'And you call them big babies?'

'What can I say?' I looped my arms around his shoulders. 'I've got a thing for penniless bartenders instead.'

Ren clicked his tongue. 'I'll have you know I'm basically landed gentry now. *And* we're the proud owners of this year's Best Restaurant in the Northwest. Third best—'

'Third best in the country, I know.' I smiled, planting a kiss on his cheek, whispering in his ear, 'So, where's my Birkin?'

'I don't know what a Birkin is, but I've got some wood to show you.' He grinned, winking.

I rolled my eyes. 'Come on. It'll take us half an hour to get across this bloody farm.'

He threaded his fingers through mine. 'Oh, it's the bloody farm now, is it? Says the woman who secured seed funding for it behind my back.'

We walked past the largest barn, its high ceilings converted from an abandoned outbuilding into a state-of-the-art gym – complete with a massive weights area, machines, and treadmills, open to PT clients, members, and hotel guests. Down the gravel path, we passed the hot yoga studio, the stables which were in the process of being turned into small offices for local businesses, and the path down to the fields where local farmers kept their sheep, grazing on the grass in the late summer sunshine.

Then, on our right, we passed the main farmhouse, now transformed into a Michelin-Guide-worthy restaurant, Magnolia, with a parlour bar and boutique hotel upstairs. The farmhouse had ivy-covered stone walls and its original windows, now restored, framed views of the orchard. Liam crafted a brilliant menu of seasonal dishes for locals and visitors alike and Kat had smashed it with the interiors, weaving in a modern farmhouse aesthetic, with terracotta floors, warm oak panelling, and mismatched vintage chairs she'd sourced from charity shops and refinished herself.

The whole farm had that charming chaos we'd come to love. Everly Heath Farm wasn't just a gym, or a hotel, or a restaurant. It was all three, stitched together with wildflower borders, reclaimed wood sleepers, and festoon lights that flickered on at dusk. There was a bit of luxury, a lot of local charm, and Ren and me woven into every inch.

'Lydia, Lydia,' Pat's nephew, Josh, our newly appointed Events Manager, came racing across the lawn in front of the Farmhouse, 'We have a problem.'

My stomach swooped. But I took a deep breath, calming myself. Ren squeezed my hand.

'What's up, Josh?'

'The power to the marquee has fused. I found the switchboard but it isn't coming back on. I'm worried we won't have any power for tomorrow—'

'Hmm. We could get a back-up generator.'

Ren pulled his phone out. 'I'll call Dad – he'll have an electrician who can come out.'

'This last-minute?' I bit my lip. 'It's Friday evening.'

Ren chuckled. 'Dad has strings he can pull, don't worry.'

I turned to Josh, who looked at us, dumbfounded. 'You two are *weirdly* calm. It's freaking me out.'

I reached out to place a comforting hand on his shoulder, which, since he was six foot four, wasn't easy.

'Josh, a few months ago, we didn't have any working toilets in the en suites.'

'And we had a pig escape on our soft launch. They ate the canapés.'

'Oh, and there was that time we had someone trapped in the

toilets in the restaurant and we had to call the fire brigade out to rescue them.'

Ren clicked his fingers. 'That *was* stressful.'

I turned to Josh, beaming. 'You're doing a great job. But this is PR, not the ER. As long as no one died, I'm not worried.'

Josh's shoulders dropped a few inches. 'Okay, I'll go and check on the linen delivery.'

'Thank you.'

'You're good at that,' Ren said, smiling, as he ran a hand down my ponytail. 'Keeping people calm.'

I blushed at the compliment. Managing people hadn't been strange at first – having people turn to me to answer their questions or have the final say on the colour of the walls. But, after a while, I found myself looking forward to leading staff meetings or annual reviews, where we could give people pay rises. My worries about my dyscalculia, my anxiety about numbers, hadn't disappeared. But Ren led on the meetings with accountants or meetings with Niall about investments and returns. I focused on the people, which had always been my strength anyway.

'Josh is a good egg. He just needs someone to turn to every now and then.'

Ren pulled me to a stop, playing with an errant hair that had escaped my hair tie.

'You're very good at your job, Sunshine. Let me say it, and let yourself hear it. Okay?'

'Okay,' I smiled.

'Come on before someone else pounces on us about tomorrow.'

Excitement bubbled in my chest. *Tomorrow.*

God, it had come around so fast.

Ren tugged me along, his long legs setting a faster pace past the packed restaurant with people enjoying their long Friday lunch.

Sleeper steps led us down to the more remote part of the farm, past a small paddock for cows, and towards the far edge of the property, where the restored apple orchard spread out in full bloom. There, between two ancient apple trees, stood an ornate archway in soft oak, woven with carved flowers and fruit. My legs moved faster than my brain, dragging Ren with me. As I got closer, I saw the detail. Lilies and citrus fruits had been painstakingly carved by hand into the wood.

I reached out, fingers gliding over its smooth, glossy finish.

'It's so beautiful,' I said. 'Kat is going to love it.'

'Dad and Liam did a brilliant job.' Ren's hand found my shoulder blade, rubbing it gently, like he knew exactly how much this meant. Weddings made me feral. It was something about the anticipation, the crisp champagne, everyone dressed up to the nines. But this wedding was even more important. Because it was family.

Kat and Liam. My cousin and Ren's brother. It meant everything to us.

And crucially, it was the first wedding Ren and I were hosting at Everly Heath Farm and we had 24 hours until go-time. I turned to Ren, looping my arms around his shoulders. His hands skimmed down to my hips, and I arched my neck, an unspoken invitation he answered with a kiss there.

'Do we have everything?'

'You know we do.'

'Are you sure?' I pulled back, scrunching my nose. 'What if we run out of bog roll?'

Ren chuckled, tucking a stray hair behind my ear. 'We've still got that lifetime supply you got from Costco, Sunshine. We're fine.'

'And the bridal suite?' I pressed. 'What do you think? I know we haven't finished the painting in that corner of the bathroom. I can do that tonight. It's not all perfect—'

'Honey.' His voice dropped, low and lovely. 'Kat loves that room. She designed it, remember? She'd accept bare plaster in there if it meant she could soak in that roll-top tub and look out over the farm. Everything's ready. We're ready.'

A smile crept across my face.

'We are, aren't we?'

'You betcha. Liam's got his surprise—' he nodded towards the archway, '—but I've got mine.'

'What are you plotting?' I asked as he led me through the trees to the far end of the orchard. Quiet. Remote.

There a bench sat, one I'd never seen before.

Ren took a seat on the bench, fingers tracing the edge of a small brass plaque on the back.

IN LOVING MEMORY OF LILY HUNTER. ALWAYS WITH US.

I stood still, fingertips grazing her name.

'It's beautiful, Ren.'

'Well,' he said, voice thick, 'she'd hate to miss the occasion. So I figured… she could sit here.'

My eyes burned. I cupped his face, tears slipping freely now. Then I sat beside him, both of us looking out at the spot where, tomorrow, Kat and Liam's family and friends would gather to celebrate their love.

He shifted, gaze steady. 'Let's do this next year.'

'What? Organise another wedding?'

'Ours.'

My eyes shot to Ren, eyes wide. Then I narrowed them, a teasing smile playing on my lips.

'Is that supposed to be a proposal? Because proposing the day before your brother's wedding – the wedding we're hosting – is a massive red flag.'

Ren smirked in that way that let him get away with anything. 'Not a proposal. Not yet. I'm just saying – let's do this next year. We can keep it smaller than Kat and Liam's. We don't need a hundred and fifty people. We could keep it low-key. You and me. Peggy. Some family.'

'You think we can get away with *just* family? The whole of this nosy town would riot.'

Ren shrugged. 'Not their wedding.'

I narrowed my eyes. 'You've been thinking about this, haven't you?'

His smirk softened into something more thoughtful. 'Hard not to imagine it. A perfect day. Family, friends, good food, love.' His gaze settled on me, and my stomach dived. 'And I already have a speech prepared.'

I huffed a laugh. 'Oh, really? Not proposed yet, but you've prepped the speech?'

'Yep.'

'Go on then,' I challenged. 'Give me a sneak peek. Then I *might* say yes.'

His expression shifted – sincere, steady – and suddenly I wished I hadn't asked, because I wasn't sure I could handle whatever came next.

'Lydia.'

My heart skipped.

'Lydia,' he said again, lifting my knuckles to his lips. 'You are the brightest light in every room. You're pure sunshine. Even on my cloudiest days, the sun's still there, because you are. I knew, even when we were six. I knew it the moment you looked at me. You've been in my life for what feels like forever, and I want you there beside me until I take my last breath.'

My chest tightened. My throat burned.

'Well, fuck,' I whispered.

Ren barked a laugh, head thrown back. Then he cradled my jaw and kissed me, soft and sure.

'Is that a yes?'

I blinked up at him, heart pounding. 'I think you already know it is.'

I kissed him, pouring every ounce of feeling into it. When I pulled away, I pressed a finger to his chest.

'But you better give me a proper proposal, loser.'

Ren's grin turned reverent, eyes deep and warm – like home. 'I promise.'

And he made good on that promise just six weeks later.

Acknowledgements

This book was the scary second album, and I couldn't have done it without the brilliant support system cheering me on.

As always, my first thanks go to my lovely parents for supporting and encouraging me through these mad creative endeavours I'm forever pursuing. Your steadfast belief that I can do this – paired with your dogmatic insistence that you simply have to *do the work* – has carried me more times than I can count. I'm in awe of you both, daily.

To my writing friends and buddies – Aurora and Olivia – and the new pals I made along the way: Emma, Philippa, Meg (TY for the marketing support too, queen!), and all the authors who've slid into my DMs to natter about this weird, wonderful career we've chosen. I appreciate you more than you know.

Thank you to everyone who has cheered me on – reviewers, Bookstagrammers, and BookTokers who've taken the time to post videos and reviews about *Fix Them Up* and *Take a Hike!*. Special shoutout to Dani and Libby, who have also become friends. It really does mean the world to authors.

There's a whole team who work tirelessly to get a book into your hands, and the crew at Bedford Square couldn't be more passionate. Thank you to my lovely editor, Rebecca, for championing my books and for your love of the romance genre. And thank you to the rest of the team for everything you do behind the scenes – I see you.

To my incredible agent, Saskia, who is always excited to

hear my hare-brained ideas (usually cooked up on far too much caffeine and not nearly enough sleep). You're a real force, and I'm so grateful to have you in my corner.

Last but never least, thank you to my husband and our lovely pup, Paddy, for keeping my spirits up. Love you both.

About the Author

Maggie Grant is a neurodivergent writer who crafts romance with heart, wit, and a dash of spice. When not writing, she's likely to be sipping wine and devouring romance novels. She lives in Stockport with her husband and their dog, Paddy.

@maggiegrantauthor

Bedford Square Publishers

Bedford Square Publishers is an independent publisher of fiction and non-fiction, founded in 2022 in the historic streets of Bedford Square London and the sea mist shrouded green of Bedford Square Brighton.

Our goal is to discover irresistible stories and voices that illuminate our world.

We are passionate about connecting our authors to readers across the globe and our independence allows us to do this in original and nimble ways.

The team at Bedford Square Publishers has years of experience and we aim to use that knowledge and creative insight, alongside evolving technology, to reach the right readers for our books. From the ones who read a lot, to the ones who don't consider themselves readers, we aim to find those who will love our books and talk about them as much as we do.

We are hunting for vital new voices from all backgrounds – with books that take the reader to new places and transform perceptions of the world we live in.

Follow us on social media for the latest Bedford Square Publishers news.

@bedsqpublishers
facebook.com/bedfordsq.publishers
@bedfordsq.publishers

bedfordsquarepublishers.co.uk